THE DEVIL DRIVES A JAGUAR

SUZANNE DOWNES

*For Sian
with best wishes

Suzanne
Downes*

COUNTRY BOOKS

Published and distributed by
Country Books
Courtyard Cottage, Little Longstone, Bakewell, Derbyshire DE45 1NN
Tel: 01629 640670

ISBN 978 1 898941 75 0

First published 2002
Reprinted 2008

British Library Cataloguing in Publication Data.
A catalogue record for this book is available from the British Library.

This book is a work of fiction.
Names, characters, places and incidents
are either products of the Author's imagination
or are used fictitiously.
Any resemblance to actual events,
locations or persons living or dead,
is entirely coincidental.

Printed and bound by:
Cpod, Trowbridge

ABOUT THE AUTHOR

Suzanne Downes is the youngest of ten and has lived all her life in Stockport, except for two years in Australia when she was a child.

She was educated at Stockport Convent High School for Girls and Stockport College.

Her first marriage ended in divorce and she now lives with her second husband in Woodley.

She has three children and one grandson.

As well as writing Suzanne enjoys reading, music, travel, gardening and has been studying Italian in her spare time.

She is Membership Secretary for Bredbury St Marks Cricket Club, but more than anything else except writing, loves spending time with her family and friends.

Author's Note

Even though I am the youngest of ten children, I would just like to reassure the reader that my real father, Joe Sullivan, was nothing like the evil papa Jacob Watkins in this story. He was a wonderful man.

And though I can't claim to have had an idyllic childhood, nor was I ever tempted to poison my sisters!

Writing can be a very therapeutic substitute.

CHAPTER ONE

"You're not going."

It wasn't a request, but a statement and I was filled with a fury I could scarcely contain. Suddenly I knew that he had spoken to me as though I were his possession for the last time.

"Oh, yes I am," I answered as evenly as I could, "And what is more, it's extremely unlikely I'll be coming back."

There was a silence on the other end of the line, then harsh laughter, "Don't be ridiculous!"

Ridiculous. Yes, that was the word that described me. Ridiculous for ever having thought I was in love with the arrogant prick who was now turning the telegraph wires blue with a mainly four letter rendition of all my faults. I held the telephone away from my ear and grimaced at Joanna, my flatmate, who was sitting on the sofa, nursing a glass of wine and grinning joyfully to finally hear me answer the 'green-eyed viper' back. Her silent support gave me the strength I needed to cut swiftly across his tirade,

"Grow up, Brendan, for God's sake. I'm going – and I won't be leaving a forwarding address."

He slammed the phone down on me, leaving me shaking with the aftermath of my anger and the infuriating knowledge that I should have been the one to do the cutting off – his balls, preferably! Still, never mind, I had had the last word.

I went over to the sofa and accepted the proffered drink from Joanna.

"That went well." I said weakly.

"I gathered he wasn't best pleased," she said wryly. She hugged me swiftly, then added, "But do you really mean it this time? We've been here so many times before, and he's always managed to talk you around again."

"Not this time. I've had as much as I'm going to take from him. Aunt Lil doesn't know it, but she's given me the perfect excuse to escape."

"It's hardly an escape, is it? Going into the depths of Derbyshire to nurse a sick old lady."

It was then I began to worry that I had made the wrong decision – not over Brendan, that had been coming for months, but I had been too afraid of being alone in London to admit it to myself – but of going back North. I tried to tell myself that this was always the effect Brendan had on me, making me unsure of myself, eroding my confidence in his subtle way, but still I began to question the wisdom of my decision.

To have taken my full holiday entitlement to travel to the Peak District to visit Great Aunt Lillian, whom I had barely seen since childhood (our paths tended to cross only at Weddings and Funerals these days), was not one of the more sane and sensible acts of my admittedly impulse-ridden existence.

But Lillian's letter, poignant in the unsteady formation of the once-strong hand, had struck deep. Memories of childhood summers, always filled with endless sunshine when recalled, had drawn me irresistibly back. Lillian had made no attempt to hide the fact that she was dying, not asking for sympathy, but help. She had, she said, several loose ends to tie up, but could no longer hope to sort them out herself. Could I possibly...?

I could – and fully intended to do so. Joanna was right, in a way, that I wasn't really the ideal candidate to dispense tea and sympathy to Lil, but she needed me – and that meant more than anything else just then.

I shrugged, appearing much more confident than I felt, "You may have a point, but nursing Lil will be a picnic compared to being Brendan Tulliver's girlfriend. Anyway, if I know Lil, she'll still be fitter than I am, even with cancer."

"I hope you are right. I don't see you as much of a Florence Nightingale, no matter how much you think of your Auntie. When did you say you last visited her?"

I was mildly irritated by her cynicism and it showed in my tone when I answered, "Okay, okay. I fully admit I haven't been as attentive as I ought to have been – but it's not easy going 'oop North' without having to see my mother as well. Lil completely understands why I've been avoiding her."

"I'm sure she does, but I still think you are bloody mad. Dropping everything and haring off to Derbyshire is not one of your more sane decisions, is it?"

"Compared to what?" I asked, a trifle bitterly, "Crap job, rotten boyfriend, grotty flat?"

"Thanks a bunch. This is my flat too, you know."

"Yeah, sorry. Half a grotty flat."

Joanna shook her head in mock despair and laughed, "Oh, you're going to be a great comfort to a sick little old lady. Tact and diplomacy are definitely your most outstanding characteristics."

ℰ   ℰ   ℰ   ℰ   ℰ

It was a long drive, but the twisted spire of Chesterfield Church told me that I was getting near. I drank in the views as a connoisseur drinks fine wine, savouring every nuance. The dark and craggy Pennines are not to everyone's taste, but it lifted my spirits as nothing else ever could. I wondered why I had allowed stupid things to keep me away for so long.

There was still some way to go and it was over an hour later that I turned the car into the hedge-enclosed lane which had not altered at all in the twenty years I had been away, and probably not in a hundred before that. My teeth rattled in my head as the front wheel sank into a pothole with a bump that had more than likely wrecked the suspension.

Lillian's house stood on a projecting fold of heather-strewn hillside, old, grey stone, weather beaten and seemingly etched out of the crags by two hundred years of biting Pennine winds. Stone-lintled and oak-beam supported, it stood inviolate. Even the lane did not go right up to the house, harking back to the days when it would have been a horse that approached the door. The car would have to be abandoned on a gravelled lay-by on the lane and the last few yards traversed on foot.

As I dragged my bag from the back seat and slammed the door, I felt a warm, familiar sensation of homecoming. How I had always loved this house, with its feeling of age, yet cosy welcoming warmth. Nothing bad could ever have happened here, no evil stained the stones or marred the atmosphere. I never felt like this when I walked up my mother's neat, brick-paved path.

To my amazement, Lillian herself answered the summons of the great cast iron knocker on the oak door. Despite my bravado in explaining the situation to Joanna, I must admit I had half expected the old lady to be confined to bed, but on second thoughts I should have known better. Lillian possessed something of the craggy strength of the hills that had always been her home. The house had only had piped water and electricity for the last fifteen years. Before that Lillian had managed as her ancestors had, with a hand worked pump in the kitchen, drawing up the pure Pennine waters from hundreds of feet below ground. Her only form of lighting came from oil lamps. She'd never had gas and wasn't likely to. My father, in a moment of generosity had contacted the gas board for her in the late eighties and had been appalled at the amount of money they wanted to run a pipe up the hillside. As he grumpily pointed out to the teenaged salesman, Lillian could have bought a small bungalow for that amount of money.

No, Lillian wasn't going to give in that easily. She had run the small holding single-handedly after her husband died, never asking for help of her numerous relations – until now. And I admit I felt honoured and also slightly smug to be the one chosen for the task.

Much later, when a good old-fashioned farmhouse tea had been consumed, we were companionably settled before a roaring fire and I felt the moment had come to find out precisely what it was my aunt required, "So, Auntie, how are you really? No, sorry, stupid question. You would hardly have asked me to come out here if you were bursting with health, would you?"

My aunt gave an old-womanish cackle of laughter, "Bless you, Libby, it's no wonder I've always preferred you to the rest of the family. You are so like me, it's frightening. Always straight to the point, no hedging."

"I call a spade a shovel, if that's what you mean," I admitted with a grin, not at all displeased to be compared to the woman I had always admired, even as a child, "Now, stop trying to change the subject and tell me what sort of things you are going to need me to do."

"Now don't get carried away with the idea that I'm some sort of an invalid, young lady," she countered briskly, "I haven't asked you here to do any nursing. You have something much more important to attend to. You've to finish something I started, but was side-tracked from when your uncle died and I had to run this place alone."

"I hope it's not a jumper, I can't knit – and I'm not learning at my age, not even for you. Can't sew either, so if it's one of those huge, embroidered table-cloths…"

The older woman laughed again, "What do you take me for, Libby? I was a women's libber before the term was ever invented. Your Uncle Frank used to do all the knitting in this house. He made a lovely warm sock, but your grandma had to turn all the heels for him. He used to save up dozens of half-finished socks for her to do the hard bit, when she came for a visit."

I barely even remembered Uncle Frank, he had died so long ago. Lillian must have been a widow for almost as long as she had been a wife. I took a long look at the old woman's face, glowing and animated in the firelight, and I thought I had never seen anyone who looked more alive than Lillian did in that moment.

"All right, it's not knitting, so what is it?"

"It's a sort of family history. I want you to finish it for me."

My heart almost literally sank, I felt sick with deflation. I had rarely been more disappointed – the graphic, if unpleasant word "gutted" sprang to mind. If there was one thing I hated about being in a job which gave access to a computer, it was the way people always wanted you to write their life story for them. It wasn't my forte and it made me feel mean and uncomfortable to have to admit that no matter how riveting a biography might be, I had no interest in writing it – not that I was above pinching the occasional anecdote for my own personal use – but that was hardly the same. Now, to make things even worse, Lil, for whom I would usually do anything, was asking me to write a family history. In my opinion there was nothing more dull than tracing the lives of those who could not possibly be of interest anyone but their own descendants. People just didn't realize how very rare it was to find a pirate or a murderer, an inventor or a Prime Minister lurking amongst their antecedents. It was like that regressive hypnotism – not everyone could be Henry VIII or Cleopatra, someone had to be servants, farmers, sewage-workers. More than likely my own family would be a long line of grocers, blacksmiths and yeomen, with an occasional Alderman thrown in, if I was lucky.

"Lil," I protested feebly, "Don't do this to me, please. Don't dump me with a long-winded 'now let's meet great granny, who had seventeen children and ran her own bakery when her husband died of the plague'."

Lillian was unmoved by the plea or by my obvious reluctance, merely tapping me, her recalcitrant great-niece on the hand with mock-annoyance, "Don't be so disrespectful, Missy. The plague was long gone by your great grandma's time. Your grasp of history is appalling. The trouble is you always think you know best – well, allow your old Aunt to know a thing or two. Perhaps the knowledge that my own great Aunt was hanged for the murder of three members of her family would be of some interest to you."

"Murder!" I was stunned, and rather horrified. My own cowardly reluctance to try regression had been seated in the pessimistic certainty that with my luck I would turn out to have been Jack the Ripper or Attila the Hun and would never be able to live with myself again. My mother had kept that skeleton firmly in the cupboard – and I couldn't honestly say I blamed her.

Lillian smiled smugly, "You seem a little more intrigued now, my dear."

I granted Lil her moment of triumph – to tell the truth, I was too astounded to say anything. In theory it was every aspiring writer's dream to have something so juicy to investigate, but in fact, the more I thought about it the more I was finding the reality rather chilling. To be so closely related to someone who had killed her own flesh and blood – and not just one of them, but three.

"Are you sure about this?" I asked eventually, when I had composed myself sufficiently.

"Oh yes. I have the newspaper cuttings."

"God! Does my mother know about it?"

"She does indeed. In fact, she's the one who is protesting the loudest. She doesn't want it to come out. It doesn't suit her purposes to be related to a notorious murderess."

I had a sudden vision of my immaculately dressed, Tory-loving mother and smiled grimly. It had almost driven her nuts when I had expressed my socialist tendencies, imagine what a killer in the family must have done to her.

"Okay, I admit you've now claimed my interest, but why do you need me? If you've got the newspaper cuttings, then that must be the full story."

"I don't think so. You see, she wasn't at home when she was arrested. She had been sent here, to live with her grandmother and to get over the deaths of her sisters. All I have is the story of the trial, and it is obvious from reading that, she was never given a chance to defend herself."

"You think she was innocent?"

"I don't know what to think, to be honest – but I've always had a soft spot for the underdog – and this girl was about as under as you can get. Even if she did do it, I couldn't honestly say I blame her."

"What do you mean?"

"For a start off, she was the youngest of ten, so they called her Decima. I mean to say, how cruel can you get? That's the equivalent of giving her a number, not a name. You are just number ten, that's all you mean to us." There was such passion in her tone, such a wealth of sympathy and understanding, that I was touched.

I scanned her face with renewed interest, "You really like this girl, don't you?" Lillian looked surprised for a moment, then thoughtful.

"I suppose I do. I can't say I condone her poisoning her siblings, but I sort of understand it. If it was today, she'd be helped, not hanged."

"But, in the end, what does it really matter? She's long dead, and so is everyone else connected with the story."

Lil looked straight into my eyes, "If she didn't do it, Libby, she deserves people to know it, no matter how many years have passed. Would you want

12

the world thinking ill of you for all eternity?"

There was no arguing with that. I was the sort of person to go back into a shop and apologise to the counter-staff if I thought I had been a bit sharp. No wonder Brendan had found it a simple matter to ingratiate himself time and time again. I couldn't have borne the milkman to think ill of me, never mind the whole human race – and forever.

"All right, I agree. Where do I start?"

"Read what I've discovered, then take it from there. I'm afraid I came to a dead end."

"How much of a dead end?" I asked warily, aware suddenly that I could become obsessed with this story, then find, frustratingly, that nothing more would ever be revealed.

"You'll find that out when you read my stuff."

❦   ❦   ❦   ❦   ❦

That night, in my oak-beamed bedroom, with firelight flickering from the old cast iron grate, but thankfully an electric lamp next to the bed, I listened to the wind whistling past the corners of the house and groaning in the chimney like a live thing, sending the occasional puff of wood-smoke back into the room, then I plumped up my pillows behind my head and began to read.

I was quite impressed with Lillian's style. She had begun in a very business-like manner, trying to present the facts and collate the evidence, but she soon drifted into a more narrative mode. Decima had certainly struck a chord with Aunt Lillian. And as I read, late into the night, despite my utter weariness, the girl began to come alive for me too, so much so that every word seemed not new, but like old, awakened memories, as if I had known it all before and had merely forgotten ...

❦   ❦   ❦   ❦   ❦

Decima was born in 1836, the youngest of ten children, to Maryanne and Jacob Watkins of Stockport. Unusually for the time, none of the children died in infancy and by the time Decima was fourteen, several of the siblings were married and producing children of their own. She had been a late addition to the family and was considerably younger than the rest. Her parents seemed to have found it profoundly embarrassing to have had another child at a time when they ought to be settling into grandparent-

hood. *She appears to have endured a rather unhappy childhood, full of childish, though serious, ailments, including measles which left her partially deaf. Her father was a typically strict Victorian father who expected unreasoning obedience, and her mother was sickly and inclined towards invalidism – probably as a defence against being forced to have more children. Decima seems to have been a biddable little soul, more than happy to be a doting aunt to her older siblings' progeny, until the day her older brother brought home one of his comrades. He, probably as a reaction to his father's strictness, had run away and joined the army when Decima was only eight or nine, and from then on she saw him only when he was granted furlough. Meeting Richard Allingham changed her life. She was just eighteen and she fell deeply in love. Before any real romance, developed, however, Decima was hastily despatched to her grandmother, who was living here at Hill Farm. In those days it was more of a manor house, which had been purchased by Mr. Watkins to house his mother-in-law, whom he did not particularly want in the vicinity of his own home. The grandmother took it upon herself to confide in Decima that Richard had asked for her hand, but had been refused. He left and was to be killed in the Crimea a matter of months later.*

It seems to have been this incident which tipped Decima over the edge. When she returned home she was sullen and unhappy. After Richard's death, there were several occasions when the entire household was struck down with bouts of sickness. Even though most of Decima's sisters were married, they either lived with their parents still, or in houses only a few doors away. It was not uncommon for several households to share such tasks as cooking and washing. Decima seems to have been used as something of a useful maidservant, falling, even though so young, into that peculiar Victorian invention the 'maiden aunt' – the one who was never expected to marry, who would always be there to be of use to her ageing parents and older siblings. Over the next few months three of the older sisters died, their deaths being attributed respectively to consumption, food poisoning and gastritis. Decima was sent once again to the grandmother to recover from the shock of these deaths and that of her lover. It was here that the police came to arrest her. Within six months she had been found guilty of poisoning her siblings and was duly hanged, never having spoken a word in her own defence. She was just twenty-three years old.

14

I wanted to read on, but my eyes were closing with utter weariness and I realized that it was long after midnight and I was suffering from the effects of the long drive. I laid Aunt Lil's manuscript aside and leaned over to switch out the light – not, unfortunately to sleep very much. I didn't know if I was over-tired, or over-emotional after the day I had endured, but I couldn't get Decima out of my mind.

It was all so horribly tragic. Twenty-three was no age at all – and what a way to die. But then, dying by poison wasn't any better. I supposed it would be arsenic – the Victorian favourite. If I remembered my history that involved vomiting green bile. And all because she had been denied the man she loved! Nowadays, she would probably be diagnosed as having PMS and get away with twelve months probation.

It was on that thought that I finally fell asleep, only to jerk wide-awake in what seemed to be only a few seconds later.

The room was filled with the sort of grey light which heralded the dawn and it seemed I had been asleep longer than I had thought. I wondered what had woken me; there was no noise. Not a sound in the house. No gurgling pipes, no creaking of expanding floorboards.

I was too hot; sweat was pouring off me, trickling uncomfortably between my breasts, and sticking my night dress to me. I suddenly realised that the bed covers had somehow tucked themselves underneath my body and were pulling uncomfortably tight about my neck and chest. I could hardly breathe, but when I lifted my hands to try and free myself I found myself tightly bound and I began struggling in a slightly wild panic. I simply couldn't move the offending covers, they seemed to grow tighter the more I pulled at them.

For a few seconds I wriggled and tussled, getting more and more heated and ever so slightly hysterical, until suddenly I gained my release. The blankets flew back and I sat swiftly up, trying to laugh at my stupidity. How childish to get into a fright just because a loose sheet had tangled itself around me. Now I knew why everyone in the country had long ago swapped sheets and blankets for duvets. Everyone except Aunt Lil.

I lay back down, relieved to feel the cool air on my hot body, but sleep had now deserted me completely. For the first time since I was a little girl, I sat by the window and watched the dawn come up over the Pennines.

❧

Chapter Two

When I finally staggered into the kitchen that morning, arrayed in my oldest, warmest and most comfortable dressing gown and down at heel slippers, my eyes barely open and gasping for coffee, I was appalled to find my Aunt had company – male company, at that.

Since I was going through one of my periodic men-hating phases, due in no small part to Brendan Tulliver, I quickly decided that whoever he was, he was just going to have to put up with my embarrassing appearance. I was determined not to flee like a schoolgirl, red-faced and humiliated, so I sank into the nearest chair, ran my fingers through my thick, unruly auburn hair and smiled blearily at him, "Good morning."

"In the country, Miss, this is very nearly afternoon." inserted Aunt Lillian tartly, "I suppose it would be pointless to ask how you slept – you look as though you didn't."

"Not much," I admitted, "Is there any coffee?"

"I was just about to make David some – you haven't met David Wright, have you?"

"Oh God! Don't tell me I'm meeting 'Mr. Right' dressed like this." I joked, then immediately regretted it – what if he didn't see the humour and started to think I was on the prowl.

He grinned, rising to his feet to offer his hand, "I can't say my ex-wife saw me as Mr. Right – not towards the end, anyway." he said, as he shook my hand.

Reluctantly I had to admit I liked his smile; it turned his blue eyes mischievous and showed his nice, straight teeth to advantage. I guessed he must be a little older than me, perhaps thirty five to my thirty, the tell-tale grey at his temples and wrinkles at the corners of his eyes giving him away, but he looked good on it. I thought he must work outdoors, because his skin had a healthy tan, which spoke of wind and weather rather than a sun bed. I shook his hand and returned his smile, telling myself severely that I was off men – even men who were tanned and muscled from working outdoors, and who made a point of declaring their availability in their first sentence.

"Are you a farmer?" I asked, gratefully accepting a mug of coffee from Lillian.

"No, he owns a very large and profitable garden centre and landscape gardening business – we call him Capability Wright," inserted my aunt proudly. David Wright smiled wryly at me and said, without a trace of rancour, "Now, why do I feel as though I'm being hawked to the highest bidder?"

"Don't worry," I said grimly, "I'm not even at the auction."

As soon as I said the words, I realized how very rude and ungracious I sounded, but I was determined not to care – though it didn't stop me from feeling vaguely relieved when he laughed and said, "No need to ask if you are related to Lillian."

Aunt Lil cuffed him lightly round the ear, "Don't be impertinent."

He caught the gnarled old hand and kissed it, "Well, I've seen for myself that you're all right, so I must get back. Goodbye Miss...?"

"Libby – just Libby."

"Like Just William?"

"Whatever. See you around, Mr. Right."

When he was gone, I watched Lillian over the rim of my coffee mug for a minute before saying, "What was that all about, dear Aunt? Are you trying to match-make for me?"

Lillian laughed, "With David? You keep your hands off, he's my beau."

"I never knew you were into toy-boys."

"I'm 'into' that one, as you phrase it. He drives up here twice a week to make sure I don't need anything, bless him."

I was more convinced than ever that Lillian was plotting, but I said nothing more, merely thinking, OK Lil, you've convinced me he's a nice guy – but so what? They all are, until the going gets tough.

Once I was bathed and dressed, I came back downstairs to find my aunt had cleared away the breakfast dishes and had gone outside to feed the chickens – all that was left of the small-holding which had previously been alive with sheep, goats and the odd goose. I suppose I vaguely regretted the changes which age had forced on her, but I was rather glad my duties were not going to include 'mucking out' and milking. The goats had never been my favourites, even as a child. I had always found them smelly and inclined to be aggressive, especially when there was food on offer.

Since Lillian seemed to have everything in hand, there did not appear to be much for me to do, so it did not take much to persuade me to nip back upstairs, grab the notes on Decima Watkins, and curl up in a big, old fashioned rocking chair. I had scanned Lillian's notes and now turned my attention to the newspaper reports of the trial.

Nothing I read changed my mind at all. Decima was painted as a manipulative, spoiled brat, who had reacted violently when thwarted. She appeared to have no conscience at all at putting her young nephews and nieces in danger from the poison; food and drink seemed to have been indiscriminately doctored. If the prosecution was to be believed, Decima had begun her campaign of hate almost as soon as she heard of Richard Allingham's death, and there were occasions when the whole family fell ill, even Decima herself, though, as it was emphatically pointed out by the learned Counsel, most poisoners are intelligent enough to know that they have to be seen to suffer along with their victims in order to deflect suspicion. No one, it seemed, had much of a good word to say about her. Her remaining brothers and sisters told of childish tantrums which were frightening in their intensity and of a quiet determination to always get her own way. Her mother and father admitted they had trouble controlling her, especially after she met Richard. Only her grandmother refused to utterly condemn her, but she was so overwrought by the whole affair that she barely seemed lucid and according to the papers, she died not long after her granddaughter was sentenced to death.

I stopped reading and rubbed my tired eyes, stretching and yawning. Why on earth was Aunt Lil putting me through all this? Decima was a classic case. Youngest child, pampered and spoiled, then reacting with anger and a desire for revenge when she didn't get what she wanted most in life – her man. I really couldn't understand why Lillian had such a soft spot for the little monster, "Spoiled little brat." I murmured under my breath.

A small noise made me jump. It sounded like something hitting the wooden floor beside me. Intrigued I hoisted myself upright and glanced over the arm of the chair to where I thought the noise had originated.

I could scarcely believe my eyes. As though it had just been dropped there, a copper coin was spinning on its edge on the polished floor, and even as I watched it, the momentum faded and it fell over with the characteristic speeding up of its spin just before it stopped. The most astounding thing was not that it seemed to have come from nowhere, but that it was an old penny, four times larger than our modern coins and as bright as the day it was minted, but with Queen Victoria on its reverse and not Queen Elizabeth II.

Instinctively I glanced up, trying to see from whence the coin had fallen, but there was nothing above my head by the white expanse of distempered ceiling. The nearest beam was several feet away, but I saw it and heaved a sigh of relief. Of course, the penny must have been dropped between the bedroom floorboards years ago and had now, due to vibration of some sort, just fallen past the beam and onto the floor, through a gap in the age-shrunken plaster.

There couldn't be any other explanation. Years and years of slamming doors, and raising and lowering sash windows had been moving the coin fractionally until at last gravity had won the day and it had fallen free.

As though to prove my point, Lil chose that exact moment to come back into the house, allowing the door to crash closed behind her, "Brr! There's still a nip in the air, for all it is April. Fancy making a cup of tea, love?"

I was only too glad to move away from the chair, though I would never have admitted it for the world, not even to myself. Somehow I didn't want to touch the coin, but even as I looked down at it I found my hand reaching out and picking the thing up from where it lay, glinting in the spring sunshine which flooded through the square-paned windows. It was so warm that I was shocked, expecting it to be cold. It felt as though it had been clutched in a child's hand. Now, why should I think that? I knew nothing about children, really, not coming much into contact with them. I just suddenly remembered how I had used to clutch my pocket money for dear life, terrified that I might lose it between home and the shops and thus be denied the myriad of delicious treats it could buy. When I had reluctantly handed it over in exchange for the sweets, it had felt just like this, hot and clammy from a passionate little fist.

"What's that you've got there?" asked Lil, seeing me looking down into my open palm.

"An old penny. I just found it on the floor."

Lil was already putting on the kettle, "An old one? You mean dirty and old?"

"No, old as in Victorian."

Lillian laughed, "I wonder where that turned up from? I have a box of old coins and other bits upstairs, but it's at the back of a cupboard somewhere."

"I thought it must have fallen between the floorboards upstairs and just worked its way free."

"Very probably," answered Lil vaguely, "Let me have a look at it." She held out her hand and I gave her the penny, almost pleased to have rid myself of it.

19

"That's in good condition. I bet it's worth something. 1859 – amazing to think how old it is."

I didn't bother to reply. Truth to tell, I didn't feel I could. Aunt Lillian had probably forgotten, but with my reading still fresh in my mind, I knew that 1859 was the year Decima Watkins had been hanged.

🍏   🍏   🍏   🍏   🍏

By mid afternoon, I had forgotten all about the penny. Well, I tried to tell myself I had. Lillian had suggested we make bread, and I was transported right back to my childhood. I rarely cooked at all in London. There were too many convenient places to eat and I always seemed to have something much better to do with my time. It was one of Brendan's main gripes. He seemed to think I ought to do that thing of being a whore in the bedroom and a chef in the kitchen. He told me sourly, with no redeeming hint of humour, that I was a whore in every room in the flat, but a chef in none of them.

Soon the house was filled with the delicious aroma of hot, yeasty rolls and my mouth watered when I thought of sinking my teeth into still-warm bread, smothered in golden, melted butter. I had home made bread and crumbly, white Cheshire cheese for my lunch and couldn't remember a time when I had enjoyed a meal more.

The phone rang whilst I was up to my elbows in floury dough and Lillian went into the hall to answer it. She returned with a message.

"That was David Wright. He asked you out to dinner tonight."

"I'll bet he didn't. You asked him, didn't you?"

Lillian smiled, "Whatever makes you think that?"

"Never mind. Anyway, you can ring him back and tell him no. I'm too busy – and I didn't come here just to go off gallivanting and leaving you all alone!"

"Oh, don't you worry about me. I'll be fine. He'll be here to pick you up around seven thirty."

I gave in graciously but was determined not to dress up for the meal with David Wright – better not let him think I was even vaguely interested in him. I had quite enough on my plate without the added complication of a man I didn't fancy chasing me. I was half-angry with Lillian for dropping me in it by arranging the dinner date and trying to organize my life for me.

However, my innate sense of neatness and style would not allow me to go along with my first instinct of wearing my old jeans and a baggy sweat-

20

shirt – that's being a Virgo for you. Can't stand a mess. I showered then slipped on my favourite midnight blue shift dress, leaving my shoulder length hair simply brushed back off my face, still damp. It would dry by itself as the evening wore on and I couldn't be bothered to get out the hairdryer.

Lillian pursed her lips with disapproval; "You'll catch your death of cold, going out like that."

A knock at the front door put paid to any further discussion, "Well, there's my date, so I'll have to take my chances. Let's hope his car has a heater."

I was mildly irritated when the door was opened to reveal David dressed in jeans and a sweatshirt. He looked me up and down, but surprisingly made no comment on how I looked. I had been ready with a sarcastic riposte had he been naff enough to make some trite remark about me looking nice, but I was rather piqued when he said nothing at all, merely smiling in a friendly manner and asking,

"All ready to go?"

"I'll just get my coat and handbag," I replied, a little stiffly.

"What about you Lillian? Where's your coat?" he asked, his attention completely taken by my aunt. I stared at him, open-mouthed. He had not asked me out at all. He'd invited both of us. He really was just being neighbourly. Thank God I hadn't taken him seriously, or I would be looking a real idiot now.

Lillian pushed him as forcibly as she was able, "Get away with you, you wretch. I don't dine out these days, and you know it."

"You should. You needn't worry, you know. We would all pretend not to notice when you got your zimmer frame out of the car!"

Lillian shrieked at the implication, "You cheeky so and so. I may be in my nineties, but I can still walk unaided."

She was still complaining when she thrust us out of the door, but I could see she loved every insult he heaped playfully upon her.

We walked down the lane in silence and when we reached his car, though he unlocked the passenger side for me first, he didn't attempt to open the door for me, or help me in. If he had I would have been annoyed, but when he didn't, I was still irritated. He executed a practised three point turn, which spoke of great familiarity with the road, the headlights sweeping across the enclosing hedges, then the car bumped off down the lane, he pausing only to ask, "Are you warm enough?"

"Yes, thank you." I half hoped my stiff reply would provoke him into

21

asking me what was wrong, so I could give him a lecture on his lack of respect for my great aunt, but he seemed quite content to accept my response.

"Good. I hope you weren't expecting anything flashy tonight. We are just going to the little local Italian restaurant. All the really posh places are too far afield to bother with."

"Italian will be fine, thank you."

He gave me a sideways glance, grinning broadly, "Are you always this polite?"

My lips twitched in spite of myself, I mean, how do you resist a comment like that? "No. Are you always that rude?"

"To Lillian, you mean? Always! Don't let it bother you, she loves it."

"I could see that."

"Then what's the problem?"

I suddenly realized there wasn't one.

The restaurant was just the sort I liked, small and cosy, full enough to be atmospheric, but not over-crowded and full of smoke and chatter, as most places in London were. He was evidently well known there and was greeted warmly. I felt myself being perused, but not in an unpleasant way – they just wanted to know who I was – and probably if I was up to Mr. Wright's usual standard.

Our table was tucked away in a quiet corner, but not so far away from the other diners as to be embarrassingly intimate. I found myself quickly relaxing. A glass of house white and I felt positively expansive.

"I wonder how many of your conquests you've brought here?" I asked with a giggle, then stopped, horrified, wishing I could have bitten out my tongue! God, what had possessed me to say that out loud? I knew nothing about the man.

He smiled, entirely unabashed, and replenished my glass, "All of them," he answered frankly.

Of course that reply merely made me want to ask exactly how many that encompassed, so I took another sip of wine to plug my mouth and prayed for the starters to arrive.

"How long are you planning to stay with Lillian?" he enquired politely, but I had the distinct impression he could plainly see my discomfiture and was revelling in it.

"I've taken all my annual leave of three weeks, but when that is up, I shall have to do a rethink."

"I'm told you are a journalist."

"Nothing so exciting. I'm a PA with pretensions to a real journalist."

"How do you find London?"

"Straight up the motorway and there it is." The giggle which accompanied this witticism alerted me to the fact that I'd better ease off the vino.

He grinned widely, more, I suspected, at the state I was in than amusement, "Okay, I'm obviously doing very badly here – you choose the next topic of conversation."

Suddenly serious I looked at him, "Do you mind if I say something?"

"I'm hoping you will – or it could turn out to be a very boring evening."

"No, I mean something personal. I just feel the need to make my position clear. Of course, I may be way off, and you can take great delight in shooting me down in flames, but I just want you to know that there's no way I'm even slightly interested in you – I'm sure you're a nice guy and all that, but I've just finished a long term relationship and the last thing I'm looking for is more complications..."

"I understand completely," he said, not in the least put out by my candour, "In fact, if it makes you feel any better, you can pay for your own dinner."

For a minute I thought he was annoyed and was being deliberately nasty – posh London types always seemed to take a rebuff, not matter how politely framed, as a personal insult. I opened my mouth to give him back as good as he gave, then I caught the glint in his eye and we both began to laugh, "All right, all right! I'm a big head for thinking you were chasing me. I apologise for mistaking friendliness for a chat-up line and now we have set all that aside, we can get on with dinner."

He grinned, "No, really, I do understand. I felt the same way when my marriage broke up. I couldn't have touched another woman with a barge pole."

"I don't suppose you could have found one who would have wanted you to!" I said.

"Sad but true. Anyway, let me reassure you, I'm not on the trawl either. I drop in on your aunt because I like her, but I'm too busy getting my business up and running to expend energy on a long-term relationship. I asked you out tonight because Lillian left me with absolutely no choice whatsoever."

Having tried my utmost to fend the man off, I now found I was horribly offended to find that he hadn't been remotely interested in me in the first place.

"Thanks a lot," I said huffily, "Do you have any more smacks in the

23

mouth to offer, or is that my lot for tonight?"

"What?"he looked vaguely startled.

"It's all very well telling me you don't want a relationship, but to admit I'm one of the women who require a barge-pole."

He laughed good-naturedly, "That's not what I meant and you know it. God, you women are hellish creatures. You are a very attractive young lady, and I'm honoured you agreed to have dinner with me, but I don't have any dishonourable intentions towards you. Does that just about wrap everything up neatly for you?"

I was slightly mollified, "It will be when I have ordered the most expensive thing on the menu". I said.

"Order what you like," he said baldly, "We've already agreed you are paying for your own."

I couldn't help it, childish as it was, I threw a piece of bread stick at him, "Very amusing." I said, but I was smiling in spite of myself.

CHAPTER THREE

Lillian was in bed when we arrived back. David had insisted on accompanying me up the lane, for which I was secretly grateful. London habits were still too strong upon me for me to want to risk walking up a dark road on my own at midnight. I was, of course, aware that the chances of there being a mugger or a rapist on this particular lane were fairly remote, even so, I was glad of the sound of his firm tread beside me – and even more grateful that he didn't do anything so utterly tasteless as try to hold my hand, or worse still link arms with me.

When we reached the door, purely out of politeness I said, "Do you want to come in for coffee?" To which he replied, deadly serious, "Would that be wise, do you think? I wouldn't want you to get the wrong idea."

"Wrong idea about what?" I asked suspiciously.

"About me. I wouldn't want you to think I'm easy. Accepting coffee after the first date."

"Oh, shut up and get inside."

He perched on a kitchen stool and watched me as I made the drink, unnerving me slightly, though I would not have let him know it for the world.

"Only instant, I'm afraid. I must nip into town and buy a few things – most importantly a cafetierre. I don't think I can stand much more of this stuff Lillian buys. She only drinks tea so this is specially bought in for guests and it is truly foul."

"It's not that bad. I drink it twice a week and I'm not dead yet."

I rather wished he hadn't said that because it reminded me uncomfortably of Decima Watkins and somehow I didn't want to go to bed on thoughts of a Victorian murderess.

"I suppose it would be terribly easy to poison people who trust you," I mused quietly, hardly aware that I had spoken out loud until his exclamation of mock-horror alerted me to the fact.

"God! If that's your train of thought, I'll swerve round the coffee."

I laughed and carried the two steaming mugs through to the lounge, motioning him to follow, "Sorry, I didn't mean to say that. It's just that Aunt Lil has been telling me horror stories of a mass poisoning in Victorian times. I was just thinking how easy it really is to adulterate food and drink. Unless you had reason to be suspicious, you would just eat and drink anything you were offered, wouldn't you?"

He took his coffee and thought about it for a moment before saying, "I suppose we take an awful lot of things on trust. As you say, the easiest person to poison is the one nearest to you – unless you had already given them reason to think you might wish them ill."

"They are also the easiest to lie to," I murmured, thinking of Brendan.

"Is that the sound of a guilty conscience, or were you the one who was lied to?" he asked softly.

It occurred to me to tell him to mind his own business, but suddenly I didn't want him to think I might have been the wrong-doer instead of the wronged – that worrying about what the neighbours think again. "Lied to," I said briefly, "But let's not dwell on that, shall we? I came here partly to get away, not to relive it all."

We drank in silence for a few minutes, then he seemed to make a sudden decision, "You weren't entirely wrong about this dinner," he said quietly, "Lillian did plan it, but not for the reasons you think."

I raised what I like to think was a quizzical brow at him and said, "Go on, I'm listening."

"She wanted me to meet you – but not for purposes of romance."

"I'm very relieved to hear it, but if that wasn't the reason, what was?"

He gave a wry half-smile, "I met your sister and your mother a couple of months ago."

I laughed a trifle bitterly, "That explains a lot. I suppose Lil wanted to prove to you that I'm nothing like mum and Maddie?"

"Something like that," he admitted cagily, "I must say they did not make a particularly good impression."

"I imagine they insulted you appallingly, if I know them."

"It wasn't quite that bad, but I was made to feel like an interloper."

"That figures – but what the hell were they doing here – I presume they were here?"

"Oh yes. I don't go into Manchester unless I'm forced."

"Then why were they here?"

He took another sip of coffee, carefully weighing his words, "I don't think it is my place to tell you that – and to be quite honest, I don't know the full details, but Lillian did give me a brief outline. I can only suggest you ask her about it."

"I intend to," I told him grimly, "In the meantime, you can't leave me on tenterhooks. At least give me a clue."

"Lillian did not say much – quite rightly. It's none of my business. But I got the distinct impression it was something about signing the house over to them. Apparently they were concerned about death duties – and the house having to be sold should Lillian have to be taken into Local Authority care when she became too ill to be left at home alone."

This I had not been expecting, and my mouth fell open in an unbecoming gape, "*What?* The absolute bitches. How dare they come bullying her. I knew they always wanted to get their sticky fingers on this place, but you would have thought they'd at least have waited for her will to be read."

"I don't think they were seeing it quite that way," he protested, determined to be fair, "After all, from what I understand, the house has been in the family for several generations. It would be sad to see it pass out of your hands for the sake of a principle."

"Huh! You don't know my sister. She and mum have always hated it up here. Can you really see their silk knickers flapping in the breeze out on the hillside, having been hand-washed in cold well water? This place would be sold to some yuppie before Lil was cold in her grave."

"Actually I can't imagine either of them referring to their nether garments as 'knickers', but that is neither here nor there. I think you are over-reacting a bit," he said calmly.

I had the grace to blush slightly at having allowed myself to be betrayed into vulgarity in front of a man I hardly knew, so there was a defensive edge to my tone when I asked, "Well, have you ever seen either of them up here before?"

"No – but I've never seen you here, either."

I was stumped for a moment by this candour, then countered triumphantly, "Yes, but I'm not trying to take the house away from my aunt."

"That's what Lillian was trying to convince me of when she arranged this meal."

I was inclined to be huffy at this disclosure, "So, I've been on trial, have I? Charming! And I don't see what it has to do with you, anyway."

"Nor do I, but Lillian seems to trust my judgement, so I went along with

27

it. After all, it's not often she asks me to do her a favour – and I could hardly be churlish enough to refuse, in the circumstances."

"Hmm! And have you reached any conclusions?"

"Suffice it to say I felt I could confide in you," he said coolly.

"That's mighty big of you." My reply was anything but cool.

He put his cup down on a convenient table, "Never let it be said I did not know when I had outstayed my welcome. I'll probably see you later in the week. Goodnight."

I let him go without bothering to see him out, but as soon as I heard the door close behind him, I leapt to my feet and ran to secure the back door. I was still a little nervous of being so far from civilization and though I knew it was highly unlikely that a mad axe-man was lurking outside, waiting for David to leave the house, I still wanted to know I was safely locked inside.

I was startled by a thudding sound upstairs, then alarmed. God, I hope Lillian hasn't fallen, I thought in a mild panic, and began to run towards the stairs, calling her name softly as I went.

When I had reached the wide landing and there was still no reply I became puzzled. Surely aunt Lil had heard me call? I went to the old lady's door and tapped gently, "Lil? Aunt Lil? Are you alright?" Still no reply. I opened the door as quietly as I was able and by the stream of light which swept across the room as the door swung open, I was able to see my aunt, fast asleep in her big old double bed – the same one she had shared with her husband, and where she had given birth to the son she had lost in the war. At first I was inclined to be worried that she was so deeply asleep that she had heard neither the thudding sound, nor my voice, but then I noticed the selection of prescription medicines and pills on the bedside table and suddenly, sickeningly, I understood – understood, but was distressed. I suppose I hadn't quite realized Lil was in enough pain to be requiring that battalion of bottles. I closed the door and turned to go to my own room.

The sound of the thudding brought me to a sudden halt. It sounded just like someone falling to the ground, but it did not emanate from Lil's room, nor any room on this floor. It seemed to come from the attics. From where I was standing, I could see the white-painted panelled door which enclosed the stairs to the attics. The brass knob seemed to glisten slightly, almost temptingly, in the soft glow of the forty watt bulb Lil kept constantly burning on the otherwise dark landing.

My heart began pounding so hard that I felt sure that even Lil must hear it and wake up; I stared in fascination at the door. I knew I ought to go and investigate. To prove to myself that the noise was just the result of squirrels in the roof, or a skylight left open causing a door to bang – but I simply could not move. If this were a novel or a film I would boldly snatch open the door and stomp up the stairs, only to find the squirrels or the window – but this was real and I was a woman who had never managed to watch "Rosemary's Baby" beyond the opening credits because I had been utterly convinced something horrible was going to come out of the hall cupboard and wreak the usual blood-stained havoc.

I waited, my nerves taut and ready to send me into flight, but the sound never came again and after a few seconds I began to calm down. After all, I wasn't alone. Lil was there in the room behind me. I fought a childish desire to sneak under the covers with my aunt, knowing I couldn't do it. Poor Lil needed every bit of sleep she could get – even if it was with the aid of pills. She certainly didn't need some hysterical half-wit gibbering in the bed beside her because of noises in an old house. Weren't all old houses supposed to creak and groan in the night? That was why all those stupid horror films were set in them. I doubted even I would be scared of a ghost story set in a tower block in broad daylight. There were much scarier things than ghosts inhabiting most inner cities.

I went to my room, foolishly relieved to close the door behind me. I felt safe in here, though I couldn't imagine why. As I undressed and took off my necklace and earrings, I thought about what David Wright had told me. I could hardly believe Maddie and our mother had even been to see Lillian, but to ask her to sign the house over to them was just horrible. Lillian was no coward, and she knew she was dying, but it seemed highly unsavoury to rub her nose in the fact by asking her to give away her house before she was even gone. I could not understand how my relations had been so hard-faced about the whole thing, but the more I mulled over past slights and unpleasant incidents, the more convinced I became that they were more than capable of doing anything which would ensure their own comfort.

The trouble was I had allowed these memories to slip away from me; had forgiven and forgotten, because in London I had been mostly out of reach. Only seeing them once or twice a year had meant I had been able to let things go. I knew I should have made more time and effort to see Lil, but it would have been hard to come to Derbyshire without going the extra few miles into Cheshire to see my mother and that I certainly hadn't wanted to do. It was easier to pretend I was too busy at work to travel North at all.

I climbed into bed and switched off the lamp beside the bed, but though I felt utterly exhausted and still more than a little tipsy from the wine at dinner, sleep again eluded me. I began to brood on the way my mother and sister had ganged up on me, how I had always been made to feel odd and awkward because I did not share their interests or like their snobbish friends. Almost against my will I found myself raking up incidents that had been over and forgotten for years. It was as though I was a little girl again, snuggled into a lonely little bed after some petty quarrel with my sister, when I had been blamed and sent to my room. I felt the same over-powering sense of injustice and boiling hatred and fury. *I wish I was dead then they would all be sorry! I wish I had three wishes and I would inflict the same hurt on them as they have on me! I wish they were dead and couldn't bully me anymore!*

It was when that thought came into my mind that I sat up with a gasp of shock and fumbled for the button to switch on the light. What the hell was going on? I was acting like a five-year-old. I hadn't felt this way for years and years. I was not sure I ever had. My childhood had not been particularly idyllic – but whose was? My sister and I had bickered, but the age gap of seven years had meant that we basically moved in different circles. If there had ever been any real tension between us it had been after we were grown up, not when we were children – and the same went for my mother. I had been closer to my father anyway and had been like most kids, utterly accepting of my mother's vagaries until I had left home and met other women of a similar age and type and realized that my mother wasn't actually a very pleasant person – but it had been a slow process and not one which I had found particularly distressing.

This just wasn't like me at all. I didn't recall ever having wished anyone dead in my life – and certainly not my family.

I swallowed deeply, feeling strangely unclean and unpleasant. It was almost as though I had been having someone else's emotions running through my mind, someone else's anger flooding me with bile. I didn't like it, but I didn't know how to stop it. As soon as I stopped fighting off the thoughts that were entering my head, they came galloping back, one after the other, until I felt almost dizzy with the speed of them, and sick at the increasingly vicious turn they were taking.

Suddenly I couldn't stand any more. I threw back the covers and without even waiting to put on a dressing gown or slippers, I raced down the passage to Lil's room and dived into the bed beside her. The old lady stirred slightly in her sleep, but she did not wake. Even though I knew Lil was entirely unaware of my presence, I felt better. Lil's body was relaxed, her breathing deep and soporific. Almost before I knew it, I felt myself drifting off to sleep. The image of my mother and sister did not even enter my head, though only minutes before I had seen nothing but the two of them, their faces contorted with anger and hatred, looking at me as a pair of witches might look at a toad just before they threw it into the cauldron.

❦

CHAPTER FOUR

I could not have been more relieved when I woke up before Lillian had even stirred and was able to slide carefully out of the side of the big bed and pad off softly back down the passageway to my own room.

My night fears now seemed unutterably babyish and to have to explain to the pragmatic old lady why I had needed someone to cuddle would have been painfully embarrassing, to say the least.

I had so much to ask I hardly knew where to begin. If I was honest, I was pretty livid that so much had been kept from me and I was more than ready for a showdown, but when Lillian came down and joined me in the kitchen about half an hour later, I found myself incapable of anger. Lillian looked tired and drained – and it really was the first time the old lady had ever given any indication of being anything other than full of life and vitality. I didn't know if it was because she did look particularly bad, or it was because I had seen for myself the evidence of illness last night in the shape of those bottles of pills and potions. Whatever the reason, I knew I had to back off, for the moment at least. Instead of asking about my mother and sister, I opted for the altogether less dangerous subject of the attic.

"Tell me, Aunt Lil, is there any chance there could be some sort of a draught or open window in the attics?"

"I don't think so," answered Lillian absent-mindedly, pouring herself a cup of strong tea from the pot I had automatically made when she entered the room. I couldn't help smiling to myself at the delicacy of the bone china cup and saucer. I had found the largest mug I could on my arrival and had been rinsing and reusing it ever since. Lillian was ever a lady, even in the privacy of her own home, "Why do you ask?" she added, as she sank into her rocking chair by the Aga.

"I thought I heard some noises up there last night when I came in. Thuds and bangs, that sort of thing. I thought it might be a banging window." I did my best to sound casual, and it seemed to work. Lillian apparently noticed nothing amiss, "I don't think so – I didn't hear a thing. But if you thought that, why on earth didn't you go up and investigate?"

I nearly choked on my tea. How could I possibly justify my stupid, irrational terror to a woman who had lived alone in this isolated house for most of her life? Lillian was going to think I was a half-wit.

"Well, it was quite late. It's hardly the done thing to wander around someone else's house in the middle of the night," I invented hastily.

Lillian seemed to accept this quite happily, "There's no need to feel that way, my dear. I want you to treat the place like home."

I took a thoughtful sip of tea. With the sunlight pouring through the windows, and the warmth issuing from the fire, this really did feel like home, but how long before another one of those unsettling little incidents began to twang at my nerves again?

"You'd better go up now," said Lillian, cutting across my thoughts, "Up where?" I asked bemusedly, having totally lost the train of conversation.

"Up to the attic, of course, to see if the windows are open. If the weather should turn rainy, I don't want wet patches everywhere."

"Are you coming?" I asked swiftly, having realized I could hardly refuse to perform this service for my aunt.

"I don't think so, love, if you don't mind. I feel really whacked today, for some reason. You know where everything is, you don't need me."

I don't think I had ever been more reluctant to do anything in my life. I kept telling myself I was being childish – and I felt it was true as I climbed the stairs and made my way along the passage. Everything was so normal, so ordinary. It was just a house, after all. Old – but lots of places were old – and I had been in many a one that was older. How could I be scared of my aunt's house, when I had tripped along the blood-soaked, torture-haunted chambers of the Tower of London, for example?

I didn't know – I only knew that scared I was. The feeling that something horrible was going to jump out and shock me persisted all the way along the landing to the very door or the attic stairs. It took all my courage to reach out my hand and grasp the brass knob.

Of course nothing happened. I climbed the stairs, slightly steeper than those on the first floor, and uncarpeted, but otherwise perfectly ordinary. They didn't even creak as I stepped on them.

The attics, as I had vaguely remembered, were another suite of rooms, but with the classic sloping ceilings. I recalled Lil telling me that they had housed servants in her grandmother's time – only a cook and 'tweeny' –

they hadn't been that rich, only slightly well-off middle-class. And it had been appallingly cheap to enslave young girls in those days.

Each room, as I came to it, showed white-painted walls, varnished wooden doors, bare floorboards and various boxes and old bits of discarded furniture. Obviously Lillian, living alone as she did, had had no need of the extra space. The rooms had evidently not been lived in for years. Someone obviously dusted and swept from time to time, because they were not particularly dirty or cobwebby, but there was that air of neglect and emptiness which hung around rooms not used. Every window was securely fastened and there was no discernible draughts or gaps in the walls or roof which could account for last night's noises.

Neither was there any atmosphere of chill or ghostliness. I didn't think I had ever been in four more ordinary rooms. They weren't particularly welcoming, but on the other hand, they didn't repel me either. I didn't think I would care to sleep up here, but that was more down to their lack of warmth and comfort than to any feeling of dread.

I actually gave a little 'huh' of ironic laughter. What a fool I had been to be so afraid last night. Obviously all the old tales of expanding boards creaking in the night were quite true. I'd put myself into a right old state over nothing at all.

When I heard my mobile phone ring, I automatically reached for my shoulder-bag to retrieve it, then realized I didn't have my bag with me – why would I? It was downstairs, by the chair in the sitting room, where I had left it last night. I hadn't used my mobile since my arrival; a quick call to let Joanna know I had driven safely and to tell her that I would ring again in about a week – in fact I was pretty sure I had turned it off, just in case Brendan should get any ideas about hassling me.

But the ringing was here, in this room which overlooked the hills at the back of the house. I glanced around, startled and puzzled and eventually guessed that the sound was coming from an old bureau which stood in the corner. The desk flap was shut and the key lay on the top, where once a glass-fronted bookcase must have stood. I could see the wood was a different colour and the screw holes that had secured the whole thing from toppling off.

With shaking fingers I picked up the key, turned it in the lock and, all the while listening to the persistent shrill of the phone, I dropped the flap to reveal an old-fashioned desk, pigeon-holes and all, the leather of the writing surface stained with ink, the gold-tooling faded by years of wear – and there, utterly incongruous, its discordant note still rending the quiet air, lay my mobile phone.

I grabbed it and ran.

❦　❦　❦　❦　❦

I was half way down the second flight of stairs before it occurred to me to answer it, but too late. As my trembling fingers quested for the right button, the ring cut abruptly off. I looked to see who had been the caller and when I recognized Brendan's number, I gave a disgusted snort, glad to have missed the message. He was the last person I wanted to speak to, especially in my present state of mind.

Lil looked up as I walked into the sitting room, "Well?"

"Well what?" I asked, still-shaken and perplexed. Lil stared at me as though I were a half-wit, "I thought I was the one who ought to be hurtling towards senility. Were there any open windows up there? You know, the reason why you went up to the attic in the first place."

"Oh! Oh no. Everything was shipshape – tell me, Aunt Lil, when was the last time you were up there?"

"Couple of weeks ago, why?"

"I found my mobile phone up there. I thought perhaps it had been ringing last night and you put it up there because you didn't know how to switch it off." This had been the theory I had formulated on the way down the stairs. I was stunned to find myself almost praying that it was true.

"I didn't even know you had a mobile phone – though I suppose it is obvious now that I think about it. You young people have all the latest mod-cons, don't you?"

"But if you didn't put it up there, who did?" I asked quietly.

Lillian laughed, "It probably fell out of your pocket whilst you were walking about. Either that or it was the poltergeist."

I wasn't laughing, "Do you have a poltergeist?" I asked breathlessly, then hastily amended the question – after all, I was supposed to be a mature adult who did not believe in anything that could not be scientifically proved to exist, "I mean, do you have a lot of odd incidents that you can't explain?"

"You always do in a house this old. But I usually put it down to my own failing memory, to be honest. Who's to say I didn't leave the keys in the fridge, or my slippers in the coal-shed?"

She meant it. I could see that she was entirely unfazed by the incident. But then she did not know that the phone had been lying inside a locked desk.

35

"Have you finished reading about Decima yet?" enquired Lillian, after a few moments of silence. I had been lost in thought and had to drag my attention almost painfully back to my aunt, "What? Oh no, not yet. I've read your stuff, but I didn't feel like trawling through the court case, to be perfectly frank. It's bad enough reading modern court cases, but the old-fashioned language makes it even more of a bind."

"You are still not convinced of her innocence, are you?" asked Lillian softly. I felt the moment had come to be honest, "No, I'm not. She seems to me to be a classic case of Munchhausen by proxy! Not that I know much about these things. I can't understand why you are so sure she was innocent. Nothing I've read so far has made me doubt the judgement of the court."

The words were barely out of my mouth when a tremendous crash upstairs made me start violently, "God! What the hell was that?"

Even Lillian looked a little concerned, "It sounded like a piece of furniture falling over."

"A bloody big piece," I asserted. The whole house had been shaken to its foundations by the noise. The china on the dresser had actually rattled and one cup that lay on its side was still rolling slightly on its saucer.

"You'd better go and inspect the damage," said Lillian.

"Are you not coming with me?" I asked, a little fearfully.

"Do you want me to?"

"Yes!"

We went up the stairs together, Lillian leading the way. I was sorry I had insisted on being accompanied when I noticed the old lady had to lean on the banister and rest for a few seconds half way up. When we reached the landing, we found the source of the noise. A large picture had fallen off the wall and lay face down on the floor, broken glass spread far and wide beneath and around it. Even though it was a sizeable portrait, at least five feet by four, and heavy with Victorian plasterwork on the gilded frame, I could not believe the noise it had made when it fell.

Lillian hoisted it upright and looked at the picture, "No real damage done, just broken glass. Odd it should have been that picture, though."

I looked at the Victorian worthy, vaguely familiar from my childhood, noting the grim visage and wealth-expanded waistline, "Why? Who is it?"

"Your great, great grandfather – Decima's darling daddy. He sent her to the gallows without a second thought."

"I don't blame him, if she killed several of his other children. Ouch!" This last exclamation was forced from me as my foot shifted and a shard of glass stuck into the side of my slippered foot.

"What is it?" asked Lillian, glancing at me.

I could scarcely reply. I had made the mistake of looking down and the sight of a large sliver of broken glass sticking out of the side of my foot had sent me dizzy and sick. I sank slowly down onto the top stair and lowered my head between my knees, "I think I'm going to pass out, Lil..." I admitted weakly.

I came round to find David Wright carrying me out to his car.

"Where ... are we going?" I said, trying to lick my dry lips so that I could speak more clearly.

"A and E," he answered tersely.

"I don't need that," I protested weakly, "It's only a little cut."

"It's not, you know. I haven't even dared pull the glass out. So what ever you do, don't knock your foot against anything. I'll try and get you there as quickly as I can, but it's a good drive and the rutted lane is going to be difficult to negotiate without jarring you, so hang on."

I could see further protest was useless, so I allowed him to lift me into the passenger seat, then I lay my head back and closed my eyes. To be honest, I still felt rather weird. When he spoke to me, his voice sounded as though it was coming from far away, and my eyes didn't seem to be focussing properly. Just for the moment, it was easier to go with the flow and let things happen to me without a struggle.

The next few hours passed in a blur. I vaguely remembered the drive, especially the potholes in the lane, which, as he had warned, tossed me from side to side, even though he drove at a ridiculously low speed, and seemed to force the glass further into my flesh with every bump. It almost felt as though the glass was hot, for it was a burning rather than a stabbing sensation and I was on the verge of fainting again by the time we reached the main road.

Fortunately we had chosen a time of day when the casualty department at the local hospital was enjoying a lull, so I did not have long to wait to be seen – not that I cared very much at that point. I let him carry me in, then sat with my eyes determinedly closed, partly to avoid the temptation to take another look at my gory injury, but mostly to discourage David from making conversation. I was still stinging from our parting conversation the night before, added to which I now felt a complete fool for having not only hurt myself, but then fainting like a big wimp. He left me lying on a trolley while he went to get himself a cup of coffee. When I heard the rattle of the curtains opening, I assumed it was him coming back and opened my eyes cautiously. It was not David, but a young doctor – and, just my luck, I thought bitterly, he had to be tall, dark and gorgeous. Why did you always meet the best men when you were feeling dreadful and looked as though you were half-dead?

"What can we do for you?" he asked heartily.

"Well, liposuction would be nice, but failing that, how about removing that lump of broken glass from my foot?"

He grinned in a friendly way, "It would be my pleasure – and I wouldn't bother with the liposuction, if I were you. Definitely not necessary."

He drew on his rubber gloves with that snap that always made me jump, then gingerly lifted my foot to get a closer look, "Very nasty. You'll be lucky if you haven't nicked a tendon."

"Thanks."

There followed a period of tedium whilst they discussed the next stage in my treatment, then down to x-ray. More waiting for the results, then a pain-killing injection followed by yet more waiting for it to start to numb my foot. David was the soul of patience, leaving when required, and coming back to keep me company during the waiting times. When the doctor finally came back to remove the glass David decamped hastily, so I decided to ask him a few questions. I told myself it was to keep my mind off the sickening feeling of knowing the shard was being drawn slowly out of my flesh and the poking around in the wound to make sure there were no bits of glass left in there, but I knew there was more to my curiosity than I was admitting.

"Tell me, doc, do you know anything about Munchhausen syndrome?"

He threw me a slightly startled glance, "You don't think you know anyone who has it, do you?" he asked cautiously.

"God, no!" I thought quickly, then came up with a plausible, if not strictly true excuse for my question, "No, I'm a writer, and sitting here has started me thinking about a possible plot line. I thought I might as well pick your brain whilst I had your undivided attention."

He smiled, "When you are no longer my patient, we can take that thought further if you like."

God, what a time to start flirting. I managed a weak smile back, "I'll think about it when I'm back on my feet – now, about Munchhausen ..."

"Well, it's an extremely rare condition, centred on the desire for attention."

"Do you think it existed in Victorian times?"

"The eighteen hundreds? I suppose it must have, but I don't think it was recognized in those days. I'm not entirely sure when it was first written up, but I can find out for you if it is important."

"No, the actual date doesn't matter. I just wanted to know if there was any evidence that it was a modern disease, caused by environmental pollutants or something like that."

"I hadn't read anything to suggest that."

"So, if a young woman in Victorian times was hanged for poisoning several members of her own family, then Munchhausen could have been a factor?"

"It could – but I have a theory that quite a lot of historical poisoners were in fact entirely innocent."

It was my turn to look startled, that word "innocent" seemed to keep coming back to haunt me – actually, on second thoughts, I didn't much care for the word "haunt", either.

"What do you mean?"

"Well, we now know there are many virulent food-poisoning bugs, but things were much simpler then. What you couldn't see, didn't exist. I wonder how many of the poor souls were hanged just because they were resistant to salmonella or botulism, but those around them weren't. The idea was if you were the only one who didn't die, you must have killed all the others. Very unfair, in my view."

I looked at him for a moment, but his attention was back on my foot and after a moment he said triumphantly, "All done. You just need the nurse to stitch it, then you can go home – but try to keep your weight off it for a few days."

"I thought you said I didn't need liposuction."

He laughed, "Take my word for it, you don't."

"Thanks – for the compliment, the treatment and the information."

"No problem. Hope to see you around." With that he was gone.

A couple of hours later I was on my way back to Lil's with David, my bandaged foot held stiffly out in front of me, my wrecked and bloodied slipper clutched in my hand. I didn't know why I had held on to it. The nurse had given it to me when the doctor had cut it off, with much tutting and expressions of sympathy. It had seemed churlish to hand it back and so I had gone back through x-ray (to make sure there were no bits of glass left in the cut) and suturing with the damn thing clutched in my hot little hands.

When we finally reached the car and he saw it resting on my knee he grinned in a friendly way, "Are you planning on cleaning and sewing that up and using it again?"

"God, no!" I said in disgust.

39

"Then allow me." He took it off me, opened the car door and tossed it into the nearest wastepaper bin.

"Thank you."

"My pleasure. Now, is there anything you require, or shall I drive you straight home?"

"It's hardly home. But, yes, back to Lil's, please."

He lifted a quizzical brow at me, "Do I detect a note of reluctance? I thought you liked being at Lillian's."

I very nearly confided in him about all the odd things that had been happening to me, but even as I opened my lips, I decided I couldn't bear to make a fool of myself again that day, "Oh, I do. It was just the thought of having to clear up all that broken glass. Especially on one foot."

"Don't worry about it. I'll do it when we get back – my business can run itself for a couple more hours."

"God, I'm so sorry. You must think me appallingly ungrateful. You've obviously dropped everything to come to mine and Lil's rescue and all I can do is whinge."

"It's okay. Don't be so touchy. I wasn't getting at you, you know – and I think I might whinge if I had a glass dagger plunged into my foot."

I was extremely startled by his choice of words, for they seemed to reflect a train of thought which I had been trying to deny for the past few hours, "What made you say that?"

"What?"

"That dagger thing, as though it was done on purpose and not by accident."

"What are you talking about? It was just an expression, something that popped into my head. I didn't mean anything sinister by it."

"Oh."

"Is there something you are not telling me, Libby?"

"No, of course not. How long will it take us to get back?"

"About forty five minutes."

"Can we get on, then? I'm absolutely starving. I haven't eaten since this morning."

"Do you want to stop and grab a bite somewhere?"

"No. Lil will be worrying – perhaps some other time, though."

"Sure. Hold tight, then, and I'll see how fast I can get you back."

"Just don't kill us in a car crash. I never want to see the inside of another hospital for as long as I live."

"I don't think you can guarantee that," he said reasonably, putting the car in gear and pulling away from the kerb.

"Why not? If I'm careful, I shouldn't need a hospital again."

"What about when you have babies?" he asked jovially.

I blushed to the roots of my hair and when he glanced sideways to see why I hadn't replied, he grinned unkindly and subsided into silence himself.

❦

CHAPTER FIVE

Back at the house, Lillian was waiting anxiously and almost ran down the path to meet us when she saw us from the window; David hovering uncertainly as I struggled up to the house, determined to use my crutches and not be carried again. I had had quite enough of playing the swooning Victorian miss. Unfortunately that comparison brought my thoughts neatly back to Decima Watkins, and made me curiously reluctant to go back into my aunt's house. I covered the feeling by being particularly jolly about my recent experiences, telling Lil gleefully about the handsome young doctor.

David listened impassively, then offered to go and make the tea whilst Lil settled the invalid into a comfy chair, my bandaged foot on a velvet cushion on à rush woven stool.

"How is it feeling now?" asked the old lady, as I sank gratefully into the chair and heaved a huge sigh.

"The numbing stuff hasn't worn off yet, so it's fine for the moment. But I bet it will sting later."

"I imagine it will. That was a daft trick, I must say. I still can't understand how you managed to spear yourself."

"Neither can I – by the way, David said he would sweep up the glass for you."

"He's a good boy, but I've already done it. I'm not as helpless as you two seem to think."

"I think nothing of the kind," I protested immediately, "On the contrary, I think it's probably me who's helpless. It looks as though I'm going to be stuck in this chair for a couple of days at least."

"Good, then you'll have no excuse not to finish reading about Decima."

David entered the room at that moment, bearing the tea tray, "Who is Decima?" he asked.

I tried to send a warning glance to Lillian, silently requesting that she did not tell David about our investigation, but Lil was looking in the other direction, "Hasn't Libby told you about our family mystery?" she enquired in genuine surprise, "I thought she'd have regaled you with the full story."

"Libby hasn't told me a thing," said David, in a curiously neutral tone.

"Oh! Oh well, it's something and nothing really. Just after my husband died, there seemed to be a sudden rash of elderly relatives going the same way, so I thought I ought to get their store of memories before it was too late – I think it was probably a way of coping with my grief – taking my mind off things, you know. Anyway, very reluctantly, they admitted we had something of a black sheep in the family. It seemed my great Aunt Decima had been hanged in the mid eighteen hundreds for poisoning several of her siblings. Intrigued, I started to read up about it and the more I delved, the more convinced I became that she hadn't done the murders. Sadly, what with the farm work, and other commitments, I never got any further than that, but in the last few months, it's started to play on my mind again. I know I can't leave things in limbo, so I've asked Libby to help me get to the bottom of the mystery."

David listened to this without giving any indication of his feelings on the matter, but I found myself cringing at the thought that he now knew I was descended albeit indirectly – from a hanged killer. For the first time in my adult life I found myself feeling vaguely in tune with my mother. Mum was right. These things were best left hidden in the shadows of time. There was something dreadful about knowing someone close had slain another human being. I was mortified and could barely bring myself to meet David's steady gaze.

"Fascinating," said Mr. Wright, after what seemed an eternity of silence,

"What's so fascinating?" I heard myself saying bitterly, "How would you like it if you found out Jack the Ripper was your granddad?"

Neither Lillian nor David seemed to hear the tremendous rapping sound emanating from the attic above their heads. I started violently when it began, then cold fear gripped my stomach when they both totally ignored it and it became increasingly obvious they couldn't hear it. The noise was aimed at me. The frantic, steady thrumming was for my ears alone – either that or I was going completely mad.

It stopped as suddenly as it had begun, but still it seemed to echo in my ears, as loud noises sometimes do, even after the have ceased. Because I could almost still hear it, I began to unconsciously analyse what it had sounded like. Drumming heels on a wooden floor – suddenly I was hauled back in time, to when I was four or five. I had wanted something – so desperately that I had not been able to cope with the overwhelming feelings of anger and frustration. I had lain down on the floor and begun to kick my legs. Then I had found myself almost lulled by the rhythmic pattern of sound I had created – drumming my heels on the parquet floor of the hall – until it had been brought to a swift conclusion by the dealing of a sharp slap.

"Oh God," I whispered.

David glanced at me, his face showing concern, "What's wrong?"

I painfully dragged my attention back to the present, looking at him in confusion, hardly aware that I had spoken out loud, "What?"

"Is there something wrong? You've gone very white. Do you feel ill?"

I drew in a deep breath, struggling to keep calm; "It's my foot. I think the numbing stuff is wearing off. It was suddenly rather painful."

He rose to his feet, "You could do with a rest. I'll pop back tomorrow, but if you need anything in the meantime, don't hesitate to ring me."

"Thanks – but I think you've done enough for one day."

"It's no trouble." With that he was gone.

Lillian looked askance at me, "What was all that about?"

"What do you mean?" I was overcome with weariness and apparently it showed. I closed my eyes and could barely get the words out of my mouth. Lillian at first was inclined to pursue the matter, but then she evidently decided to leave it. Perhaps she too had noticed how pale I was – I certainly felt pale, anyway.

I heard her get up and walk quietly out of the room, but was so utterly exhausted that I could not even summon the energy to open my eyes and witness the departure. I was too tired even to think, though it did strike me as vaguely odd, the speed with which this lethargy had over-taken me. I began to drift into that lovely, warm half sleep, where you knew the world was still there, but nothing contained within it really mattered. I was in what I laughingly call my 'happy place'. A sunlit field full of swaying grasses and beautiful wild flowers. It had begun when I had fallen into the current fad of meditation – listening to a cheesy relaxation tape, "...imagine you are in a field of poppies, surrounded by the light..." I had often wondered what would happen if someone suddenly yelled, "Go into the light!" You'd probably drop dead on the spot.

Then I wasn't in the field any longer. I was in a corridor, a long, dark passageway – dank. That was the word. It was cold, cold and wet, but not an outdoors sort of wet. The moisture seemed to seep from the walls as if it were underground, but more than that the atmosphere was dank too. It was as though misery and despair oozed from the dirty bricks along with the water.

As I walked along this interminable way, I felt my head sink lower, as though borne down by the weight of the anguish which assailed me on every side. It was then that I noticed my clothing. I wasn't wearing my jeans and those dinky little boots I had paid a small fortune for – nor was I limping on my bandaged foot. My toes were just visible with each step I took, encased in soft black leather, the eyelet holes with tiny jet buttons showing beneath the hem of a long, black silk dress, the soft frou-frou (how the hell did I know a word like that?) clearly audible above the tap of my heels.

Suddenly there was daylight ahead, but when I looked up I saw my way was barred – literally barred by a great iron gate. It swung open to reveal an open square, surrounded by imposing buildings and as I stepped out I found myself blinking and wincing against the pain of the transition from darkness into light. It took several seconds before my vision cleared sufficiently for me to see where I was and then the terror began to rise in my breast.

There were people there – a silent crowd, whose every eye was upon me, burning into me with hatred and accusation. I couldn't look at them and turned away, but that was even worse, for off to my left there stood a tall gallows, the nooses swaying slightly in the breeze.

I felt someone approach from behind, felt myself seized by rough and uncaring hands, then pinioned securely with leather straps. I wanted to scream and struggle, to fight off the man who was binding me – even though I couldn't see him, I knew it was a man, for I could hear his laboured breathing and smell his sweat. I had the sudden, horrified certainty that he was enjoying what he was doing, that he got some perverted kick from my helplessness.

A hand in the middle of my back forced me to walk forward to the steps of the wooden dais and I stumbled, almost falling on my face, without my hands free to steady myself. I looked up, the misty sunlight telling me that it was early in the morning. Then I was at the foot of the steps and again I could see my feet as I climbed. How highly polished were the little shoes – and how tiny.

At the top other hands gripped my arms and shoulders, manoeuvring me into position, then my feet were strapped together, the voluminous folds of the dress carefully gathered in. Why was I just standing here, letting them do what they wanted? Even when the noose went over my head, catching my nose as it fell, seeming to scrape the delicate flesh with its roughness, I did nothing, said nothing. No screaming, no fighting, no cursing, no struggle, just an overwhelming feeling of sorrow, of emptiness, despair and lethargy.

45

A voice behind me spoke softly to me, "In the name of God, in whose presence you are about to appear, I adjure you to make your guilt known."

I answered in a voice that was not my own, "Before God, then, I die innocent."

Then the floor dropped from beneath my feet and I was plunged into a dark and terrifying abyss.

With a gasp which was almost a strangled scream, I jerked awake. God, what a horrible dream.

Even as I looked about me, seeing the still glowing embers of the dying fire, the afternoon sun lighting the room with its warm redness, the old familiar pictures on the walls, the soft comfort of the cushions on the chair in which I sat, I could not shake off the emotions the dream had left with me. I wanted to weep. To cry and cry until I had no tears left.

And more than that I wanted revenge. Greater than my sadness there was wave after wave of anger – the raw, wild heat of overwhelming fury.

I had never felt this way before. I seemed to hate everyone – everyone I knew, everyone I didn't know. I wanted to smash their smug faces, destroy their comfortable lives. If I could have risen from my chair and torn the room apart, I would have done. I would have rent cushions, delighting in the vision of their spilled fillings, like the innards of gutted animals. I would have smashed glass and china, trampling their beauty beneath my little, leather-clad feet...

It was this thought that brought my mind back to reality. I didn't have little, leather-clad feet. I was a good size six – and only then at a vain crush. And at that moment one foot was swathed in bandages.

"Aunt Lil!" I roared, suddenly afraid to be alone, "Aunt Lil! I need you!"

When Lil came in she must have been astounded to find herself dragged into a panicked embrace by her hobbling niece, "Help me into the kitchen, Lil. I need a drink."

"I can bring you a cup of tea in here, dear," she pointed out reasonably.

"No! I'm not staying in here – and I need more than tea." I said, scrambling towards the door as fast as my bandaged foot would allow.

❦

CHAPTER SIX

When I had sunk two large glasses of wine in quick succession, the dream began to fade, though I could not completely shake off the feeling that I had actually been experiencing Decima Watkins' last moments on earth. I knew it was stupid, unlikely, very probably impossible and just the product of a tired brain filled with prescription drugs, but still the emotions persisted.

The trouble was it had been all too horribly real. I had never before had a dream where I had been so aware of the sensations of heat and cold and the smells associated with the places I was seeing. It was the cohesion of the scenes, following on, one after the other, in perfectly regimented and sensible acts – like watching a television programme or a film.

Always in the past my dreams had been piecemeal at best, positively jumbled and mad at worst. I didn't recall ever having a dream that told a story with any logical sequence. Half the time the action changed swiftly from one place to another, containing faces I didn't know, but who represented people I did.

The only thing I didn't understand was the fact that there had been a crowd of people watching me (or was it her?) walk to my death. I had always thought hangings took place in private – and indoors, surely? Hadn't they always nailed a note on the prison door, telling the gathered ghouls outside that the sentence of death had been carried out – usually at some ungodly hour of the morning?

I had wanted to ask Lillian, but couldn't find the words, so instead, once my nerves felt steady enough, I had gone back into the sitting room and pulled an encyclopaedia off the shelves.

Under the word 'hanging' I had found what I had been looking for – but it prompted more questions than it answered. It seemed public hangings had only ceased in 1868, prior to that the gallows were exposed, situated outside the prison walls, and often more than one execution took place at a time. It was not uncommon for a crowd of thirty thousand or more to gather and witness the death throes of the criminals – including women and children. I could scarcely believe what I was reading, but it was true, every word. Both Dickens and Hardy had apparently attended executions in their youths and both had evidently been profoundly affected by the experience.

Decima would undoubtedly have kicked her life away at the end of a rope observed by a horde of onlookers – her own family might very well have been in attendance.

I closed the book, feeling slightly sick. I had thought the antics on shows like Jerry Springer had been the depths to which some people would plunge in pursuit of kicks. Apparently parading your innermost secrets before an audience of millions was nowhere near as exciting as taking the wife and kids to see a young girl hanged by the neck until she was dead.

It was my intense pity for Decima that made me pick up the sheaf of notes again. Perhaps she had killed her sisters, perhaps she had not – but the utter despair and humiliation of those final moments made me recognize the need to know the truth, once and for all.

"Decima Watkins was indicted at the Assizes on April 23rd, 1859, for that she, on various dates on and around October 1856 to November, 1858, feloniously and unlawfully did administer to and cause to be administered to Phyllida Burton, nee Watkins, Charity Nevins, nee Watkins, and Jemima Stillman, nee Watkins, certain deadly poison (to wit arsenic) with intent the said persons to kill and murder.

The case was started by Mr. Fairfax Aylward, barrister, after which Mr. Jacob Watkins, father of the accused, took the stand and deposed as follows:

"I state that the prisoner here held is my youngest daughter, Decima Watkins. Her age is twenty-two years and she is unmarried. On or around the 18th October 1856, she was requested by her mother to make and serve tea to three of her older sisters, who were visiting. She did so and within hours all three and their mother were taken ill with stomach cramps and sickness. On this occasion she remained unscathed, but it seemed all the others had taken milk in their tea, but Decima had taken lemon. On several occasions thereafter various members of the family were taken ill after eating or drinking in our household. Decima herself was mildly ill on two occasions, but never with the severity which affected her sisters. The following year saw the deaths of Charity and Jemima. Decima was apparently devastated by their loss and was sent into Derbyshire to visit her

grandmother to recover. Phyllida was taken ill whilst she was away and died also."

Upon being asked how Decima could possibly be responsible for the death of Phyllida whilst she was not even in the same county, Mr. Watkins replied that Phyllida had been ill since the last occasion which had killed her sisters and had never recovered."

I reached for a pen and paper. I wanted to collate this information in a way which I could understand more easily. All these 'thences' and 'thereafters' were making me dizzy.

I wrote down the names of the siblings first – and fine old-fashioned names they were, too.

Adelaide, Percy, Jabez, Phyllida, Charity, Aloysius, Martha, Jemima, Job and Decima. Of those, only Decima, Percy and Job were unmarried and without offspring. I knew, from family history, that I was descended from Adelaide on my father's side and Lil from Martha. Percy took very little part in the story since he was in the army and was away for most of the time. His major contribution to events was to bring home Richard Allingham on one of his furloughs. Until she met Richard, it seemed Decima had been quite content with her lot in life. She had reportedly adored her young nephews and nieces, and had been happy to act the part of maiden aunt.

If Allingham had been a friend of Percy, he was perhaps quite a few years older than Decima and I found myself wondering if he had returned her affection. It could have been, of course, that she had a schoolgirl crush on a man who didn't even know she existed.

I found myself scanning the pages to see if this question could be answered. It was – in a way.

Mr. Watkins was asked, during cross examination by Mr. Horton Brookes, for the defence, *"Had your daughter ever shown any inclination towards disobedience before these incidents, sir?"*

"On the contrary, she had been exemplary. Her mother and I rarely had cause to chastise her. She was shy to the point of being irritating! She had the usual cross words with her brothers and sisters, as might be expected in any family, but the older she grew, the more insular she became. Frankly her mother and I had decided that she was altogether too sensitive to be allowed out into the world. It was our intention to keep her at home and to protect her from the sufferings she must surely endure if ever the day came that she was to leave the haven of our home."

"Is it not true that she was in fact forced into this role in life, and did not choose this way? Punishment was swift and terrible should she ever dare to show her true feelings!"

"If you are seeking to suggest that I am somehow at fault for disciplining my children, then I suggest you look no further than the dock to see how youth can be corrupted when it lacks a firm hand! Decima should never have been allowed to consort with Richard Allingham! I trace all our woes to his advent in our lives! Sadly it did not occur to me that Decima was old enough to engage the interest of a man of his age and background! Would to God that he had been killed before he had the opportunity to seduce my daughter!"

This comment caused one of the few reactions observed in the defendant. For the most part of the trial, she sat with her eyes demurely lowered, her hands neatly folded in her lap, but when her father spoke these words, she raised her eyes and looked at him with utter loathing.

Mr. Brookes appeared not to notice his client's demeanour, but instead pursued the comment made by the witness, "Are you stating, sir, that your daughter was involved in an unsavoury liaison with Major Allingham?"

Mr. Watkins' countenance grew ruddy with a mixture of annoyance and humiliation, "Certainly not!" he blustered, "I meant 'seduce' in a much broader sense!"

"I know of no other meaning of the word, sir. Pray enlighten us!"

"I meant that she was encouraged away from the path of righteousness, ordered to defy her parents and deny her duty!"

Mr. Brookes consulted his notes, "It is true, is it not, that you were instrumental in having Major Allingham sent back to his battalion, effectively preventing his marrying your daughter – and, as a tragic consequence, sending him to his death?"

Decima leapt to her feet and leaned upon the rail in front of her, a sob escaping her lips and her eyes burning into her father's face. He avoided her glance and seemed relieved when the warder gently forced the girl back into her seat.

"It is quite true, sir, and I might add, I have no regrets! Major Allingham had no right to try and entice my daughter away from her family. Her future had been decided – and marriage did not enter into our plans! Decima's duty was to serve her parents, not to think of her own selfish whims!"

Brookes seemed genuinely horrified by this pronouncement, "You seriously expected that poor child to deny her every desire and ignore her very natural instincts merely for your convenience? You fully intended to prevent her ever marrying and having children of her own?"

"As her father I had every right to decide her fate! She was fully occupied with the care of her siblings' children, and later her nurturing instincts would be utilized by my wife and myself when age overwhelms us! If she had possessed one scrap of family feeling, the slightest amount of honour, any other course would have been unthinkable! Does not the Bible tell us, 'honour thy father and thy mother'? What honour has she done us now?"

Mr. Brookes looked at the man with a contempt which almost equalled his young client's, "No further questions, My Lord."

Phew! I thought, I had been held almost spellbound by this exchange between the man who was trying to save Decima and the man who had fathered her. Of the two, I definitely preferred Mr. Brookes. He really seemed to care what happened to the girl – and to understand why she had ended up in the dock. Almost against my will, I was beginning to understand it too. I had started this investigation with the greatest reluctance, convinced that the law could not have been wrong and that Decima Watkins had deserved to face the consequences of her actions, but now I was not so sure. The kid really did seem to have everything against her. Not allowed to show her temper, not allowed to voice, or even have, an opinion, and finally not even allowed to fall in love and get married. No wonder she had gone off her trolley! If indeed she had. Perhaps Lillian was right. Perhaps some other member of what seemed to be a severely dysfunctional family, had dosed the tea with arsenic.

Just a minute, had it been arsenic? I couldn't actually recall whether I had read that or merely assumed it. It was a fair assumption, after all. Arsenic had always seemed to feature in Victorian melodrama. And if it was the world-famous poison, where had she obtained it? Hadn't there been safeguards put in place to prevent so many poisonings? What year had the Poisons Register come into being?

I pulled the encyclopaedia off the shelf again, this time the word 'poison' was the target. Yes, I had been quite right. The Arsenic Act of 1851 had decreed that anyone selling arsenic had to record the sale in a book, following a set pattern. This action had to be performed immediately, before delivery of the poison could be completed. Arsenic had to be distinctively coloured (usually with soot) to help in its detection if it was used criminally. The purchaser, or a witness to its sale, had to be known to the seller. Summary conviction and a fine to a maximum of £20.0.0. was the penalty for not conforming. It didn't sound like much now, but I assumed it was a hefty sum in 1851.

Decima's alleged crimes had taken place between 1856 and 1858, so she must have abided by the poison rules – so where did she get the poison – and had it been arsenic?

Frustratingly, just as I was beginning to shuffle through the papers to see if I could find out, my mobile began to ring.

Odd, because I could have sworn I'd left it turned off – anyway, more from habit than anything else, I picked it up without looking and answered it.

"Hello, darling, feeling any better?"

Damn! Brendan. Why the hell hadn't I checked to see who it was before answering? Well, I might as well speak to him now that he was through, but it would definitely be the last time.

"Hello, Brendan – and don't darling me. What do you want?"

"That's not very friendly, my sweet. I only want to know when you are coming home. I think we've had enough of this silly display of temper now, don't you?"

"Brendan, I'm only going to say this once, so listen well. We are finished, over. For good. I may come back to London, but I won't be coming back to you, is that clear?"

There was a short silence, then his oily tones slid down the phone towards me, "So, it's going better with Farmer Bill than I thought. How quaint."

For a minute I couldn't quite believe what I was hearing. He knew about David Wright – Farmer Bill could not possibly refer to anyone else – and anyway, I hadn't seen another man. I felt faintly sick, "Where are you, Brendan?"

"Right outside your door, my sweet. Want to let me in?"

"Not really."

"I think perhaps you better had."

I didn't really have much choice in the matter, did I? I knew by now that Brendan was perfectly capable of sitting outside the house all day if necessary – and should he decide to get drunk, more than likely he would start to smash windows and uproot shrubbery. Brendan never directed his violence towards human beings, he was too afraid of getting punched back, but the latent menace was always there, just simmering below the surface, so there was always that hidden fear that one day he might lose control and direct his blows where he really wanted them to land. I couldn't subject Lil to a scene.

Dear God, what had I ever seen in the maniac? He'd been so utterly charming at first, that lovely Irish lilt to his voice, the sea-green eyes! He'd hidden his true personality well. And then, of course, once men like him have you in their power, the slow, sure, subtle erosion of your confidence begins. The arguments, the apologies, the promises to atone, then suddenly every quarrel is your fault – you are so hard to live with, no other man will ever put up with your sulks and your tantrums. It doesn't help when you have a mother and a sister who agree with every word he says. When everyone who is supposed to love you starts to criticize your every action, it doesn't take long to convince you what a horrible person you are.

I still don't know how I suddenly found the strength to break away. Perhaps it was when Lillian made it obvious she wanted me, above all the others, to spend her last days with her. That small kindness finally produced the crack through which the flood could suddenly burst. Things had suddenly become very clear.

As soon as I opened the door, it was obvious nothing had changed for him. He greeted me with that lop-sided grin, half-arrogant, half-apologetic – he really knew how to turn it on. He must have bonked the Blarney Stone, not just kissed it.

"Lovely Libby. How I have missed you."

"Bollocks! Brendan, why don't you just sod off back to London and leave me alone?"

"Couldn't do that sweetheart. Don't you know yet that we are soul mates? I was meant for you – now how about a coffee. It's perishing out there. What the hell you see in these God-forsaken hills, I'll never know."

"Keep your voice down. Aunt Lil is having a rest."

He grabbed me around the waist and pulled me against him, "Good, that gives us time to renew our acquaintance in the time-honoured fashion before she gets up..." He tried to kiss me, but found my lips firmly folded against the assault. I pushed him away, "How many different ways do I have to say it before you understand, Brendan? I have left you. I am not coming back. It is an ex-relationship. Dead, expired, pining for the fjords!" I shouldn't have joked, of course, because he found it an excuse to laugh, give me a swift hug, then sit down and gesture towards the kettle,

"Tea or coffee, I don't mind which."

I made him one of Aunt Lil's foul cups of coffee.

"How did you find me, Brendan? I'm damn sure I never told you where Aunt Lil lives."

He sipped the coffee and made a wry face, "Your sweet sister, of course.

53

Who else would tell me where you were? Certainly not that Hell-cat, Joanna – and speaking of your dear relations, you had better gird your loins for a visit. She and your mum are firing up their broom-sticks even as we speak. You've been a naughty little girl Libby. The whole family had agreed that Lillian needed to be sent to a hospice before you put your oar in and agreed to come and nurse her."

"Not the whole family. I'll bet dad was on my side."

"Since when has your father's opinion ever mattered? Anyway, I venture to suggest he's rather busy, entertaining his dolly-bird in the South of France."

"Elaine is hardly a "dolly-bird", as you so chauvinistically put it. She's forty if she's a day – and a very nice lady. I don't blame dad for taking her on holiday – and it's not as though he and mum are still married, is it?"

But I could have done with his support. Not that I would admit to Brendan that I was in any way worried about a visit from my mother and sister. They were formidable when they pooled resources – especially when there was money at stake – and money there was. I knew this sudden concern for Lil had nothing to do with her, but everything to do with the house we were now sitting in. They were desperate to have it signed over to them before Lil died and the whole place had to be sold to cover death duties.

That was something else that had become blindingly clear over the past few days. I was still mulling over this information when I suddenly became aware he was speaking again, "What?"

"I said, I hope you're not fooling yourself that Lil has any other motive in inviting you here than to use you. It seems she trawled around the whole family, cousins, nephews, nieces and all, before she found you were the only one willing to come here and look after her."

I didn't believe him – of course I didn't. Lil didn't have a dishonest bone in her body. When she said she'd asked me because she loved me, she had been speaking nothing but the complete truth. But I also knew that in my lowest moments his words were going to come back and haunt me – and what was more, he knew it too.

"I'd like you to leave now," I said coldly.

"A shag is out of the question, then?"

"Completely!"

I couldn't believe the overwhelming sense of relief I felt when he finally sauntered out of the door. I was shaking like a wind-blown leaf when I sat down again and when I caught sight of my face reflected in the glass door

of the dark-wood corner cabinet, I saw I was as white as parchment –
parchment? Where the hell did that word come from? I wasn't even sure I
knew what parchment was. Some sort of paper, I supposed, but not the sort
of word I was accustomed to using. Just imagine that in a busy office. "Do
we have any fax-parchment?" I really was going nuts – slowly but surely
completely bonkers.

❦

CHAPTER SEVEN

Lil slept for ages and I was soon bored with my own company. I had to be honest; I didn't really want to read any more about Decima. She was starting to freak me out. Whichever turned out to be the true story, I didn't like it. Either she was a spoilt bitch and a cold-blooded murderer, or a sad little victim, ganged up on by her whole, supposedly loving, family, and hanged, in public, for a crime she didn't commit.

Any way you viewed it, this was not going to be a story with a happy ending.

In the end I hoisted down the encyclopaedia and looked up the Crimean War. I might as well find out what happened to Richard Allingham anyway.

"Crimean War (1854-56) This was a war fought in the Crimean Peninsular by Britain, France and Turkey against Russia, whose expansion into the Ottoman Empire sparked off the conflict. Among the Anglo-French victories was the battle of Balaclava, where a 'thin red line' of red-coated Scottish Infantrymen repelled the Russian forces, eventually sending them into retreat. In the same battle the British Army sustained heavy losses in the Charge of the Light Brigade. At Inkerman, British and French troops withstood a Russian assault and inflicted heavy casualties. The Russians were defeated after a long siege forced them out of the port of Sebastopol. The campaign was marked by incompetent leadership on all sides and by disease, which claimed more lives than the fighting. Florence Nightingale cared for sick and wounded British soldiers in the Crimea, using innovative techniques that remain at the heart of modern nursing practice."

Poor Richard. He was either struck down in battle – possibly even as one of the "Six Hundred" in the Charge of the Light Brigade (was it six or five, I could never remember?) or worse still he died of some disgusting sickness miles away from home with only the Lady with the Lamp for comfort, obviously never knowing that the love of his life was going to choke to death on a gallows less than three years later.

I began to wonder what sort of soldier he was, how old he had been, where he had lived and how he and Decima had met. I knew her brother had brought him home on furlough (leave, we would call it now) but I imagined that with her father and mother watching her every move, it could not have been easy for them to snatch any time alone together.

I glanced back over the short paragraphs which encapsulated so much misery and suffering and thought how strange it was that words which were names of places which the majority of British people would never see – and indeed hadn't even known had existed – had now become so familiar to our modern ears. Balaclava had a very different meaning now – awkward head-gear designed specifically to make small boys look extremely foolish. And Inkerman and Sebastopol were the names of many a terraced street in the Industrial North of England.

Was it really for this that so many men had died? So the box covered in chintz at the end of the bed could be called an ottoman? It was all so meaningless now, but then it had been worth fighting and dying for. No wonder Decima had been bitter. She had lost the man she loved to a war she probably didn't understand in a place she'd never heard of, and all because her mother and father wanted an unpaid servant. I suppose in that way, it even made sense that she had killed her sisters and not her parents. Let them be deprived of the ones they loved, to live on for years and years with the pain of separation, just as they had condemned her to do.

The banging upstairs began again. I was momentarily startled, then gathered all my courage and said out loud and to no one in particular, "OK, Decima. I get the message. You don't like it when I remind you of what you did. Well, be patient, perhaps one day you'll convince me like you convinced Lil."

Lil walked in at that moment, "Who are you talking to?" she asked, looking around in a puzzled way.

"No one. Had a good snooze?"

"Not bad. I thought I heard voices earlier. Has David been round?"

"No. Brendan turned up – uninvited and unwanted. Maddie gave him your address."

"That was nice of her. I thought you had told her that you and Brendan had split up?"

"I had. But if she sees a way of making my life difficult, she's going to seize it. He did give me one useful piece of information before I threw him out. Apparently she and mum are planning on visiting us. It might be as well to be prepared for a tempest."

Lil smiled grimly, "Don't you worry about them. I've spiked their guns good and proper, did they but know it."

"Why, what have you done?"

"You'll see."

With that she refused to be drawn any further on the subject, so I turned my attention to the tragic Richard Allingham.

"Do you know anything about him, Lil? Even though he was dead before the murders began, he still holds quite a big clue as to what happened and why."

"Actually I found out quite a bit about him. He was a huge catch for the likes of Decima. Son of the local aristocracy and worth a fortune. They were devastated when he was killed and held Decima entirely responsible. According to them he would never have been in the war if it hadn't been for his romance with her. His family home isn't very far away from here – I think perhaps the affair flourished when she was sent to her grandmother to get her away from him. Her father thought he had gone back to the army, but he wangled some sick leave and followed her up here."

"You mean she was here, in this house, when she fell in love with him?"

"I believe so, yes. They met in the house in Manchester, but they got to know each other here."

"Does anyone in the family still own the Manchester house, like you still have this place?"

"No, that branch of the family fell on hard times and it was sold many years ago. When the Watkins family had it, it was very posh, but the area, like the house, declined rapidly. It was pulled down about ten years ago and I believe there is now a supermarket on the site."

"So Hill Farm is the only place left that has any connection with Decima."

"Apart from Havering Hall, yes."

"Havering Hall?"

"The name of what was the Allingham country estate. It's still in the hands of a family now, not the National Trust or anything, but they open to the public a couple of days a week during the summer."

The name rang vague bells, but I was sure I had never been there, "Is it open now?"

"What's the date? April 10th – yes, I think it is. Why don't you ask

David to take you? It will do you good to have a day out."

I smiled at her obvious machinations, "Two reasons – the man has no more interest in me than I have in him – and I still can't walk properly."

"Take a wheelchair – you'll gain endless sympathy."

"I'll think about it."

The truth was, now that I knew the house existed, I was desperate to get there – and David would make a useful companion. I stewed for an hour, then rang him. "I don't suppose you could spare me a couple of hours one day this week, could you?"

There was short silence, then he said, "Is it something particularly urgent? Around Easter time is one of my busiest periods. Everyone wants to get their bedding plants in."

I tried not to betray my disappointment, "Oh, I see. I'm sorry. I never thought you might be busy. Forget it, it wasn't important."

Another silence, then he seemed to make a decision, "Wednesday is half-day closing. Will the afternoon be long enough?"

"I should think so, but you'd know better than me. How far away is Havering Hall?"

"About ten minutes from you – but why do you want to know?"

"I need to go there – and I was thinking you might be kind enough to go with me."

"Gladly – but the word 'why' springs to mind once again."

"I'll explain it all when I see you. I mustn't keep you from your work. Shall we say one o'clock on Wednesday?"

"Unless you are planning to buy me lunch, you can say two."

"One it is then," I said facetiously, then wished him a cheery goodbye before he could argue.

❦   ❦   ❦   ❦   ❦

He seemed to be in an odd mood, very quiet and noncommittal when I tried to make conversation, so I left it until we arrived at the pub, when he wasn't concentrating on his driving and I could argue with him if I should feel the need – and there was something about his off-hand attitude that told me I might.

I waited until we had our drinks and had found a table before I asked lightly, "So, do you still want to know why I need to go to Havering Hall?"

He shrugged, "No doubt you'll do as you always do and tell me just as much as you want me to know."

I know my mouth dropped open in amazement, but I quickly gathered my wits, "Just a minute. Where the hell did that pompous little speech come from? I seem to recall us agreeing that we were going to put this friendship on a strictly frivolous footing. That means you have absolutely no right to expect me to tell you anything at all – and I have no right to expect you to want to know."

He was annoyed, a muscle twitched in his cheek as he clenched his teeth, "That was before you decided to involve me in your machinations."

"Machinations." By God, we were all hurtling back to the nineteenth century now, weren't we? "What on earth are you talking about? I just asked you to give me a lift to a local stately home because I can't drive myself. How did that suddenly turn into an evil plot to entrap you?"

"Look Libby, I'm a fairly ordinary bloke – what you see is what you get – and I don't much care for being used. If you want to make your boyfriend jealous, find some other mug to do it, OK?"

"Boyfriend? What boyfriend? I told you I had split from him, never to return. I don't lie and I deeply resent you intimating that I do."

"Well, if you are telling the truth, you don't seem to have made it terribly clear to him. He came round to my place yesterday and offered to pour weed killer over my prize specimens if I didn't stay away from you. You can imagine I wasn't best pleased."

I felt as though the wind had been knocked out of my lungs by a physical blow, "Brendan has been to see you?" I managed to gasp.

"Yes, stunning isn't it – after all, according to him, that is just what you were aiming for. He says you've done it before and no doubt will do it again. You like the excitement of these romantic little games you both play."

Now I felt sick. What sort of a nut case was Brendan making me out to be? No wonder David was appalled. He must have thought I was a PT of the highest order. And knowing how plausible Brendan could be, I realized I was going to have a hard job convincing David that I was no such thing.

"Look, I don't know what that Irish charmer has been telling you, but this is the truth. I've only known him for about a year and even though I was stupid enough to be taken in by him, I was never dumb enough to move in with him. My first few years in London were appallingly lonely and the only men I seemed to meet were either married or eighteen-carat prats. Brendan seemed like a breath of fresh air – until I got to know what he was really like and I've been trying to find the strength to break with him ever since – but it wasn't easy and he's apparently determined to prove that it is actually impossible."

"Then what is he doing here? He told me you had invited him."

"Well, he would, wouldn't he? Let me ask you this, if I'm still so in love with him, how is it that he's not staying at Aunt Lil's?"

"He said you didn't want to shock her with your 'sleeping together out of wedlock' stuff,"

I raised a cynical eyebrow, "Have you ever known Aunt Lil be shocked by anything?"

Suddenly he grinned, "Alright, you've made your point – but what's his game? I've always thought it a tedious business chasing someone who doesn't want to be with you. What's the point? Even if you wear them down enough to take you back, where does that get you, in the end? You can't have a relationship with only one interested party."

"I'm with you on that one – but evidently he doesn't agree. I know it sounds big-headed, but I'm starting to feel just a little bit stalked."

"Libby, my advice is that you call the police. I'd say you were being well and truly stalked."

The barmaid arrived at that moment with two steak and kidney pies with chips, so the conversation was suspended for a while and when it did resume, Brendan had been banished.

"You were going to tell me why you wanted to visit Havering Hall – you seemed very keen on the phone. I must say I was surprised. According to Lil you spent nearly all your holidays here when you were small, so I imagined you must have been there dozens of times. It is the nearest big house and country park to Hill Farm."

"I know. Odd, isn't it? But my mother was never very interested in Havering. She always preferred Chatsworth, even though we had to travel to get there. It never occurred to me to question it when I was small, but I think I might just have the solution now."

"I'm intrigued. Tell me everything."

"I'll tell you as much as I want you to know, sir, and not another word." I answered, in a sly dig at the previous conversation. He grinned amiably, "OK, I apologise. I should have asked you first before leaping to conclusions – but you try facing an irate lover who is threatening your livelihood and see how logically your mind works."

"Oh don't worry, I know how convincing my EX-boyfriend can be. Anyway, let's forget him. I want to tell you about Richard Allingham."

"I didn't know you knew him," he responded, looking surprised.

I laughed, "Don't tell me you do or I'll be really freaked out. He's been dead since the Charge of the Light Brigade."

He looked astounded for a moment, then his face cleared, "Oh, I see. You mean a different Richard Allingham, of course – not the present owner of Havering Hall."

"Never tell me it's still owned by the Allinghams. Aunt Lil said it was still in private hands, but I had no idea the name had stayed the same. No wonder my mother wouldn't go near the place. I bet the feud is still bitterly fought! Not that I'd know anything about it. I'm rapidly learning that no one in my family ever tells me anything – except Lil, and she's almost left it too late."

"Would you like to stop rambling and fill me in?" he asked, in mock weariness.

I gave him a brief outline of the connection between my murderous aunt and the antecedent of the owner of Havering Hall.

"I wonder if Rick knows about this," he said, when my tale was told.

"Rick!" I couldn't help my revolted exclamation, "What a dreadful shortened version of Richard. I hope to God Decima never called her lover anything other than Richard. Rick is almost as bad as 'Dave'."

He looked sheepish, "Oh, dear! Please don't expect Rick to call me anything else."

"God, Rick and Dave! You sound like a bad sixties folk duo. Anyway, how do you know him? I thought he was aristocracy and you a mere business man."

"Snob!" he accused equably, "The class barriers are slowly coming down, you know, even in the barbarous North. We play cricket together, and I provide the thousands of bedding plants he uses every year in the Hall gardens. No need for the Masons when you've got cricket."

"Is he likely to be in residence now?"

"With the Season almost upon us? Of course. He'll be oiling his willow even as we speak."

"I don't even want to think about the mental image that conjures. Any chance of you introducing me to him?"

"No problem, if he is around – but if you are right and the family feud really is still in place, how are you going to persuade him to talk about your Richard and Decima?"

"I'm a writer, aren't I? It's amazing how people open up when you say those magic words."

"If you say so. It would have the opposite effect on me."

"Let's hope Rick is less taciturn, then. Are we having coffee or shall we get off to the Hall?"

"We'll be offered drinks by Rick, if he is about."

"Right, then show me to the man who would have been some sort of a cousin if Decima had been allowed to follow her heart."

He was much struck by this, "Good God! I suppose he would be. Imagine being related to Red-eye Rick."

It was my turn to be intrigued, "Why Red-eye Rick?"

"Cricketers humour – his capacity for drink is legendary – and he's no 'Dead-eye Dick'."

I presumed that meant he wasn't a very good shot, but I was really none the wiser. With a shrug I drained my glass of now-warm white wine and followed him out of the pub, wincing as he missed cracking his skull on the low doorway by a millimetre. Evidently he had been here before.

By common consent we didn't discuss the Allinghams or Decima on the way to the hall. Leaning towards safety, I spoke of the weather, "The tops of the trees are thrashing about. It must be getting windy out there."

"Umm, good drying weather," he said vaguely.

I laughed scornfully, "Oh, like you'd know anything about laundry," I said cynically, rather annoyed that he should be sexist enough to think that washing and drying clothes would be the limit of my interest in the weather.

He looked blank, "I was talking about Cricket Pitches, actually. You need a good strong wind to clear the wicket when you've had a week of rain."

I don't think he understood for a minute why this sent me off into hysterical laughter!

❦

CHAPTER EIGHT

Rick Allingham proved to be a real charmer. If he resembled the Crimea Richard in any way, I didn't blame Decima for falling for him. He was the archetypal tall, dark and handsome. If he had a fault at all, it was a slight stammer, but even that had its own particular attraction. It made everything he said seem to be carefully weighed before being imparted, making the most mundane of utterances hold a sincerity that was refreshing. He was probably just as big a blagger as every other man I'd ever met, but at least he appeared to mean every word. It was nice to be told I was a 'lovely creature' by someone who sounded as though he really was stunned by my beauty. Of course David ruined it all by raising a quizzical eyebrow and saying, "Come off it, Red-eye, didn't you use that line on Sally Symthe last month – and she's got a face like a horse."

"Thanks a lot!" I protested, "I have to say, Dave, I much prefer Mr. Allingham's polite fibs to your truth." I turned my smile upon the latter, hoping to convince him what a nice young lady I was, so that the stories of my Richard would flow. He grinned back, "T...take no notice of him, L...Libby. He's never forgiven me for running him out last season."

"And dropping several of my catches. I don't know how you keep your place on the team."

"Easy. I pay for the maintenance of the Pavilion, along with the groundsman's wages. Now, young lady, what can I do for you? Dave mentioned something about you being a writer."

"That's right. I happened to be toying with the idea of doing something – a novel perhaps, or a TV script, with the Crimean War as a background. I couldn't believe my luck when David told me you had an ancestor who fought in it. I don't suppose you have any information about him, do you?"

His eyebrows shot up, "Good grief! Now you have managed to s...surprise me. Dave knew about the C...Crimea?"

"I'm a man of many parts," interjected David huffily, "And much as you hate to admit it, I did go to school."

"Well, it is hard to credit it, Dave. You give so little indication of even rudimentary intelligence."

"Richard Allingham?" I reminded him gently, before this boy's rivalry really got out of hand.

"You even know his name?" he asked, "My word, you are a thorough researcher, aren't you? Yes, I have the honour to be named after my Grand Uncle, hero of the Siege of Sebastopol. And it would seem you are in luck. As I recall, Uncle Richard was a prolific writer, who kept campaign diaries throughout his army career. If you are really interested, you may borrow them to read – but I would have to consult the rest of the family before I could allow his name or experiences to be used for publication. I personally shouldn't mind at all to have Sean Bean swashbuckling his way through a battle under the name of Allingham, but some of the ancients might object."

I hoped I didn't look as excited and stunned as I felt. Even a serious writer wouldn't be this astounded to be presented with written words by the very man she was seeking to investigate. I tried to remind myself not to get too bowled over. After all, Rick had said 'campaign' diaries. It would more than likely be a dry as dust collection of army reminiscences with no mention of his love life – be it with Decima or anyone else.

"That would be wonderful – and rest assured, I wouldn't dream of using a word without consulting you first. I'm only too aware how generous you are being."

"Think nothing of it, my dear. Let's face it, you are probably the only person who has shown the slightest interest in the poor fellow in the last hundred years. He seems to have been something of a black sheep, from what I can gather. Some sort of a disastrous love affair, then off to be killed without redeeming himself by being a glorious hero. Not the sort of behaviour we expect from our relations, I must say."

I almost choked when he mentioned the love affair. Don't let my face betray my knowledge. I prayed silently. The fling with Decima evidently wasn't forgotten or forgiven, so I wouldn't do myself any favours in admitting I was related to her.

I had to be patient, though, and it was no easy task. He showed us around the house and grounds first – not quite Chatsworth, but large and imposing enough. Stone-portico, floor-to-ceiling windows, a ballroom, book-lined library and Italian sunken garden. I barely took it all in, I was so eager to get to the diaries.

65

We took tea in the Green Drawing Room, which took its name from the Japanese jade panels on the fireplace and the green furnishings. Apparently there was also a Red Drawing Room (Italian pink marble) and the Chinese Salon (black lacquer work). Rick assured us the green room was the cosiest. Cosy wasn't exactly the word I would have used to describe it. I was terrified of touching anything. It was like taking tea in a museum exhibit. Silver tea set – with sugar lumps, if you please. And bone china so thin I could almost see through it.

It was stupid, I know, but when he finally led us towards the library, to collect the diaries, I was trembling. I'd been having enough trouble hobbling around on my crutches, but now I was shaking so much that I was convinced the damn things were going to slide from under me on the polished wooden floors and I was going to end up sprawled at the feet of Richard Allingham's great-great nephew.

Casually, as we crossed the great hall, Rick nodded towards one of the huge portraits that adorned the walls, "There's your man, by the way. Major Richard Allingham, VC. Posthumous, of course."

"I thought you said he didn't die a hero," I managed to squeak, my head tilted back to get a better view of Decima's lover.

"Oh, he was there, that was enough to warrant the medal, I think. I don't remember anyone telling me he did anything particularly courageous."

I looked up at the portrait and saw a man whose face I immediately liked. He wasn't as classically handsome as I had been imagining. Actually he had quite an ordinary face, friendly and open. He looked like the sort of man you could trust, who would always be there for you when things were tough, but equally who could have a laugh with you in the pub when things were fine. His hair was dark, his eyes brown and kind. He had a fine nose, delicate nostrils and a strong chin, but overall his demeanour was strong and honest, loving and somehow sincere. Looking at the features of a long-dead soldier, I found myself hoping that Decima really had loved him and that she hadn't sent him to his death with a carefully hidden broken heart.

"How old was he when he died?"

"About thirty five, I think. He was quite old to still be in the forces, but I understand he was told, in no uncertain terms, to volunteer for service in the Crimea. Whoever the girl was, his family were pretty keen to get him away from her."

I didn't say anything. I was too busy with my mental arithmetic. Thirty-five. No callow boy, then, draw into an unwise alliance by the sight of a pretty face. That meant he was at least fifteen years older than Decima when they met. So why the resistance to the marriage on both sides? Surely his family must have been grateful that he was finally prepared to settle down, even if it was with a girl of lower social standing. And as for the Watkins' – what possible objection could they have to an alliance with one of the richest and most aristocratic families in the district? It didn't make sense. Oh well, maybe the diaries would cast some light on the subject.

There were enough of them, when Rick began to pull them off the shelves in the study – they were all beautifully bound in morocco leather, but whether he had bought bound notebooks, or they had been re-covered later, I had no idea. They were all dated in periods of approximately five years, the dates tooled in gold on the spines.

I very nearly missed the most important one of all when Rick pulled it out, then thrust it back, saying dismissively, "Oh, that's his private notes, you won't want that. You are only interested in the War, aren't you?"

"Oh, shove it in anyway," I said as casually as I could, "A bit of background to his character will always be useful."

I caught David's grin, but scowled at him not to give me away. He took the books and carried them to the car, with me trailing behind him like a hungry puppy following her owner home from the butcher, knowing there's a bone in the shopping bag. It was as much as I could do not to dribble with anticipation.

Saying goodbye to Rick and promising to take care of his property was an almost unbearable strain, especially when he began to chat me up and hint after a date. I was almost ready to agree, just to get rid of him, them I remembered Brendan and backed off hastily. The last thing I needed on my conscience was this lovely building being reduced to a pile of smouldering rubble thanks to my jealous ex.

"I'm not really fit for any more outings just at the moment, thanks, Rick. My foot is throbbing horribly now. I'll be in touch when I've finished my reading and perhaps we can go for a drink or something then?"

Of course he accepted the rebuff with grace and I heaved a sigh of relief as we swept around a curve in the drive and he was lost to sight.

"Nice guy, isn't he?" asked David, glancing at me sideways, then returning his eyes to the road ahead.

"Very nice."

"Pity he's gay."

I must have looked shocked, for he began to laugh heartily. For some reason I was furious with him, "You are such a liar."

"I swear to God I'm not."

"Then what was the point of him asking me out?"

"It makes his mother happy if he occasionally turns up in London with a pretty girl on his arm."

"I don't believe you."

"Believe it or not, it doesn't make it any less true. But he is a lovely guy – and the cricket club groundsman thinks so too."

I really didn't know if he was pulling my leg or not. I usually congratulated myself on knowing if a man were gay or not within minutes of meeting him, but Rick gave out no vibes one way or the other. I decided it didn't really matter anyway. Why should I care? The only reason I needed to know for sure was if I planned a romance with him – and I certainly didn't.

All I was really interested in at that moment was getting home and starting to read Richard Allingham's diaries – especially the one Rick had said was private. If Richard really had been in love with Decima, surely he would have written about it somewhere. Thank the Lord the aristocracy have houses big enough to allow them to keep everything.

In suburbia those notebooks would have long since been consigned to the bonfire or a skip. I was sure there was nothing left behind by poor Decima. Judging from the way her dear family had treated her, they would have slung her few pitiful bits and bobs into the cesspit before she had been cut down and placed in a box.

Richard Allingham might be my last chance to find out what this great-great Aunt of mine had really been like.

❦   ❦   ❦   ❦   ❦

Aunt Lil met us at the door with the news that there was a power cut in progress, so we had better get ourselves organized before the light faded, otherwise any tasks would have to be achieved by the light of candles. I was astounded she was taking the inconvenience so calmly, "Does this sort of thing happen often?" I asked incredulously.

"All the time," she assured me cheerfully, "You get used to it."

David was looking a little more concerned than her, "I'm going to have to get back, Lil, so phone me if there is anything you need. I really need to make sure the emergency generators have kicked in. If there is a heavy frost tonight, I could be in big trouble with my seedlings."

I sort of hadn't realized that he was going to leave so abruptly and I surprised myself by being a bit disappointed he wasn't going to be around when I started to read the Richard Allingham journals. I bit back the first words that sprang to mind and forced myself to speak with normal friendliness, "Are you going? Oh, well, thanks so much for the introduction to Rick and I'll let you know if I find anything interesting in the diaries."

"You do that. No doubt I'll be back before long. See you, Lil."

I watched him walk down the path, feeling slightly wistful, then gave myself a mental shaking up and went indoors.

Of course, because I now wanted nothing more than to curl up in a chair and read, I found I had loads of other things to do first. Lil was convinced the power wouldn't be off for long, but we had to prepare for a siege, just in case. I had to haul in logs and coal for the fires, feed the chickens and make sure they were secured for the night in case the local fox came calling.

Typically the Aga in the kitchen had gone out and I knew this particular old model was the very devil to re-light.

Before long I was covered in perspiration and soot, my hands black and my mood blacker. No matter what I did, the blasted thing wouldn't light. I must have raked it out and started again at least three times, and still nothing. The fuel all felt icy cold to my touch and before long my fingers were stiff and clumsy with the chill. If I hadn't known better, I would have suspected that all the fuel had been doused in freezing water – but it couldn't have been, could it?

Lil came into the kitchen, pulling her cardigan tighter about her shoulders, "Heavens above, Libby! You are making a meal of that, aren't you? Stir your stumps girl, or we'll be left in the dark without any heat or means of cooking."

For the first time ever, I lost my temper with her, "If you think you can do any better, you light the bloody thing," I snapped. She looked vaguely surprised, but not particularly annoyed, "All right, all right. No need to get testy. Give me the matches."

Wouldn't you know it, the moment she put a match to the edge of the newspapers the whole thing went up in a crackling, merry blaze. I could have cried. To her credit, Lil said nothing at all, merely put the kettle on to boil.

I went upstairs to have a bath before the final rays of daylight died behind the hills, then remembered that if there was no electricity, then there was no emersion heater and therefore no hot water. I managed to wash my hands and face in cold water, but I still felt grubby and cold and decidedly unhappy.

Still, never mind. I had the journals to read. And I fully intended to spend the next couple of hours doing nothing else.

❦

CHAPTER NINE

I didn't recall ever having read anyone else's diary in my life before. I've never even been one of those people who read books in the form of diaries, fictional or otherwise. Just not my cup of tea – and I don't know why, because they don't come much nosier than me. But there you are. I've just never found a diary that struck me as being interesting enough to read. After all, they are pretty personal, aren't they? I'd rather read a biography – at least that way you have the chance of getting a vaguely balanced view.

A few lines into Richard Allingham's journal and I was a convert. It was fascinating.

I made myself read a few pages of the war diaries first, intending to savour the personal journal for later, like leaving the most succulent morsel on your plate so you can finish the meal on a high note.

The story that emerged was one of misery, privation, illness and horror, coupled with disastrous leadership and crass military errors – the story of all wars, I suppose, but this was different. It was written in the words of a man who was there, on the front line, watching the whole sorry mess unfold before his eyes.

There was one major difference in Richard, and that was the lack of blinkered optimism. He wasn't there because he was seeking glory. He hadn't wanted to go. He didn't believe in the cause they were fighting for and he recognized the folly of his superiors. He did his duty, he cared for his men and he fought to get them the things they needed, but at the base of it all, he was in complete despair.

Frankly my heart bled for him.

And I knew his descendants would never allow his thoughts to be published. His lack of respect for the military and the proper amounts of 'derring do' would never pass muster with those who sought to glorify war.

His notebooks being shelved for all those years wasn't just about his affair with Decima. It was also to do with his own clear-sighted view of the misery and ultimate uselessness of battle. One whisper of his opinions and his VC would never have been presented.

"Ask any man why we are here – what we are expected to achieve – and he will shrug his shoulders, 'it's our duty, sir, that's all I know'!

I look around me and I see men wandering aimlessly about the camp. Cholera has broken out and spreads like wild fire. The men are pale, shivering ghosts, with no will left to fight – not the Russians, but their own failing bodies, the life is draining from them even as I watch. Clouds of flies are everywhere and the weakest of the sick cannot even raise their hands to brush them away. There is little enough to eat – lack of proper organisation with the supplies – but we are all too exhausted to prepare and eat even the small amount that there is and so it is cast aside and left to rot in the dust, covered in flies and beetles.

Too ill and despairing to dig fresh latrines, we are forced to bide in the vicinity of the foulest of smells, and the sight of unburied carcasses, scavenged upon by huge rats is enough to turn a healthy man's stomach, let alone one who has dysentery!

I am in complete despair. How can our leaders let their men suffer thus? The fighting has not yet even begun in good earnest, only a few small forays and small exchanges of desultory gunfire. Perhaps the Russians know that all they need do is wait for long enough and our troops will be so decimated with illness that they will have no need to engage in battle! Are men's lives so cheap that they can be sacrificed thus? If they must die, could they not be given the honour of dying on the field of conflict instead of this humiliating, painful end?

To escape the misery those that are managing to stay in reasonable health have taken to drinking the coarse, strong brandy that can be had cheaply from the local towns. Part of me cannot blame them for their weakness, but I cannot help despising the resulting drunkenness and brawling. My only desire is not to be here amongst men with whom I have nothing in common! It is my own vision of hell, this loss of everything of grace and beauty that I hold dear. I do not mind so very much the dirt and the discomfort, the hunger and the privation, but why must men descend lower than beasts when they are denied the trimmings of civilization? I can only thank God that I had the foresight to deny my sweet Decima the wish of her heart, which was to accompany me as other women have done. I would not have her associate with even the best of the camp followers, and alas circumstances would have dictated that she would have been debarred from the company of the Officer's wives. At first I was angry that they would have dared to judge us – what, after all, do they know of us? – but now I am merely grateful that she was not forced to endure this misery..."

I almost jumped out of my skin when the telephone suddenly trilled. Damn the modern world! Just as I was sinking into the nineteenth century, the present had to intrude.

My irritation and impatience must have been clearly reflected in my tone, for David Wright began his conversation with an apology, "Am I disturbing you? I'm sorry. I just thought you ought to know that either your power cut is very localised indeed, or you've got a blown fuse. Everything is fine here and according to the staff, it has been all afternoon."

For some reason I found that extremely disconcerting, "You mean this isn't a power cut at all?"

"Probably not. Do you want me to come up and check your electricity supply for you?"

Of course I did – desperately. So why did I go all proud and feminist? Your guess is as good as mine. Probably because I didn't want him to think I was a wimp and a useless girlie who couldn't fix a fuse.

"There's no need for that. If Lil and I can't mend a fuse between us it will be a poor show. We'll be going to bed soon anyway. I'll call on you in the morning if I have no luck."

"Are you sure?" He sounded a little worried and I wondered why.

"Positive. I'll speak to you tomorrow."

"OK. Goodnight, Libby."

"Bye David." Why did I sound so jaunty? I didn't feel it. The very thought of being in this house all night with no lights terrified the life out of me.

My finger hovered over the dial – Lil still had an old fashioned phone – but I couldn't bring myself to ring David back. He would think I was such a twit if I did. I fought with myself for several seconds, weighing the idea of a candlelit vigil against the amused look on the man's face when he arrived loaded down with his macho tool kit and his male superiority.

Lil poked her head around the door, "Supper's ready – did I just hear the phone?"

"Yes, it was David Wright. Apparently it's not a power cut, just us with the problem. I don't suppose you know how to mend a fuse, do you?"

"Of course I do. I've lived up here all my life, and alone for over thirty

72

years. But there is a difficulty with the notion of fixing it tonight."

My heart sank, "What's that, then?"

"The fuse box is in the cellar, but it's set so high up on the wall that we'll need the step ladder to reach it – and that is outside in the barn, which is the last place I used it."

"Couldn't I stand on a chair or something?" I asked, not relishing the idea of stumbling around the dirty old outhouse in the dark.

"You can't stand on anything – you're still on crutches, remember? And I'm sorry, but I'm really not up to standing on a chair at my age. It will have to wait until tomorrow. I must say I'm surprised David didn't offer to come up and fix it for us."

"He did. I told him not to bother."

She gave me what can only be described as an old fashioned look – you know the sort. The one that said, "Oh, I see!"

I elected not to rise to the bait, "What's for supper?"

"Stew," she said shortly. I couldn't help but think it would have sounded more appetising if she had called it "casserole".

We ate in the rapidly darkening kitchen by the light of a couple of candles, then washed up in half a bowl of lukewarm water. I was almost dancing with impatience to get back to Richard Allingham's journals, but Lil seemed not to notice.

"I thought we might have a game of Scrabble when you've done that," she said, as I dried my hands. I really must remember to do some shopping, I was thinking. I wouldn't dream of washing up without rubber gloves at home. My hands were beginning to feel like sandpaper.

"What?"I responded intelligently as her words began to sink into my consciousness.

"Scrabble?" she repeated.

"I was going to read," I said diffidently.

"You shouldn't read in candlelight," she answered briskly, "Very bad for your eyesight."

"Our ancestors did it," I protested.

"They had no choice – anyway, they were used to it. You're not!. Come on, don't be mean. What am I supposed to do without the telly, if you are going to have your head stuck in a book?"

After biting her head off earlier, I didn't really have a leg to stand on, did I? Literally as well as figuratively. Sadly I laid aside my plans for getting to know Richard Allingham better.

"Alright, where is it? And don't say stored up in the attic, or you are most definitely on your own."

She laughed, "What is it with you and that attic? There's nothing up there."

Nothing human, perhaps, I wasn't so sure about anything else.

Half an hour later we were in the sitting room, settled in front of a roaring fire – Lil had had to light that one too. I don't know what it was, but I had completely lost my touch with the fires that night. We had opened a bottle of wine and it was on the tip of my tongue to ask whether she ought to be drinking whilst on medication, but on second thoughts I kept my mouth shut. After all, it hardly mattered now, did it? What harm could she do herself that wasn't already done?

It was quite hard to see the Scrabble board in the flickering light of the softly guttering candles and I silently admitted that deciphering Richard Allingham's handwriting in the half-light wouldn't have been that easy anyway. He had quite a nice, solid hand, rounded and honest, rather like his own personality, I thought, but even so, reading handwriting was never easy at the best of times. Perhaps it was best delayed until the full sun shone upon me.

Lil and I picked our letters and as mine was nearest to A, I started the game. I could hardly believe my luck when the first word made itself as I laid the pieces on my little plastic tray – MALIGNS. It's not often you get a full, seven letter word straight off like that. Lil was suitably impressed and apologised that she could only manage to add ME.

I thought nothing much of it until my next dip into the sack brought forth KILL YOU. Now I was beginning to feel uncomfortable. I quickly made SKILL and handed over to Lil for her turn.

When she made GALLOWS, I was really getting ready to freak out. I promised myself if one more nasty word came out of the sack, I was packing the game in, no matter what protests Lil made. My relief when I came up with a Z, X and Q was almost palpable. It was just my imagination after all. There was nothing sinister happening, just me over-reacting, as usual.

It was still only about nine o'clock when the game ended – I won – and Lil announced her intention to retire for the night. She did look tired, but I think she was only going so I could get back to my reading.

Funnily enough when we had locked up and she had disappeared upstairs, I found that I was bone-weary too. I supposed it had been quite a long day, but I had been raring to get back to Richard Allingham only minutes before. Now that I was settled in front of the fire, the journal open on my knee, I found I could barely keep my eyes open.

I fought it, blinking and trying to focus on the written pages, but the warmth and the wine got the better of me and I was soon drifting off.

That was when the dream came back. I was back in that dank passageway again. It was an odd experience this time though, for part of my mind was still conscious and as soon as I started to realize where the dream was taking me, I tried desperately to wake myself up. I could feel my own body sweating and my gasping breaths as Libby, but I was still walking along the passageway and out into the weak daylight, being strapped up, climbing the steps to the gallows. It was doubly horrible this time because I was feeling my own emotions and not Decima's. Before it had seemed that I was detached from the events because I had known they were happening to someone else and not to me. I didn't have that advantage this time. Now it really was happening to me – and I didn't wake up when they pulled the lever. I suddenly found myself suspended in mid air, the rope burning my skin as it tightened, my throat being squeezed and constricted so that I was fighting for breath. My instinctive reaction was to try and reach up with my hands to grab the rope and heave my weight off it, but of course I couldn't. My hands were tightly bound. Next I tried to kick my legs out to try and reach some foothold so that the inexorable tightening would be relieved, but of course they were tied too – and there was nothing there beneath me anyway.

I thought hanging was instantaneous, but I was wrong. It seemed to take an eternity before the blackness began to ease the agony and in the meantime I felt every jerk of my body, every fibre of the rough rope cutting into my skin, the slow closing of my throat so that each breath became more painful and laboured. I felt I really was dying. Any thought that this was only a dream from which I would surely awake disappeared.

The blood began to pound in my head. Bang, bang, bang. The worst headache ever felt.

Suddenly I was awake but the bang, bang, bang still went on. I was gasping for breath and covered in perspiration, tears rolling down my cheeks, my hands raised to my neck, which was still stinging and sore.

Then I realized the noise wasn't in my head. It was real. Someone was knocking on the door.

I staggered to my feet, dazed and confused, still crying, half-hysterical, but still with enough sense to gasp, "Who's there?" before I would unbolt the door.

"David. I was worried. I couldn't leave you all night with no power, so I drove over."

With shaking hands I unlocked and unbolted the door, then fell weeping into his arms when he came in. He didn't say anything, just held me close for a few minutes, then led me into the sitting room, kicking the door closed behind him.

He poured me a brandy and watched me drink a sip or two before he even attempted to find out what had happened.

"Feeling better?"

I nodded, though in truth I wasn't, much.

"Then would you like to tell me what's wrong? Where's Lil? She's not..."

I shook my head hastily, immediately understanding that in Lil's present state of health, the fact of her death must always be the first conclusion anyone would jump to, "No, she's fine. She had an early night, and I, stupidly, fell asleep in the chair."

"Why stupidly? Anyone can drop off in an armchair in front of a roaring fire. In fact it's almost obligatory."

"Yes, but whenever I fall asleep in that chair," I jerked my head at the poor old rocker with a shudder of distaste, "I always have a horrible dream – well, more of a nightmare really."

"Do you want to tell me about it?"

"Not really, but I will. I dream I'm being sent to the gallows, but it is peculiarly vivid and quite honestly it scares the life out of me."

He looked thoughtful, "I can understand your being upset, but it's really not that surprising, since you fill every waking moment with your investigation into your relation's unhappy life."

"Oh, I know why I dream it – but it doesn't mean I have to like it, does it?" I felt, and probably sounded, hoarse. I suppose it was that which made him look more closely at me. Suddenly he leaned forward, picked up the candle and lurched towards me, his face a picture of astonishment and deep concern, "What the hell have you done to your neck?"

I was startled and lifted a self-conscious hand to my throat, "Why, what's wrong with it?"

"You look like you've been clawed by a cat or something. Your skin is red raw!"

I felt my mouth drop open in an extremely unbecoming gape.

❦

76

CHAPTER TEN

After the initial shock wore off, I pulled myself hastily together, "I must have scratched myself in my sleep when I dreamt the rope was tightening. I know I wanted to, but in the dream I was tied up."

He looked unconvinced, but answered, "Very probably. Look, you sit here and drink your brandy. I'll go and fix the fuse, then we can have a proper look at you and see if you need medical attention."

"Of course I don't – it just looks worse in the candlelight. It can't be that bad, it doesn't hurt much."

"But it does hurt?"

I admitted it did. He raised one eyebrow, but said nothing more. He stood up, "Will you be OK while I go and get my torch from the car?"

"Sure. But Lil said the step-ladder is in the barn – that's why we didn't fix the fuse ourselves." Suddenly I didn't want him to think I was a complete half-wit. I couldn't believe now that I had thrown myself at him like an hysterical drama queen. What was I thinking of, acting like that?

"Don't worry about that, I'll stand on a chair or something."

He went off and I took a huge swallow of brandy. I noticed my hands were still shaking and the booze burned my throat as it went down, but even so I was glad of it.

Within about ten minutes the lights were shining out and it was almost as though nothing untoward had ever happened. I heaved a huge sigh of relief, then remembered my injury. I had to see just how badly I had scratched myself, though I could scarcely believe I could have done any such thing in my sleep. I peered into the big mirror which hung over the mantle. My neck really was a dreadful mess. The surrounding redness was beginning to fade a little, but that only made it look worse, because it made the deepest marks look for all the world like the grooves which would be left when a taut rope bit into skin. I was horrified, but I sternly told myself that I did have sharp,

77

well-manicured nails and they were bound to leave nasty marks on the delicate flesh of my neck.

When I heard David coming back up the cellar steps, I hastily sat down again, trying to look casual.

"Right, let's have a look at these scratches," he said, as he walked back into the room, throwing his torch onto the sofa.

"No need," I said hastily, "It's fading now."

He took no notice, but gripped my chin between strong fingers and tilted my head back. He seemed to examine my throat for ages before he let me go, "I don't think you need a doctor, but you ought to bathe it in salt water or something. You've broken the skin in one or two places."

"I'll put the water heater on and have a hot bath, that should help."

"Good idea. Well, I'll leave you to it, then."

I stared at him and before I could stop myself I heard myself saying, "You're going?"

"That was the general idea, yes."

My horror must have been clearly reflected on my face because he looked amused and somewhat resigned, "Do you want me to stick around until you've had your bath?"

"Yes please."

"OK. Do you mind if I find myself something to eat? I was on my way to the pub for a pint and a pie when I suddenly felt the urge to come up here and make sure you two were alright."

"I'm glad you did. And if you are making something that isn't too hard to swallow, I wouldn't mind joining you. Suddenly I'm starving."

It was about half an hour later when I came back down, wet hair slicked off my face, my dressing gown collar turned up to hide the marks on my neck. I had had a good look at them in the steamy bathroom mirror and they were a mess, not just scratches, but bruises beginning to form as well. The last thing I wanted was for David to see them again. I just wanted to forget the whole incident and didn't think I could stand a long and pointless inquest into the cause. I was sure there must be a logical explanation, but what it could be, I had no idea – and an illogical explanation didn't bear thinking about.

He'd made scrambled eggs – his on toast, mine not. Funnily enough it was just what I fancied, good, old fashioned comfort food, straight from the nursery. I tucked in gratefully, though complained that the coffee he had made to go with it meant I would be awake half the night.

We said nothing for a few minutes, just ate hungrily, but when the edge had been taken off his appetite, he ventured quietly, "Libby, don't you think all this is a bit odd?"

I knew exactly what he meant, but still I looked up and said, "All what?"

"The things that have been happening in this house. The way you keep hurting yourself, for a start. Are you always this clumsy?"

He couldn't have picked a word that would rile me more. Being the youngest in any family meant that the first few years of one's life were plagued by a lack of dexterity when compared to older siblings. Of course you couldn't crayon inside the lines as well as your big sister, you couldn't hit a cricket ball, get a hoop over a stick, read as well, run as fast, swim as far. The eternal cry was, "Look what you've done. You're so clumsy, so stupid, such a liability. We would have won that game if it hadn't been for you."

"I am not clumsy." I said stiffly, in a clear little voice. To grant him his due, he immediately recognized the danger signals, "No, not clumsy," he conceded hastily, "That was an unfortunate choice of word, but you have been particularly accident-prone since you arrived. I've been wondering if, subconsciously perhaps, you feel that the task you have taken on is too much for you. After all, you are very young and inexperienced to be nursing a dying woman. Do you think perhaps this is your body's way of telling you that you really shouldn't be here?"

Normally I would have been as mad as hell to hear some stranger tell me that I wasn't up to looking after my own aunt – but after the thoughts I had been chasing out of my head all evening, his explanation seemed a lot more palatable than the one I was refusing to acknowledge.

"I suppose you could be right. I must admit I'm enjoying being with Lil at the moment, but deep down I'm dreading the end coming. She's flagging visibly now and I would be a liar if I didn't say that I don't relish the thought that she might die whilst we are here alone."

He reached out and briefly squeezed my hand, letting it go immediately. Though the gesture was swift, it was curiously comforting.

"I don't blame you. Nobody would. Why don't you just admit defeat and let those who are paid to do it look after Lil at the end?"

If only he knew how I longed to do just that. This house that I had once loved was now scaring the life out of me. I was terrified of being there with Lil, even more afraid of being there with a dead body. But I had made a promise.

"I can't, David. If I desert Lil now, she'll die in a hospice, surrounded by strangers. She's never asked anything of me before and all she wants now is to die in her own bed, between her own four walls. She was born here, married and gave birth here, grieved the loss of her son and her husband here. If I don't stay, neither can she. I can't do that to her."

"No, I suppose you can't. Well, I'm fond of Lil and I wouldn't want her last weeks to be miserable, so I'll help as much as I can, but I can't be here every minute, so you really are going to have to pull yourself together and stop smashing yourself up." He grinned amiably as he said it, so these last words didn't have quite the sting they might otherwise have done, even so, I was prompted to give him what Paddington Bear would have called "a very hard stare". He laughed and held up his hands as though in surrender, "Okay, Okay. I know it wasn't your fault, but can I suggest you don't fall asleep in the chair again? You did say you only have the hanging dream when you nod off down here?"

Fall asleep in the chair? I was never, ever sitting in the chair again, let alone sleeping in it.

"I think I can guarantee that!"

"Good. Now, is there a spare bed in this house? I'm whacked and I have to get up early in the morning."

❧ ❧ ❧ ❧ ❧

A light tapping on my bedroom door woke me from a deep – and thankfully, dreamless – sleep.

David popped his head around the door as I blinked in the light that flooded in behind him from the landing. It was still dark outside.

"Sorry to wake you, but I really have to go now. I'll let myself out, there's no need for you to get up. I'll give you a ring later."

"Alright – and David, thanks for everything."

"No problem. Bye." With that he was gone and the room was in darkness again. I lay back, thinking about the events of the night before. I couldn't help wondering what would have happened had David not arrived when he did. When I started to recall the nightmare, the images were just as vivid as they had been during the experience and I began to shake uncontrollably. My teeth were chattering in my head and my hands trembled so violently I could barely grip the bedclothes, but grip them I did, and cast them back. I was going downstairs to make a cup of tea and turn the television on. That would drive away the demons. I defied anything to be scary with Breakfast

TV going on in the background.

I looked in on Lil on my way past her room, but she was still zonked out.

When I walked into the kitchen and switched on the light Brendan was sitting there, a cup of coffee in his hand. I almost jumped out of my skin when I saw him, but quickly got a grip of myself. The last thing I intended was to let him know he had frightened me so I bit back the inevitable, "God, you scared me." and substituted, "What the hell are you doing here?"

"Good morning to you too, Libby."

"Get out!" I wasn't even going to try and be conciliatory. The man was a pain in the arse and I wanted him gone.

"When I've finished my coffee," he said calmly. I decided to simply ignore him. I went to the Aga and picked up the kettle to make myself a drink too. A sudden thought assailed me, probably because of all the odd things that had been happening around the house, like my mobile phone mysteriously appearing up in the attics. It hadn't occurred to me before, because I hadn't known Brendan was around, but that was just the sort of sick prank he would find immensely funny. If he had found some way of getting into the house, he would love to freak me out with silly tricks.

"How the hell did you get in here?"

"Lover boy left the back door unlocked when he left," he said coldly, putting his mug down on the scrubbed oak table, "I can't say I think much of your taste. He's only lacking a corn stalk sticking out of the corner of his mouth."

I was assailed by so many different emotions I didn't know which one to voice first. I swallowed deeply and tried to gather my thoughts. Oddly enough the overwhelming feeling I had was not to hotly deny the fact that I was sleeping with David Wright, but the horror that David should think I was lying when I had said Brendan and I were finished – and what else could he possibly think, when my nutcase ex turned up at my house before dawn, as though to sneak in for a quickie before my aunt woke up?

"You spoke to David?" I asked hoarsely.

"Oh, yes. I always exchange pleasantries with the country bumpkin who is shafting my girlfriend." he spat with vicious sarcasm.

That made me see red, "For fuck's sake, Brendan! What does it take to get through to you? I am not your girlfriend. And if I was bonking David, it would have sod all to do with you."

He was on his feet and across the room before the last syllable had died away. He grabbed hold of me around the throat with one hand, thrusting me backwards so that the edge of the work top dug into the small of my back,

"I'm getting a little tired of your silly games," he said quietly. It was odd how his calm tone was so at variance with the violence of his actions. It was more frightening, actually, making me feel that he was still in control of himself – but only just.

I winced as his fingers tightened slightly on my throat and that stopped him in his tracks, because he knew he wasn't really holding me tightly enough to hurt me. He pressed his body against mine, so I couldn't move away, then released his grip on my neck so that he could pull down the collar of my dressing gown. Obviously the marks were still there and hadn't faded because his face went white, "You filthy bitch! Love bites all over your neck and you've have the utter gall to tell me you didn't sleep with the bastard."

I was terrified, but I was damned if I was going to let him know it. I forced a slight smile to my lips, "I didn't say I hadn't slept with him – just that it is none of your business if I did."

That was a mistake. He slapped me in the face with his full strength. I don't think I'd ever experienced such pain. I felt as though the side of my head had exploded. Tears spurted from my eyes and I gasped with shock. I had learnt over the past few months that Brendan was a vindictive swine – but I never thought he would hit me. I never thought any man would hit me. I wasn't the sort of woman who became a victim. I was independent, feisty, confident. Men didn't hit women like me. They hit pathetic, clinging women, didn't they?

After the shock died away and my ears stopped ringing, I was mad. Furious. If he could hit, so could I. I lifted both hands and started flailing wildly at him. I got a few good slaps in before he managed to grab both my hands and fling me across the room. I landed in a heap on the floor, my dressing gown flying up and revealing the legs of the warm pyjamas I was wearing – it's not my usual night attire, but it's bloody cold in the Peaks, even in April. I was astonished to hear him laughing, though admittedly there was air of desperation behind the mirth, "God, he really is a bumpkin if flannelette turns him on."

I sat up with difficulty. I felt as though I had been trampled on by an elephant. "You are such a prat, Brendan. I'm not sleeping with him – or anyone else." I despised myself for my cowardice, but I really didn't want another belt, so it seemed sensible to take the heat out of the situation. As soon as I could get him out of the house, I could call the police – but until then, I was alone with an insanely jealous man, basically at his mercy, since it was obvious he was much stronger than I. Only an idiot would have continued to taunt him in those circumstances.

"Oh, really? Then how do you explain the love-bites? Don't tell me you did them yourself with the Hoover."

"They are not love-bites. I despise the bloody things. Do you really think I'd let anyone do that to me?"

"Go on, I'm listening."

I really didn't want to go into this right now, but the important thing was that I kept him calm so that he would go away and I could call the police. I pulled myself up off the floor, so I didn't have to look at him as I explained.

"It's stupid really, but I had a sort of a nightmare. I thought I was being strangled with a rope – it was very vivid, and I must have clawed myself in my sleep, trying to get the imaginary noose off."

He approached me and I backed away, but he waved an impatient hand,

"Don't be an idiot. I'm not going to smack you again unless you ask for it. I just want to see the marks." I couldn't believe he was being so calm about it. He hadn't even apologised for the blow, but was just acting as though he had been perfectly within his rights to do it. Even so, I allowed him to come near enough to look at my neck, though I shuddered when he gripped my chin and forced my head back. He seemed to scrutinise my throat for ages before he released me, an unpleasant grin adorning his features, "Well, well, well. You are a dark horse, Libby. Why didn't you tell me your inclination was for S & M – I would have gladly indulged you – I still can."

My mouth dropped open. I didn't know what he was talking about, but the caressing, lustful way he said it warned me that I wasn't going to like what I was about to hear, "What?"

"Oh come now, my darling. Do you think I was born yesterday? Those are rope burns, not scratches. You've been indulging in a bit of solo fun, haven't you? You should have told me, I'd gladly have joined in. It's a dangerous game on your own. Michael Hutchence learned that the hard way."

It wasn't until he mentioned the rock star's name that I understood exactly what he was suggesting – and then I was utterly revolted, "What the hell are you saying – no, don't bother to elaborate. Just get out – and don't come back."

"A bit late for playing hard to get, sweetie. You've obviously been putting it about quite a lot – and you're not the innocent you've been pretending all these past months. Now I see where you are coming from, I think we could have a lot of fun. I'm prepared to forget this little hiccup, so let's just pack your bags, say bye-bye to Auntie and get back to London, where we both belong."

I drew in a deep breath. I suddenly felt incredibly unclean. I couldn't believe I had ever found this creep even vaguely attractive, "I'll say this one last time, Brendan, and then I am going to scream blue murder for my Aunt. I did not do any of the disgusting, perverted things you are thinking and I'm not interested in renewing my relationship with you. I think you are a slimy, arrogant bastard and if I never see you again it will be too soon. Now get out!"

A slight sound behind me caught his attention and his eyes left my face and travelled beyond me, the grin sliding from his lips, "I think Libby has made herself quite clear, Brendan, don't you?"

I turned my head. Lil was standing in the doorway, holding a shotgun to her shoulder and aiming it straight at Brendan's heart.

He quickly regained his composure. The grin came back and he lifted his hands in the age-old way, "Don't shoot, Auntie. I get the message. I'm going. See you around, Lib."

I burst into tears when he had gone. Aunt Lil said nothing, but held me close.

❦

CHAPTER ELEVEN

I'd recovered most of my composure when David rang later. I gave him a brief outline of the events of the morning. He went very quiet when I told him Brendan had hit me, then he asked tensely, "And did you report it to the police?" I hesitated then admitted, "No, I didn't,"

"Why the devil not? The man is a maniac! He needs taking off the streets pronto."

"I know, but there was more to it than meets the eye," I said carefully.

"Like what?"

I explained what Brendan had said about the marks on my throat, adding desperately, "What if the police had thought the same thing? I couldn't bear the humiliation. They'd hardly believe me when I told them he had belted me, if they thought I was the sort of nutter who gets her kicks from half-strangling herself. And you've seen for yourself how plausible Brendan can be. He would make mincemeat of me in front of the police."

When this explanation was met with a blank silence, I was hit by a painful and embarrassing thought. Like a douche of icy water in my face, I was suddenly aware that David was probably now thinking exactly the same thing. Why should he take my word for what had happened? He hardly knew me. His only experience of me had been various odd injuries – and plausible lies told by my ex-boyfriend.

He probably heard my stifled sob as I put down the telephone without saying anything else. When it rang again, I frantically signalled Lil to answer it.

"It's David for you. He said you must have been cut off."

I shook my head wearily, "Tell him I'm busy," I hissed, "I've gone out to feed the chickens."

"I don't lie," she whispered back, annoyed. I legged it towards the door, "Well, now you are not lying, are you?" I said and childishly slammed the

85

door after me.

My intention was to get as far away from the phone as possible so she couldn't call me back and make me speak to David, so I chose to start climbing the hill behind the house. At first I was striding out, fuelled by fury and embarrassment – how dare David Wright immediately think the worst of me? He didn't even know me. So much for his offers of friendship and help. Within about three minutes my trot had slowed to a walk, and within another two I was puffing and blowing and looking for somewhere to sit and rest – not only was I completely unfit and out of breath with the climb, my bad foot had also begun to throb again. I had been managing without my crutches, but if I carried on with this hill-walking lark, I thought I would pretty soon find myself hobbling back on them again. The hill was a lot steeper than it looked from the yard.

Luckily I came upon a convenient slab of stone set on a grassy bank – or maybe it wasn't just luck. It had the appearance of being set there quite deliberately as a seat. Perhaps I wasn't the only person over the years who had found this particular climb tough going. Anyway I sat down and looked back over the view which had previously been behind me and therefore not appreciated.

And believe me, it certainly needed appreciating. Apparently this stone seat wasn't just a place to catch your breath. It was a place to have your breath taken away again by the magnificent vista. I could see for miles – and it was beautiful. Craggy hills on either side dropped steeply down to a deep valley and I could just see the sparkle of sunlight on water at the bottom. No doubt later in the year the grey and green hills would be covered with purple heather, but now, in April, they were lightly decorated with the vibrant green of early foliage, dotted here and there with a tree bearing the white and pink blossom of spring.

After I had drunk in the view for some minutes I began to feel that familiar lightening of spirits which always accompanied the experiencing of something perfect. I'd always been like that. No matter how bad things were, no matter how pissed off I was, I only needed to see a minor miracle of Mother Nature, a great sunset, a dark sky full of stars, a particularly clear moon, and I'd start to feel better about everything. That had been lacking in my recent life. It was hard to see the stars in London against the glare of the streetlights, and to catch a glimpse of a sunset between the houses and tower blocks was a minor miracle in itself. I belong here, I told myself. This house is scaring the hell out of me, but still I feel I belong here.

As a sky lark soared above me and showered me with its fluid notes of joy, I found myself sporting a soppy smile on my face and with a swelling heart, I transferred my gaze from the far to the near.

There it stood – Hill Farm – as it had stood for generations. Grey and solid, as immovable as the hills around it. And there was Aunt Lil. I could just make out her small, thin figure through the kitchen window. Apparently she had finished on the telephone and was now busying herself at the Aga – probably making the inevitable cup of tea to warm and comfort me when I decided to go back in. Which ought to be now, I supposed. She had been left cleaning up my mess and the poor woman didn't even know what I was mad about.

I was just about to heave myself to my feet when my glance strayed from the kitchen window and took in the rest of the house. What I saw deprived me of the ability to breath or move.

There was a woman standing at the attic window. At least I thought it was a woman. She stood back from the frame, shrouded by shadows, but I could make out her pale face, and one white hand resting against the edge of the pane. She didn't gesture to me, she was as stock-still as the stone on which I sat. And she was much too far away for me to see her features, but still I felt that she could see me, that her eyes were boring into me – and that her gaze was most certainly not a friendly one. I don't know how I knew, but her animosity seemed to emanate from her in waves of spite and hatred. I had never before felt as though someone wanted me dead, or at least hurt, but she did.

I don't mind admitting I was terrified. I knew Lil was alone in the house – and I could see her even now, still bustling about the kitchen in her usual purposeful manner.

As I watched, my breathing suspended, an icy horror gripping my stomach, the woman at the window slowly faded away. She didn't move, she didn't walk away, but suddenly she wasn't there any more.

As though released from a spell, I was suddenly mad as hell. Who the devil was it, wandering around my aunt's house as though they owned the place? Letting themselves in just to play stupid, frightening pranks on two lone women. I was damn sure I was going to catch them at it. I leapt to my feet and began to run down the hill, utilising that strange, ungainly gallop where one leans backwards so as not to pitch headlong down the slope.

The sound of a car braking on gravel brought me up short. It was astounding how clear the sound was in the still air, because the parking lay by was a good three hundred yards beyond the house, but I could hear the car doors slamming and the voices of the visitors ringing out. I couldn't hear the words, but I recognised the voices. Oh God, my mother and Maddie. The figure in the attic was immediately forgotten. I had to warn Lil that the Witches of East Cheshire were about to descend on us.

Of course it was all very civilized to begin with. I managed to get to Lil with just seconds to spare and she reassuringly squeezed my hand and said quietly, "Don't worry, my dear. I've spiked their guns good and proper."

I wondered again what she meant by that, but didn't have time to ask before mum and Maddie came strolling in without even the courtesy of a knock on the door. They were talking about some bitchy saleswoman in an expensive shop in Alderley Edge or Altrincham, or somewhere similar and only broke off to greet us as they would a pair of troublesome children who were blocking the path.

My mother drew off her gloves. She always wore gloves and in winter a hat too. She seemed to think she was in a 1950's movie most of the time. As far as she was concerned the progress of the human race stopped in 1960 and never improved thereafter. My mother was true to the old adage, "If you can remember the '60's you weren't there!" She remembered them all right, but she never took part in them.

She held her face sideways for me to kiss her cheek, which I dutifully did, then she said, "Lillian, how are you?"

"Oh, about the same, Marjory – you know, still dying."

I hid a grin but mother evidently wasn't amused, "I don't really think there is any need to dwell on that, is there?" she asked icily.

Lil shrugged, "Not much else for me to dwell on, my dear. Still, we'll see how much better you do when your time comes."

Seeing that she was getting nowhere fast, my mother changed the subject, not hastily, that wasn't her style, but with determination, "I hope Elizabeth has been making herself useful to you."

"Who's Elizabeth? Oh, you mean Libby. Yes, we're getting along grandly, thank you. Now, did you want anything in particular, or is this a social call?"

Mother wasn't about to be hurried, "A cup of tea would be welcome. It's rather a long jaunt up here, you know."

Lil went off to make the tea, I tried to follow her with the cheery, "I'll give you a hand, Lil," but mother's perfectly manicured hand was laid on my arm as I passed her, "Lil is perfectly capable of brewing a pot of tea," she said, "I want to see my baby. Don't run away."

That ought to have sounded affectionate, but unfortunately it didn't. I felt my stomach contract as she touched me. This was ridiculous. She was my own mother. Granted, the last few years had been a bit tough on both of us, as I had realized she wasn't the mother I wanted and she that I certainly wasn't her idea of the perfect daughter, but this was too much. I was feeling as though a slightly watered down version of the spite from the woman at the window was sneaking its way towards me, slithering across the floor like a snake – and coming directly from the woman who had given birth to me.

I forced a smile, "I wasn't running. I just like to keep an eye on Lil, in case she has a funny turn."

"What a quaint expression. The only funny turn Lil ever had was when she was born both contrary and stubborn. And I find it hard to believe you are going against your mother's wishes, and aiding and abetting the silly old dear in her dementia."

I bit back the angry retort and managed to say calmly, "Lil doesn't have dementia, mum. She just wants to die in her own house. There's nothing odd in that, is there?"

"There is when doing so may deprive her family of its birthright. Refusing to sign Hill Farm over to me is nothing short of wicked. She knows we can't possibly afford to pay death duties on this place. It will go out of the family for the first time in several generations."

"And you are planning to live here, are you?" Lil's voice came from the doorway. My mother whirled round and smiled at the older woman, "Lil! You startled me. Not lost your propensity for creeping up on people, I see. Well, now you have heard what I was saying, we might just as well bring everything out into the open. No, I wouldn't live here all the time, of course I wouldn't, but it would make a very nice weekend retreat or holiday home – anything is better than it falling into the hands of strangers."

I knew she didn't mean it. She hated it up here. The South of France was more her style. No doubt she would hang onto the place for a couple of years, to keep up appearances, but then some excuse would be passed around the family making it utterly necessary for the house and land to be sold – to the highest bidder of course. My mother had no sentiment. She wanted and needed money – a lot of it. I just hoped Lil knew it too, and wouldn't be swayed by the guilt mother was trying to load on her.

"My dear Marjory, I've told you before and I'll tell you again, Hill Farm has been left in safe hands. When my will is read, you will find out which one of you I deemed fit to inherit."

"But if you merely leave it in a will, there will be extortionate death duties to pay. You have no direct descendants. There is no doubt the house will be sold and what little sums there are left will be divided between a dozen or more cousins. How sensible is that? One signature on a piece of paper and Hill Farm will be safe for future generations – and I will pay for you to have the best care possible in the hospice of your choice."

"Why so squeamish about me dying here, Marjory? I wouldn't be the first person to expire here – nor do I expect to be the last."

"Oh, we know all about that," burst out Maddie suddenly before my mother had chance to say anything else. It was as though she couldn't stay out of the conversation for another second without bursting, "We hear there was nearly a little tragedy the other night."

Lil looked confused, but my heart sank. I hoped Brendan hadn't been talking to Maddie, but I very much feared he had.

"What do you mean?"

Maddie walked across to me and before I could stop her she pulled down the roll neck of the jumper I had worn deliberately to hide my throat, "Dear Libby had a little mishap, didn't you Libs? Do you really trust a suicidal woman to take care of you, Lillian? How much use is she going to be when you are confined to bed, in agony, and she's hanging from a beam in the attic?"

I dragged myself from her grasp, "You bitch!" I whispered, "I'll never forgive you for this." She laughed, "Oh really? Do you think you'll be around for long enough to extract your revenge?"

"That's enough, Madeleine," interjected my mother calmly, "I'm sure Brendan was right when he assured us that Libby was going through a bad patch because of their splitting up. Nothing of the sort will occur again, though, as a mother, I really feel I must make my concerns known to Social Services. They can hardly continue to allow this travesty to go on. Lillian lives alone in an extremely isolated house and her own company is a severely depressed girl. It's a tragedy waiting to happen."

Lillian was at her most dignified, "I don't pretend to understand what you are talking about, Marjory, or you Maddie. But I do know that there have been no suicide attempts in this house. The only time Libby has been out of my company, she has been with another person, so she could not have tried to hang herself, as you seem to be suggesting. You can tell Social Services – or any other damn services – what you like, but I am not a child and I will not be dictated to, by you, them or anyone else. Now, get out of my house before I throw you out."

Mother was scarlet with rage, Maddie was still grinning vindictively at me, but they left. I'll say that for them, they never outstay their welcome.

We stood by the back door together until we heard the angry swish of gravel under the wheels of a car reversing too fast, then we went back indoors to drink the well-stewed tea Lil had made for our guests.

"Would you like to tell me what happened?" said Lil, gesturing towards my neck.

"You won't believe it, but I'll try," I answered grimly.

❦

CHAPTER TWELVE

Lil's expression gave no indication of her emotions when I had finished my tale. I had no idea whether she believed me or not, but I found myself praying she would. It seemed that everyone about me was having no difficulty at all in crediting this story of self-inflicted injury. I was even beginning to wonder myself if I wasn't losing my marbles and had done something whilst asleep or unconscious. Anything else just seemed too far-fetched and ludicrous to contemplate.

She was quiet for so long that it began to play on my nerves, "Lil, please say something," I begged, "I don't think I can cope with much more of this."

"I'm sorry, love, I'm just trying to take it all in. You have to admit it's a pretty odd story. And I can't help feeling responsible for everything."

She looked so worried that I was immediately prompted to put my arm around her and give her a quick hug, "Don't be daft. How can it be your fault?"

"Well, it was me who put all these weird thoughts in your head, wasn't it? You are so sensitive and imaginative, I should have known stories of murder, hanging and unrequited love were going to give you nightmares."

I felt ridiculously relieved, "You think it is just nightmares, then? You don't really thinking I'm being ... haunted, I suppose that's the only word to use, though I feel stupid even voicing it."

I'd have felt better if she had laughed when I said it, or immediately rushed to deny the possibility, but she looked me straight in the eye and said softly, "You know, Libby, the nearer I get to dying, the more I hope there really is an afterlife. How can I pretend that I don't think there are stranger things in Heaven and earth, as the saying goes. And I've got to say that if anyone has the right to be as mad as hell over how life treated her, it's Decima Watkins."

"That's all very well, Lil, but why the devil should I take the brunt of her fury? I've not done a bloody thing to her – on the contrary, I've been investigating her case."

"Yes, but you don't really believe she's innocent, do you?"

She had me there. I was still at the stage of being open-minded – and quite frankly, if it was the shade of Decima who was giving me nightmares and injuries and horrible frights, then she wasn't exactly convincing me she wasn't a vindictive bitch who was more than capable of murdering her sisters in cold blood.

I gave myself a mental shake. This was ludicrous. I didn't believe in ghosts. If there was any such thing, then they were some sort of hiccup in time, which enabled the psychic to catch a glimpse of a fleeting moment of the past. To believe that they were physically able to inflict damage on living flesh was the stuff of B movies from the seventies.

I forced a laugh – and it sounded forced, take my word for it. "I don't believe in ghosts," I said, more loudly than I had intended. Lil smiled, "The Marquise du Deffand, in the 18th Century summed it up perfectly for me, Libby. She said she didn't believe in ghosts, but she was afraid of them."

I think that summed it all up for me too.

"But what do we do about it all? My first instinct is to run – like the wind, as they say. But if I do that you will either be here all alone – or my mother will get her own way, as usual, and you'll be in a hospice before you can protest."

"How do feel about calling a priest in?"

I had long since fallen away from any religious practise, but I had no objection, in theory, for the ministry to get involved. My only concern was that a priest or vicar might just think I was as batty as everyone else did.

"Do you know a nice one?" I asked diffidently.

"The local vicar is very pleasant," she said.

"I thought we are supposed to be Catholic," I said, suddenly realizing that our religion had survived for generations in the family, but was likely to end with my own peers. I didn't know a single one of my cousins who attended church except for the celebrations of 'hatches, matches and despatches' as my father used to graphically describe them.

"Well, you can have the priest if you prefer it, but he's one of the modern, 'happy-clappy' lot – nice, but no match for the mood Decima seems to be in."

"The vicar will be fine," I agreed, with a barely concealed shudder. The last Christening I had attended had been one of the new, hug-your-neighbour sorts and I had been mortified. I have enough trouble hugging people I know, never mind complete strangers.

Lil went straight to the phone and the vicar agreed to visit us that afternoon. While we were waiting for him, I went back to the Richard Allingham diaries, but this time I didn't waste my time on the battle journals. I went to the private notes. I was now desperate to find out what kind of a girl Decima really was. Richard might have been smitten, but he was bound to mention things which would give me an indication if Decima was genuine, or taking him for a ride. Infatuated men never noticed these things, but women did. I knew from personal experience that girls could be the biggest bitches, but a man who was thinking with his trousers didn't stand a chance of noticing, until it was too late.

It didn't take me long to find the year that they had met, but a reference to Decima proved elusive at first. It seemed she had not made much of a first impression. If she had raised any emotion in him at all, it had been pity.

"18th March 1853. We have been granted furlough and a fellow officer, Percy Watkins has cordially invited me to spend a few days with his family. At first I was inclined to refuse, as I do not know him particularly well, but then the thought of going home and enduring another of Papa's interminable sermons about my decision to join the army made my mind up for me! Percy seems a nice enough fellow and his family, though not top notch, seems comfortably off. He tells me he has several sisters, so a flirtation would not be out of the question. Though I had better make sure I cannot be taken seriously! Being at outs with my father over my choice of career is bad enough, but to bring home a bride who springs from the lower classes would surely kill him!

"19th March 1853. As always the journey North was uncomfortable, but Percy and I got on famously. Despite the jogging of the coach, we endeavoured to play cards. I won four guineas off him, which was inclined to make him sullen, until I offered to pay for his dinner and all the brandy he could drink! After that, I fear he had a much worse journey than I!"

"20th March, 1853. We strolled over to Percy's house after a hearty breakfast in the coaching inn. We had arrived in town too late last night to want to wake the household! And Percy couldn't really appear before his mother in his delicate condition!

All was as Percy had assured me. His brothers were good fellows, welcoming me with friendliness, his sisters all charming. The three elders were married, but still dined with their parents and siblings, accompanied by their husbands. Their numerous progeny were apparently cared for by nursemaids in their own homes, which all seemed to be in the near vicinity. They seemed an exceptionally close-knit family. It was almost disconcerting to join the merry throng as they all were so well acquainted that each seemed to know what the others were thinking before a word was spoken It seems unkind to say it when they had welcomed me so warmly, but there was something distinctly odd about their closeness. From conversations I heard, they did not have many outside friends, only Percy had left the household permanently, for even those who were married and should now have lives of their own still hovered near the family home. What is more they appeared to revert to childhood when they were together, each vying for attention by being louder and more amusing than the others. As a result dinner was an hilarious meal and the only time I have ever experienced anything like it was at school when the masters were away or even further back in my own nursery days.

There was only one who did not appear to join in. At first I did not notice her. Decima, the youngest. I supposed her to be about sixteen or seventeen, but with her grave little face and downcast eyes, she could have been older.

My attention was drawn to her when the meal was over and the gentlemen rejoined the ladies in the parlour. A game was suggested and much good-natured quarrelling ensued as to what we should play. I saw Decima heading for the door and thought it a pity she should miss out on all the fun so I said to her sister M, "Pray call Miss Decima back, she will miss the game!"

M. laughed gaily, "My dear sir, do not bother about poor Decima. She never plays games. Not only is her demeanour far too serious for our frivolity, she is also a trifle deaf and one is forever having to recall her from the land of dreams to attend to her cards or her counters. Believe me, playing with her is pure tedium!" She spoke so heartlessly that I found myself immediately in sympathy with the poor girl. How a sister could mock her deafness as though it were of no importance, I simply could not understand. Decima had reached the door, but I could see she had heard her sister's comments for she had blushed to the roots of her hair, so I could not call her back to face more ridicule. I determined to be kind to her should I be given the opportunity during the rest of my short stay."

Well, Decima certainly didn't sound like a man-eater. I felt ever so slightly sick at this first peep into the home life of the girl. It wasn't much, but there was a heartlessness there, a callous indifference to her affliction and her dignity. To denigrate her in front of a stranger – and a young handsome man, at that – was an entirely different matter to good-natured teasing within the family. That wasn't nice.

Lil looked in, "We'd better have some lunch now. We don't want to be still at the table when the vicar comes to call."

I wasn't hungry, and looked longingly at the books spread out on the table in front of me, "Coming Lil," I said obediently, thinking, "If she brought me here to investigate Decima, why the hell doesn't she leave me alone to get on with it?" But of course I said nothing and trailed after her into the kitchen.

It was fortunate she had suggested we eat when we did, for the vicar arrived just as we were washing the dishes. Lil ushered us into the sitting room, presented us with a tray of tea and biscuits, then took herself off for a lie down. As she had bustled about making the tea, I had taken the opportunity to peruse his face and pretty well liked what I saw. He was about forty, I guessed, which somehow comforted me. The thought of telling my tale to some smooth-faced enthusiast whose voice had barely broken was not a pleasant one. His dark hair was a little grey at the temples and the crinkles at the corners of his eyes were caused by a kind smile.

"Now, Miss … er … I'm sorry, your aunt didn't tell me your name,"

"Call me Libby,"

"Very well, Libby, I'm Thomas Hills – call me Tom. Now, what did you want to see me about?"

I gave him a potted version of the events over the past few days, including the marks on my throat and the run-in with my mother. He was very good, listening patiently, making no comments and asking only a few pertinent questions – not only about Decima, but about my own home life too, and my relationship with Brendan. When I finished he looked thoughtful, but neither grave or horrified, which gave me a little more confidence, "Libby, you do understand that I'm not about to do an exorcism or anything of that kind, don't you?"

"I'd rather be told you don't feel you need to."

He smiled, "Just at the moment I'm not sure I do. But I'm more than willing to tell you what I think – one doesn't join the Ministry unless one has a covert affection for the sound of one's own voice. Do you want me to go on?"

"By all means. I can take it on the chin." I wondered what the heck he was talking about, but I was intrigued.

"I don't have much time for amateur psychologists, but in my job you can't help but pick up a few insights over the years. I'm no shrink, so don't think that what I'm telling you is necessarily the truth, but I feel you identify much more closely with Decima Watkins than you believe you do."

"Go on, I'm all ears," I hoped I didn't sound as cynical to him as I did to myself. Identify with a cold-blooded murderer – I think not.

"You say you don't think Decima was innocent of poisoning her sisters – but I suspect you are very much afraid that she did commit the murders. And that if she was capable of such callousness, then maybe you are too."

"Are you saying I'm hiding murderous intent?" I tried to sound light-hearted, but I admit I was a bit shocked. This was forthright – even from a man who had been given permission to be straight.

"Certainly not. I'm saying that Decima did not get on with her family, she felt an outsider, rejected by them and in her turn rejecting everything they stood for. You openly admit there is little love lost between yourself and your mother and sister. They seem to 'gang up' on you, share secrets and confidences from which you are excluded. They enjoy each other's company whilst you cannot wait to get away from their society. You seem to feel they see you as insignificant, your opinions unimportant. In that you and Decima are similar. But it goes further. Decima blamed her family from parting her from the man she loved – so do you."

"I most certainly don't love Brendan."

"I didn't mean Brendan, I meant your father – every girl's first love – and I don't mean that in an unpleasant way. Naturally I am not suggesting anything untoward in your relationship with your father."

"Good!" I said shortly, "Because there wasn't. And isn't. He's just a nice guy – too good for the likes of my mother. Why do nice men always go out with bitches?"

"That's another realm of psychology altogether, my dear. If you don't mind we'll explore that some other time. And I'd venture to suggest my wife is very far from being a 'bitch' as you so eloquently phrase it." He smiled as he spoke, so I was sure he hadn't taken offence.

"Maybe you're not a 'nice guy'." I ventured slyly, then added "That's fine by me. Well, so far you are not making perfect sense, but I'm prepared to be open-minded. But how do you explain the hanging dream and the rope marks?"

"The mind is a very powerful thing. If you are feeling angry enough with your mother to subconsciously wish her harm, perhaps you have also punished yourself by inflicting the same fate on yourself as was inflicted on Decima. You have, after all, been spending most of your time thinking,

97

breathing and studying her."

"But the marks and the bruises are real. The mind can't produce physical harm."

"Can't it? The stigmata springs to mind."

That did give me something to think about – and I wasn't sure it was any more comforting than imagining that I was being haunted by a malicious ghost.

❦

CHAPTER THIRTEEN

When Tom left I mulled over his words for a few minutes, then dismissed them and went back to my study of the Allingham diaries. I found it very difficult to accept that I might feel subconsciously murderous towards my family. Yes, they bugged the hell out of me. Yes, they made me feel excluded – in fact I didn't just feel excluded, I was excluded, but I really didn't think I wished them dead – struck dumb on occasions, but not dead. There was, however, one niggling doubt. I recalled, only too clearly, just how livid I had been when they started to threaten and bully Lil. For one single split second there, if I had had a weapon, I think I might almost have been able to use it. The vicar's musings were, perhaps, a little too close for comfort.

Richard Allingham falling slowly in love with Decima was much more soothing.

21st March, 1853. I rose early this morning. Force of habit, I'm afraid. Would that I could shake off the shackles of army life as easily as Percy seems to! He has no difficulty in being a slug-a-bed! I wake before seven and cannot be still. Usually it is something to regret, but not today! Today I was not the only person to be abroad with the servants. Decima met me at the breakfast table at eight. Since we the only two there, she had no choice but to converse with me, though I could see that at first it was extremely painful for her. Her cheeks took on the hue of two rosy apples and she could barely lift her eyes to mine. I soon set her at her ease, speaking to her as one might to a skittish horse or a frightened child. Recalling what her sister had told me yesterday I made sure I spoke clearly, but was not so unkind as to raise my voice excessively or to correct her when she misheard me – in truth, I said nothing that was important enough to bother correcting. We merely discussed the weather, the food we were eating, and her multitudinous family. The only time she showed any animation on this latter subject was when she told me of her nephews and nieces – they, at least, treated her with affection and respect. Not that she complained of ill treatment at the hands of her siblings. Her silences were far more telling than a long list of their wrong-doings.

As she became more comfortable in my presence, she began to introduce topics of conversation herself and I was rather surprised to find how very intelligent she is. It seems that her childhood delicacy has made her somewhat isolated from the interests pursued by her sisters – who seem inclined towards the physical, being neck-or-nothing riders to hounds and sportswomen in general. Her inclination has always been much more cerebral. She reads extensively – often books which her father, had he known she possessed them, would have swiftly confiscated! I found her enchanting. A curious mixture of naivete and worldliness!

We chatted for so long that presently we heard the advent of the rest of the family descending the stairs and gathering in the hall, so I turned to her and said quietly but clearly, with what I hoped was a winning smile, "I should like to continue our discussion, Miss Decima, pray escape with me before the horde is upon us!"

She looked a little shocked, her little pearl-like teeth sinking guiltily into her lower lip, "I ought not..." she began and looked worriedly at me. She has the loveliest eyes, green with flecks of brown and gold and this was the first time I had seen them clearly, for always since our first introduction she has kept them lowered demurely, shielded by the longest, blackest lashes I have ever seen on a woman. I suppose it was merely my fancy, but I swear when our eyes met that first time, the breath was suspended in us both. I know I was stunned by the impact of her glance – and by God, I hope she experienced the same! If she did not, I have lost my heart in vain!

"Be quick!" I murmured, "Will you come with me or not? The enemy is at the door!"

Suddenly she grabbed my hand and we fled together through the door at the rear of the room which gives on to the passageway which leads through a green baize door to the kitchens. We managed to evade the servants, who were busily going about the task of bringing trays of food and drink to the dining room. We hid in a doorway until they had passed us, then she led me on through another passageway, through a door and out into the stable yard.

All was quiet out there. Decima told me that the outdoor staff would be gathering in the servant's hall ready for their own breakfasts after the family had been fed. Though the day was pleasant and the sun shone, hinting at the promise of an early spring, still it was chilly. I noticed she shivered slightly in her cotton day dress, for all it had long sleeves.

"Is there nowhere indoors we can go? You are cold without a shawl or cape."

"Escape?" She lifted those bewitching eyes to mine again, "But we have escaped!"

I did not bother to correct her, merely saying a little more loudly, "Shall we go into a stable? You are cold."

She nodded swiftly as she understood me and with a swift glance about her, to ensure we were not observed, she hurried towards the darkened doorway of the nearest loose box, her full skirts swinging like a bell with the motion of her hips. It was all I could do to drag my eyes away from her tiny waist and the tendrils of auburn hair which hung down her back and follow her into the safety of the stable. It was dusty and half-dark in there, huge cobwebs were strung across the exposed beams, but she appeared not to notice. She sat on a bale of hay and did not object when I sat beside her, but I saw the blood had stained her cheeks once more and her eyes resumed their contemplation of her demurely folded hands. I had so much I wanted to say to her – and not a word with which to say it! When I did find my tongue at last, my utterance was so simple as to be embarrassing – at least I thought so. She seemed quite happy to merely hear my voice; "May I call you Decima?"

"Of course, if I may call you Richard."

"It is my name! Richard Algernon Allingham at your service!"

She began to laugh – an enchanting sound, "Oh dear me! Algernon! That is almost worse than Decima!"

"I'll have you know, young lady, Algernon is a very old Allingham family name!" I pretended wounded dignity, but found it hard not to join her laughter, so infectious was her merriment.

"Well, when you have a son," she said, completely unabashed, "pray do him the service of calling him something else!"

"I suspect I will have the wisdom to leave the naming of my offspring to my wife!" I assured her. Her face grew suddenly serious; "Did you say your wife? You are married? I'm sorry, I must have missed that piece of information! I fear I miss more than is good for me!"

I laughed at her sudden conversion into a prim and proper young lady and prevented her rising and leaving me by catching hold of her hand, "I have no wife – yet, Decima! I meant my future wife!"

She did not withdraw her hand from mine, but stood in front of me and perused my face with fascination, "I think you must be quite old not to be married," she said, "Your mama must despair of ever seeing a grandchild!"

"She does, but I dare swear she will not be held in suspense much longer."

"You have someone in mind?" she asked, her small white hand lying comfortably in mine, her green eyes looking directly into my own, "I think perhaps I have," I replied, and kissing her fingers I rose and led her back into the house."

I had to stop reading for a moment to catch my breath. I had never really believed in love at first sight, but I had to admit, Richard and Decima gave a damn good impression of it. I was half in love with Richard myself. He was almost impossibly nice. A gentleman through and through and in every sense of the word. Any other vacationing soldier would not have given his host's young, plain, deaf daughter a second glance – but having done so, he would certainly have pressed his advantage and thrown her to the floor of a deserted stable to give her a good seeing to. I gathered she was ripe for seduction and would not exactly have fought him off – I know I wouldn't have, given half the chance. And how often in those days did a man find himself alone in a stable with a Victorian virgin? Not often, I'll be bound.

22nd March, 1853. Percy claimed my attention for most of the day today. I could hardly dismiss him in order to pursue his youngest sister, but I have never been more so inclined. Had I known the plans he had for me, however, I should not have hesitated. I had wondered, once or twice in passing, what had prompted him to suddenly become so friendly and to invite me to his home. Today I discovered the reason. It seems he has an ongoing feud with his father. It is very subtle and hidden and all the family pretend to be unaware of the tension between father and son, but I suspect they all know about it – except poor Decima, who is told nothing. She was as astounded as I when I confided in her this evening.

To return to Percy – albeit reluctantly! He has long held a grudge against his father. I know nothing of the particulars, but I understand it was the reason why he took the King's shilling in the first instance. He knew his papa would be mortified to have an ordinary soldier in the ranks and it was not long before a Commission was purchased – once Mr. Watkins had realized Percy would not be prevailed upon to leave the service. Of course none of this concerned me in the least. I had my own Commission merely to show my own father that he could not hope to continue to rule my life as he had for so long. No, this was not the issue! But for Percy to use me in his petty quarrels is unforgivable! I shall not soon forget the expression of triumph on his face when he finally confided to his father that I was the son of the same William Allingham who had recently bested him in a business venture which had cost him a great deal of money and some dignity! Percy thought it a grand joke that I had been offered unlimited hospitality by his dear, unsuspecting papa! My position in this house is now untenable. I should pack my bags and leave immediately, but then, there is Decima. I must at least speak to her alone before I leave."

24th March, 1853. I did not see Decima today. I asked after her – in as casual manner as I could manage – and was told that one of her sister's children was unwell and she was the only one who could calm the fractious infant. Somehow that made her seem even more desirable in my eyes. I began to think of her constantly, counting the moments until dinner when I might see her again. I cannot understand this reaction myself, so I hope no one ever expects me to explain it! Only two or three days have passed since I was a man blissfully ignorant of the existence of Decima Watkins. Then I saw her and felt nothing but mild interest followed by overwhelming pity. How this changed to the passionate desire I feel for her presence now, I do not know. One glance of those bewitching green eyes and I knew I had met the woman with whom I wish to spend the rest of my life. I cannot be happy until I meet her before a priest and make her my wife. God knows how this will be achieved. Her father hates the name of Allingham with a frightening intensity and mine would see me dead at his feet before he would allow me a marry a dowerless girl from a commoner's family. But both must be prevailed upon to see sense! I will have Decima for my wife – if she will have me!"

I was so deeply engrossed in my reading that I didn't notice David Wright had entered the room until he spoke, "Hello, am I disturbing you?"

"Hello," I felt myself growing horribly red as I recalled our last discussion on the telephone. To cover my embarrassment, I attempted false heartiness which fooled neither of us, but made me feel slightly more confident, "You've become quite a stranger. Afraid of what you might find hanging from the beams?"

"Not in the least. I always carry my trusty pruning knife, I'd have you down in a second."

So sarcasm was to be the order of the day. Well, I couldn't say I blamed him. How exactly did one talk to a woman whom one believed to be a suicidal maniac? "That's comforting to know. I must bear it in mind. Was there something you wanted, or is this a visit to check on my mental state?"

He pulled a chair out from under the dining table where I was sitting and sat down, "Do you think we might stop all this backbiting and have a sensible discussion? I wasn't very inclined to come out here and I might as well admit it. If there is one thing that makes me as mad as hell it is having the telephone hung up on me. My first reaction was to let you stew in your own juice, but I care about Lil and... and I couldn't leave the pair of you here alone if there really are weird things happening to you."

I had the grace to feel a little ashamed that I had misjudged him so badly – but it served him right for being so bloody obtuse. If he had put his point across more clearly, I would never have lost my temper with him.

"Are you trying to apologise and say that you didn't believe the lies Brendan was telling about me?"

"Apologise? That's rich coming from you. I haven't done anything to apologise for, and I certainly never said I believed that crazy boyfriend of yours."

"I've told you," I said evenly, trying to keep a rein on my temper, "He's not my boyfriend."

"Whatever," he snapped back.

"Why don't you just bugger off?"

"Why don't you grow up?"

Lil walked in and we both subsided guiltily. "Having a nice chat?" she asked breezily. I'm sure she had heard every word, but neither of us contradicted her, "I've put the tea on to brew, it won't be a minute. David, has Libby told you about the diaries Rick Allingham lent her? Apparently they have the full story of Richard and Decima's love affair. I've barely been able to drag her away from them since she got up this morning."

David glanced at me, "No, she hasn't told me a thing, Lil, but I'm looking forward to hearing everything over a cuppa."

Lil went off happily to bring the tea and he said quietly, "For God's sake, Libby, I'm trying my best to help you, but I'm in way over my head here. You know I want to believe you, but I'm the world's biggest cynic. I'm not even sure I believe in God and an afterlife, let alone the concept of ghosts that can inflict physical harm on living human beings. I only know that I'm sure you sincerely believe something is haunting you. Don't ask for any more than that, because I can't give it."

I had to give him full marks for honesty, if nothing else. I looked into his eyes and felt my anger fading away. What was the point in being obstinate? I didn't even believe in what was happening myself, so how could I expect him to? And if anyone needed a friend right now, it was me.

"Alright, alright! I get the picture. You're not the enemy. But even you must understand how all this is affecting me. I'm frantic with worry about Lil, my family are all plotting against us, helped by a man I hoped I would never have to see again. Just to add to the complications, I'm being frightened stiff in a house that I used to love. Is it surprising that I'm feeling a little tetchy?"

He stretched out a hand and briefly gripped mine in that gesture of his that was becoming warmly familiar, "Of course I understand, but ease up on taking it out on me, will you?"

To my complete astonishment and embarrassment, electric shocks sped up my arm. I wanted to snatch my hand away, but having just promised to be more friendly, I could not – but by God, this was a complication I really didn't need, especially as it was fairly evident from our very first meeting that he had less interest in me than he had in Lil. I tried to assure myself that I was just feeling vulnerable and soppy because of what I had just been reading. Damn Decima! She was taking over my entire life. Now I was even feeling romantic because I knew she had fallen in love with Richard.

This thought brought me up short. Of course I knew no such thing. Richard had admitted to falling in love with her – but I knew nothing of her feelings. She might have just seen a chance to escape an intolerable family home. Nothing Richard had written had given any indication that she had seen him as anything more than one of her brother's cronies.

Above our heads there was the sound of little feet pattering across the bedroom floor. We both instinctively looked up. Then I realized David had heard it too, "Was that footsteps?" he asked, his voice only just louder than a whisper.

"It was. The only trouble is, Lil is in the kitchen, there's no one else in the house – and that bedroom is carpeted with shag-pile. You couldn't hear the footfall of a man wearing hob-nailed boots."

"Oh," he didn't say anything else, but looked into my eyes. I hoped he couldn't see the expression in mine that was begging him to help me. And yet, I suppose I hoped he could.

❦

CHAPTER FOURTEEN

When Lil came back into the room, the noises upstairs ceased abruptly. David and I never referred to them again for the duration of his visit.

Lil was eager to hear what I had learnt of the meeting and subsequent romance between Richard Allingham and Decima, so I gave them both a brief outline of the story.

"Well, now we know why the romance was doomed," said Lil, when I reached the point where I had stopped reading, "It's seems hard to believe the social divide was so insuperable in those days, doesn't it? No one would turn a hair at the aristocracy marrying into the working class these days, would they?"

"Don't you believe it, Lil," said David quietly, "You should hear Rick Allingham on the subject. His mama is forever presenting him with high-society misses in the hopes he'll do the decent thing and marry into the upper crust."

"You couldn't be more wrong, my dear David," said Lil with a grim smile, "Rick's mama just wants him to get married – take my word for it, she doesn't care who she is, just as long as she is a she."

David looked a little shocked, then grinned, "You don't miss much, do you Lillian?"

"Not a thing, my love."

"Well, this gives us some insight into why Decima was denied her heart's desire, but it doesn't tell us whether or not it made her angry enough to poison her sisters. The trouble is that though Richard knew our girl, he only knew her when she was young, sweet and in love. Did she really change so drastically when he died that she could commit murder?"

The other two looked at me as I mused aloud and I knew my cheeks were burning when I felt David's blue eyes upon me, genuinely interested in what I had to say, but evidently unaware of the new emotions he was rousing in me. I couldn't understand the sudden change in me. I had thought him pleasant enough from the first and acknowledged that he wasn't unhandsome, but to suddenly veer from disinterest to breath-stopping passion was more than I could handle. I supposed it was because he had been so considerate when I needed him the most. Compared to Brendan he was the image of masculine perfection, let's face it. The thought briefly skittered across my mind like a chased mouse, that perhaps Decima was taking over my emotions again, as she seemed to have done when I was angry with my family, but I firmly repelled it. Bad enough to think I was being physically haunted by the bloody girl, without giving her credit for demonic possession.

Obviously I was just feeling vulnerable and David was the only available male. Leave it at that – altogether much safer than any other explanation – and he need never know, as long as I didn't do something stupid like throwing myself into his arms again.

I could scarcely believe it when he seemed to read my thoughts and asked casually, "Do you think we might go out for dinner this evening, Libby?"

I hoped I didn't look as shocked as I felt. It seemed to take me ages to gather my thoughts enough to stammer out a reply, "I wouldn't mind, but I think I ought to stay with Lil."

"Nonsense!" intercepted Lil briskly, "You go out and enjoy yourself. I'll be fine. I've been feeling so much better since you've been here, Libby, that I think I might find I've been crying wolf. I feel as though I can't shuffle off this mortal coil anyway until I've solved the mystery of Decima and the poison."

I smiled at her and took her hand, "If that's the case, I think we'll leave it a mystery forever."

Strangely enough, it did seem to be true. She had definitely had more energy in the past couple of days, but that could have been because I had been such a liability that she'd had no choice but to brighten up. It was rather ironic that I had given up work to come and care for her and she had spent most of my visit looking after me.

"Is it a date, then?" asked David.

"It looks like it," I agreed, trying not to sound – or feel – too eager.

"I'll pick you up at seven. In the meantime, do a bit more digging into the history books. No offence, Lil, but I have the feeling there will be no peace for Libby until Decima is either vindicated or damned once and for all."

He left and I obediently went back to my books.

25th March, 1853. I spent the whole day trying to meet with D. alone, so that I might speak my heart to her, but the task was damned near impossible. I don't know if her family have recognized my interest and are deliberately keeping her away from my society, or if that is merely my fevered fancy, but I met obstacle after insuperable obstacle. It took all my ingenuity to finally bring about a congress, which actually took place in her own room, whence I had followed her when the household were changing for dinner. I did not even knock, but merely slipped in through the door after her when she entered. Her face was white in the gloom, for dusk was upon us and she had not even had the opportunity to light the candles or the lamps. "Dear God! Are you running mad? My father will kill you if he catches you here – and me too, if it comes to that!" she whispered in genuine anguish. I took hold of her hand, "I don't care! He can shoot me like a dog, but I must speak to you!" She looked puzzled and I realized she could barely make out my words as I was forced to lower my voice below the level she can hear. I was overwhelmed by my love for her. Why should her vulnerability clutch at my heart so? I don't know, all I do know is that she seemed to need protection more than any other woman I had ever met – and I wanted to be the man to protect her.

"Decima, listen to me! I haven't much time and it is entirely inappropriate that I should be here at all. Thanks to Percy and his mindless japes, I am no longer welcome here and must leave soon. Before I go I intend to ask your father for permission to pay court to you. He may refuse, but I am relying on his ambition to change his attitude. Saving your presence, my father's son is no mean catch for the Watkins family!"

She smiled with an amusement which made me feel like a callow boy in the presence of a woman of the world, "You do have a high opinion of yourself, don't you?"

"Not at all, my sweet love! I have never felt less worthy! But if you will consent, you will make me the happiest of men! Decima, I humbly ask you to be my wife!"

"How can you do so? You barely know me. I might be a fishwife for all you know! I might be petulant, ill tempered, unchaste! You may be incurring my papa's wrath and your own father's displeasure for a shrew of a wife!"

I could not help but smile, "Are you any of those things, sweetheart?" She looked deep into my eyes for a long time before she whispered, "For you I will not be so!"

"That is all I ask. May I speak to your papa?"
She nodded and I drew her into my arms and kissed her for the first time.
At the first touch of our lips I knew I had not been mistaken! Decima was
meant to be mine as surely as the sun rises and the rain falls."

Ahh! I heaved a satisfied sigh. God, this was better than Mills and Boon. He
was such a darling man. Why couldn't men be like that these days? Mainly,
I suppose, because women weren't like Decima and her ilk. A man could
hardly offer to protect you if you were more likely to get involved in a pub
brawl than he was. Poor David had been trying – and all he'd got for his
pains was a mouthful of abuse. I told myself I had to be kinder to him from
now on. But it wouldn't be easy. I was too used to fighting my corner to
suddenly become a prissy little woman now.

*26th March, 1853. Naturally the Watkins family are too courteous to
merely ask me to leave, but it has been made uncomfortably obvious that
this is their wish. M. has been sending me languishing looks, but even she
dare not defy her father by making her true feelings known. Only Decima
has had the courage to continue in my society despite their tacit
disapproval. I know it has not been easy for her, but she has changed
overnight. No more is she shy and reticent. She blossoms with health and
happy smiles – mainly aimed at me, I'm delighted to say. I take my leave in
the morning so I asked to see Mr. Watkins today privately in his study. I
could see that he had no wish for the interview to take place, but short of
being downright rude, he could not gainsay me.*

*It was evident from his severe expression that he knew he was not going
to like what he was about to hear from me, but nevertheless I plunged in,
"Sir, I would be a fool to deny that I know my presence is no longer
welcome in your home, but I cannot pretend to know why. My father has
offended you in some way – I can do nothing about that, but I ask you now
to put aside such considerations."*

"Might I be allowed to ask why I should do any such thing?"

*"Sir, I hesitate to speak plainly after so short an acquaintance, but I have
no choice. I have come here to ask your leave to court one of your
daughters."*

*He smiled slightly, "Ah, I should have known! Well, they are a pretty,
spirited set of lasses, so I suppose I should not blame you! I suppose it is
Martha who has caught your fancy?"*

"No, sir,"

"Jemima, then?"

"No."

"It cannot be any of the elder girls, they are all married!"

"It is Decima, sir,"

His face changed as though I had spoken a foul oath in his presence, "You cannot possibly speak with candour, sir! You are cruel to mock the poor child thus!"

I was astounded at his reaction. I suppose Decima, poor plain, deaf little Decima, might not be every man's first choice, but by God, she was mine! He spoke as though she carried some dread disease, or bore some unsightly scar and I felt the anger rise in my breast, "Decima is my choice, sir! I dare you to speak one word of detriment of her to me!"

"Don't speak to me, thus, you young puppy, or I'll have my servants throw you out on the street, bag and baggage! You are indeed your father's son if you think arrogance and discourtesy will win the day for you! Decima will never be allowed to marry! She came into this world incurably marred and I will see that she passes on none of her imperfections!"

I knew I had to control my anger and calm him if I was ever to make him see reason, "My dear sir, Decima is but a little deaf! That is hardly a cause to deny her the right to marry and produce children! There is every likelihood that her offspring will be as healthy as any other child!"

"Do you think I will risk that? Decima's life is already planned. She will make herself useful to her sisters and their children. When that duty is done, she will in turn nurse her mama and myself in our dotage! Anything else is unthinkable!"

"Sir, I beg you to reconsider..."

"There will be no further discussion, sir! If there was ever the remotest possibility that I might change my mind, it certainly would not be to ally myself to your family! I can see now the sneers of your father and mother when they find that Jacob Watkins has dared to foist such a monstrosity upon their son! I will not do it!"

I have never been nearer to striking a man full in the face, only his age and my own need for Decima stopped me. I could not believe he so viewed his child. Decima was by far the prettiest of her sisters, she was also the sweetest natured, the most intelligent by far. For this one flaw of deafness she was to be condemned to eternal spinsterhood! Well, not if I had ought to say on the matter! If she had to be persuaded to elope with me, then so be it! I said nothing more to the man, merely made my formal bow and left him.

I went to my room to pack my clothes, wondering how I might have *words with Decima before I left. Now that I had made my intentions obvious, it would not be easy! As I approached the door I saw a note lying on the floor. Evidently it had been thrust under the door. When I read it my heart leapt, even though its contents were, ostensibly, unhappy.*

"My dearest love,
Papa knows all and has arranged for me to be sent away. His first thought was to send me abroad, but I have convinced him that I will be safe enough with my grandmother in Derbyshire. He knows that your home is very near, but I have told him that you are about to return to your army career and will presently be sent to the Continent yourself. This of course swiftly changed his mind about sending me to Switzerland! Percy redeemed himself slightly by confirming the contents of the orders you have been sent!
I will wait for you at Hill Farm, but for God's sake, do not let this note fall into the wrong hands or we will be undone!
Your own Decima."

I doubt I have ever packed and left a house more swiftly in my life! Of course I am not about to be sent back to Europe! I shall go home to Havering and endeavour to persuade my father that Decima should be my wife. I am reluctant to estrange myself from my family unless there is no other choice. It cannot be denied that life with Decima would be a great deal easier with the support of at least one set of parents! Papa shall meet her whilst we are in Derbyshire, and surely he cannot fail to love her as I do!"

Want to make a bet on that, Richard? I thought sadly. This pair of lovers certainly didn't have it easy. And what a beast Decima's dad had turned out to be. I already hated him from the little bit of the trial I had read, but this really took the biscuit. Did he honestly believe being slightly hard of hearing really made Decima some sort of a freak who shouldn't be allowed to reproduce? It was hard to credit such thoughts ever existed in the minds of men.

Lil came in to remind me that if I wanted a bath and hair wash before David came to pick me up, then I had better get a move on.

Reluctantly I closed the books. I was getting used to be dragged back into the present just as the past was getting interesting, but this was particularly hard. Finally I was about to learn exactly what part this house played in the romance of Decima and Richard. It would be nice to think that here within these very walls was the first place they ever made love to each other – but I would have to wait a little longer to find out.

CHAPTER FIFTEEN

David was punctual – as he always was. It was one of the better things about him. I always felt that lateness hid an arrogance that boded ill for the future of any relationship even one of friends. After all, what makes anyone think they have the right to leave you standing around twiddling your thumbs for them? It is a tacit admission that they think their time is more important than yours. I'm never late without a damned good reason and I expect everyone else to be the same.

As we approached the car on the rutted lane he said, "I've chosen somewhere quiet so that we can talk, is that ok with you?"

"That rather depends on what you want to talk about," I answered warily. I certainly wasn't up for a lecture on my mental state.

"Lil, mostly, but you too. I know I should mind my own business, but I'm worried about the pair of you."

"Look David, I'm hungry – and when I'm hungry I get grumpy. Shall we save this for after the starters?"

"Of course."

True to his word he kept up a flow of small talk, but said nothing important until we were warmly ensconced at a candlelit table, with wine and food in front of us.

"Now, even though our acquaintance is short, I've already learned that, like your aunt, you don't welcome interference, but I have to say I'm not happy about the two of you staying in that isolated house alone."

"Volunteering to come and live with us, are you?" I intercepted facetiously and was astounded when, with perfect gravity, he replied, "I think that if it was at all possible, I might just do so. But unfortunately I'm not in a position to do that. The only solution I can see is that Lil take up the offer of a place in a hospice and you find somewhere nearby so that you can visit her every day."

I was utterly appalled by his betrayal and it must have shown on my face because he immediately reached out and tried to take my hand, "Don't look like that, Libby. I really don't like it any more than you do, but there's something odd happening in that house with you and Lil there alone and I don't like it."

"I thought you didn't believe in ghoulies and ghosties," I said stiffly.

"I don't – and I don't necessarily think that your mishaps are anything to do with the afterlife. It's easy enough to break into Lil's – she's never felt the need to be overly security conscious. After all, as she says, she hasn't anything worth pinching, she doesn't keep money on the premises – but there are other reasons than robbery to break into a house."

"What the hell are you talking about?"

"Look Libby, I don't want to alarm you, or make unsubstantiated accusations, but it's easy enough to cut part way through a picture wire so that it eventually snaps. And I have to say the fuse box showed definite signs of having been tampered with. Strange noises are enough to scare anyone when they don't know the cause. I think someone is trying to drive you and Lil out of that house – but you are both so stubborn, they might just succeed in frightening you both half to death first."

"And who do you suggest is doing it?" I asked with a cold edge to my voice. Everything he was saying was making me more furious with every passing moment. I didn't know why, but suddenly it was vitally important to me that it was Decima who was haunting Hill Farm. I didn't want to believe that all the things that had happened had a prosaic explanation. This was altogether too romantic a story to have died with the demise of the players concerned in it. I knew it was totally illogical, but I wouldn't let Decima and Richard be dead and dust in their graves. I wanted them to still be around. I didn't want them to be gone – I couldn't bear them to be no more. The feeling I had now, that little pain in the pit of my stomach, the slight nausea, was exactly how I had felt when my elder sister had told me that Mother and Dad were splitting up. The scarcely contained terror that she might be telling the truth, the determination that she was saying these things just to get a rise out of me – it all came flooding back now. In a crowded restaurant, with mushroom and Stilton bake steaming gently in front of me, I felt like screaming like a banshee, "You don't know what you are talking about! You don't know anything!" I don't know how I contained myself, but thank God I did. If there's one thing I can't bear it's making a fool of myself in public. I'm one of those people who leap to their feet after a fall, swearing I'm ok whilst wincing in agony on a broken ankle.

He noticed something was amiss and ignoring my question he said softly, "Are you alright?"

"I'm fine, thank you. Do you think we could change the subject? Lil and I are not going anywhere. If you think I would break my promise to her, you are sadly mistaken. You may not have the integrity to keep your word, but I do. Still at least we now know who our friends are."

He looked hurt, "That's not fair, Libby and you know it. I'm worried and I don't know how else I can help you."

"Pray don't bother. We are perfectly capable of looking after ourselves."

"Yes, you've done a damned fine job up to now."

My eyes blazed into his, "How very typical of a man to throw feminine weakness into the argument. I fully admit there have been moments when I have been spooked, but if I'd known you were going to use them against me like this, I'd have seen you in hell before I would have given in to them. Thanks for the meal, I'll get a taxi back."

I rose to my feet but he grabbed my arm and pulled me back down, "Don't add misplaced pride to your list of flaws," he said grimly, "Eat your food. You said you were hungry. I know when I'm beaten. I apologise for everything I've said. Just be careful and promise me that you'll ring me, day or night, if you need anything. I'll just have to be satisfied with that, won't I?"

I wanted to tell him to take a running jump, but the mushroom bake suddenly sent up a whiff of aromatic steam and I realized I wasn't just hungry but completely famished, "It certainly looks that way," I said grudgingly, and tucked into my food, not missing his cynical grin, but ignoring it with dignity.

We ate in silence for a few minutes then he ventured, "I suppose I have now so utterly alienated you that you won't allow me to help with your research?"

"It all depends on whether or not you are genuinely trying to be helpful," I told him pompously. He grinned, "By God, you and your aunt Lil certainly came out of the same mould," he said admiringly, "You can't imagine how hard I had to work to get her to take my favours in the beginning."

"I think I can. What are you offering me?"

"As you know, my cricket brings me into contact with people from every walk of life and it occurred to me yesterday that I know a couple of police-men."

"I'm listening," I said cautiously, wondering where this was heading. Surely he wasn't going to suggest a police presence at Hill Farm every night? I couldn't see a truncheon being much use against ghostly footsteps.

"Well, it's not generally known, but most police forces have an archive – somewhat similar to the famous Scotland Yard Black Museum – you know, a macabre collection of things like Jack the Ripper's knife and the noose that hung Christie."

"And?" I prompted, light beginning to filter in.

"Well, it seems logical to think our local constabulary might have something left of the district's criminal past. Didn't you say Decima was living at Hill Farm when she was arrested?"

"She was indeed – but surely her family would have claimed her effects?"

"Do you really think they would? It seems to me they showed no interest in her whatsoever once she had been condemned. And if there is anything left, it might just contain a gallows confession. That would end the speculation once and for all, wouldn't it?"

I was excited. This was almost too good to be true – but I had to curb my enthusiasm. Nearly a hundred and fifty years had passed since Decima died by the hangman's noose. She might not have left anything, and if she had it had probably long since been destroyed. It was all very well keeping hold of mementoes from famous murderers like Christie, Florence Maybrick and Dr. Crippen, but why would anyone ever have heard of Decima Watkins – especially after the efforts my family had evidently made to bury her story as surely as they had buried her poor, broken body.

"Do you really know anyone who can find out for me?" I asked, in a calm manner which I was very far from feeling.

"I'll do my best – but only if you promise to let this matter go when you know the truth. I really don't think it is healthy to keep harking back to the past."

"Alright, 'daddy' I promise. Once I've written the book..."

"Book! You really have got to be joking."

"I might be – ooh, here's my steak – just as I like it. Thank you." This last was aimed at the waitress who smiled at the tone of enthusiasm in my voice. I don't suppose she had many customers who were so glad to see their meal. How could she know my excitement had nothing to do with food and everything to do with the possible existence of the final effects of a woman who was hanged for murder in 1859.

David, as usual, insisted on walking me to the door when we reached home. He stopped me as I was about to put my key in the lock, "I'd just like you to know that you are possibly the most infuriating woman I have ever

116

met, but I can't go on for another moment without doing this..." He turned me around to face him, lifted my chin with a gentle finger, then he kissed me. At first I was too stunned to respond, but not for long...

I suppose I had been expecting him to make a move for a while, despite the fact that we were both insisting we didn't want to complicate our growing friendship with romance. The thing was, it felt right. There was no embarrassment, no nerves, just a solid feeling that I belonged in his arms and would be safe there. A new departure for me, I must admit. Feeling safe was usually just about the last thing I would ever want, but there you go. How do you suppose I got involved with the mad Irishman? It just goes to show that anything is possible in this life.

Thankfully he didn't push it. He kissed me until we both felt it was getting a bit too passionate, then he broke away, "This needs talking about..." he murmured, "I'll see you tomorrow."

Part of me was unutterably disappointed that he'd stopped, the rest wholly relieved that I was not going to have to deal with these new emotions right at this particular moment.

I opened the door, watched him walk away, then went into the dimly lit house. Obviously Lil was already in bed, so I could just make myself a milky drink, lock up and trundle up to bed myself – doubtless to lie awake, wondering what the next step would now be for David and myself. Already the doubts were setting in. Why had he chosen now to kiss me? Had he really fallen in love with me, or was this a sly, manipulative way of softening me up so I would let him persuade me to desert Lil? What was his real agenda, as the business gurus say? Did he have designs on Hill Farm himself? Had he been hoping Lil would either sell or leave it to him in exchange for all his good deeds? Was he really the nice guy he appeared or was he a complete bastard, like every other man it had been my misfortune to date?

It was because I was in such a spin as I walked into the sitting room that Brendan found it so easy to dupe me – that's my story and I'm sticking to it. How else do you explain that you were such an idiot?

He burst through the door, nearly giving me a heart attack with the fright, and started to jabber in such a panic that I was completely swept away by the fear he engendered, "Libby, thank God you're back! It's Lil! She's collapsed. I've been giving her heart massage, but I don't think it's working. Come quick!"

I didn't even hesitate. It crossed my mind to wonder what he was doing in the house, but if Lil needed me, that could be asked about later, "Oh my

117

God! Where is she?"

"In the attic. She went up to see if the skylights were closed when we heard an almighty bang up there, but the stairs must have been too much for her."

I sped past him heading for the stairs, my heart was pounding and I had enough wit to regret that it was to the attic I must go, but I went anyway. This was no time for silly, childish terrors.

I cleared the stairs two at a time and when I reached the door at the bottom of the attic stairs, I didn't think twice before wrenching it open and scaling the second flight of stairs. Only when I reached the top did I turn and face him, "Which room?"

He indicated the far end, "Down there," he said swiftly. Of course, that was the only room with a light on, I could see the beams lying across the bare floorboards. I should have been suspicious then, for that room didn't have a skylight set in the roof, but a little pointy-roofed window – the same window where I thought I had seen the woman standing a couple of days before. Of course I didn't think of any of this until I had walked into the room and realized that it was entirely empty of anything except an unmade bed and a couple of broken-spindled chairs.

It was several unbelieving seconds before I could assimilate that facts and turn to face him. He was stood, his back to the closed door, a triumphant grin on his face, "Surprise, surprise!"

"You unspeakable bastard! Let me out of here right now."

"After all the trouble I went to getting you up here? I don't think so. Tell me, don't you admire my acting skills? I really should have won an Oscar for that little performance."

"Where's Lil?" I tried to keep my tone even, so that he should not know how afraid I was.

"Snuggled up in bed fast asleep as she has been for the past two hours. Really, I don't know how you stand the tedium of this place. The television reception is abysmal and watching Lil sleep is about as entertaining as cricket – but of course, your new little man plays the dreadful game, doesn't he? That's how he knows dear old Ricky. Now there's a man with a big mouth. One only has to flash one's bewitching green eyes and he sings like a canary."

"What the hell are you talking about?"

"Your darling Dave. He really needs to find more reliable friends in whom to confide, my dear. I suspect I know most of your little secrets by now. And I must say, your little love scene in the porch was most affecting.

118

I could hear more than see, I admit, but he certainly knows how to sweep a girl off her feet."

I began to slowly back away from him. I was terrified. His whole demeanour was menacing. The more he sounded normal and friendly the more underlying malice I could sense. He was furious with me. Really, truly livid and I was going to pay the price.

"Why are you doing this, Brendan? What's the point? I've told you we are finished. You were the one who was always carping and criticising, you were obviously unhappy with the relationship, so why do you want me back now?"

He turned suddenly nasty, "Don't flatter yourself, Libby. Who says I want you back? I just know you want me. I only have to wait for you to see the error of your ways and you'll come crawling back. Especially when I tell you what I have found out about your precious Farmer's boy and this place."

That made me decide to humour him – partly because I didn't want to provoke him again, but mostly – and yes, I know it wasn't particularly laudable, but I'm only human after all – I wanted to know what the hell he was talking about. His hints that David was up to no good just tallied too closely with my own recent doubts.

"I'm all ears, Brendan."

"You will be sweetheart. This is a gem. You ought to be grateful. There can't be many women around who get such a vivid insight to the mind of a lover."

"Then tell me."

"Alright, no need to be impatient. Sit down, I'm not going to bite you – though from what I've been hearing about your sexual proclivities, you wouldn't actually object to that."

"Don't start on that again, Brendan! You can think what you like, but I don't want to hear it. It makes me sick to the stomach."

He grinned and gestured that I should sit on the bed, which I did, but with great reluctance and by perching precariously on the edge of the old fashioned and extremely lumpy striped mattress.

"If, as I strongly suspect, Lil has not yet confided in you about the contents of her will, she's been playing fast and loose with you, Libby."

"You've seen her will? How?"

"My dear, I've had two hours to kill. How do you suppose I occupied myself? With crochet work? I went through her papers, of course."

"You had no right."

119

"Of course I had not – that's what made it more fun. And she deserved it for holding a gun to my head. That's not something I'll forgive or forget in a hurry."

"She was protecting me – anyway, get on with your tale."

"Where was I? Ah yes, the will. That makes interesting reading. You are going to be ever so popular with your ma, my dear. All her efforts have been in vain. Lil made this place over to you years ago. It's been held in trust for you. She's been living on your bounty and you didn't even know it."

I know my mouth dropped open, but for a long while no words came out. To say I was gobsmacked was to vastly understate the matter. When his words finally sank in, my first reaction was delight, but then I began to have second thoughts. What the hell was I supposed to do with this place? I certainly didn't want to live out here, alone. Not after my recent experiences. And from the sound of it, I wouldn't be able to sell it. A trust sounded remarkably permanent, and I knew Lil was adamant the property should stay in the family. Quite apart from which, Brendan was right, Mum and Maddie were going to be utterly livid. They would never believe Lil had done this off her own bat. They would think I had been in conspiracy with her – so much for family feeling. They would never speak to me again – and whilst I didn't object to that in theory, in practice how miserable is the thought that those who should love you the most, instead despise you? I had a tiny glimmer of how abandoned and betrayed poor Decima had felt in those last few weeks of her short life.

I dragged my mind back to the present – I was finding it all too easy to identify with Decima, but whenever I did, it nearly always heralded some creepy event that scared the pants off me.

"OK, so Lil has been less than honest, but that's hardly a cardinal sin, is it? She probably knew I'd refuse to accept the house, so she's waited until it's too late for me to object. That was misguided but not unforgivable. And where does David come into all this? He can't possibly have known what was in Lil's will, can he? Not unless he has your talent for housebreaking."

"You couldn't be more wrong, my love. He knows exactly what the situation is. You see, Lil went through a bad patch when she first found she was ill, and he offered to buy this place from her, to remove the worry of running it. She explained then that it wasn't hers to sell. David the ploughboy knows exactly who owns this little goldmine, and all the land around it, plus a goodly sum of money raised by shrewd investment."

I didn't want to believe him, but I knew he was telling the truth. That

120

horrid little pain in the pit of my stomach was back. I couldn't understand why I had been so bloody gullible. Brendan had been right all along. He was the only man around who could put up with me, who loved me in spite of all my faults.

If he had left me alone then, it might all have worked out the way he wanted it, but he had to push his luck and try to join me on the bed. When he tried to kiss me, his hands sliding inside my blouse, I was utterly revolted. David's Judas kiss was still too fresh on my lips for any other man to wipe the memory away. I started to protest and struggle, just about having the presence of mind to keep my voice down so as not to wake Lil, but still being forceful enough for him to know he had misjudged the mood I was in, "Get your slimy hands off me!"

"Come on sweetheart, you know you want to. You know you've missed me as much as I've missed you."

He began groping at the button on the waistband of my trousers. That really made me see red, "Don't even think about it, Brendan. Make one more move and I'll scream rape – because that's what it will be."

He threw me away from him as though I was obnoxious filth, "You bitch! How dare you use that word after everything we've been through together. After I have done all this, just to protect you from a man who's trying to rip you off."

I sat up wearily and pulled my clothes straight, "I'm not going to argue with you, Brendan. I'm grateful you've warned me against David, but that's it. I don't want to come back to you – I don't want any man at all. You're all bastards in your own special ways."

He calmed down immediately and the grin, momentarily missing, was back firmly in place, "You just need a little time to think about things, that's all. And what better place for you to think things through than a nice quiet attic."

As soon as I realized he intended to leave me alone in this room, the panic began to rise, "Brendan, don't be stupid. I'm tired and I want to go to my own bed to sleep. We'll meet up in the morning and discuss things then, shall we? I am grateful, really I am, but I can't think straight just at the moment. Too much has happened tonight..."

With that blasted intuition which made him such a shit when we rowed, he immediately cottoned onto my inner most fears and dreads, "You're afraid of this room, aren't you?"

"I don't know what you are talking about. Just let me go downstairs to bed."

The grin widened, "No, I think my first idea was best. There's a bed there, and it's not particularly cold. You'll be just fine up here until I come back in the morning."

I pretended no more, "Don't leave me here, Brendan, please!" I begged him, tears hovering on the edge of my voice.

He looked around and saw the discarded curtain pole propped against the wall, he picked it up and swung it above his head so that it smashed against the bare light bulb hanging from the ceiling. We were plunged instantly into pitch darkness, "Let me put the light out for you." he said with a laugh as I gasped with shock and fear.

There was one moment of brief light as he opened the door, slipped through it and closed it behind him. I heard the key turn in the lock as I shot across the room and began to hammer on it, crying and begging him to come back and let me out.

His footsteps faded away down the passageway and I sank the floor, whimpering and straining my eyes to see in the gloom.

Never had I been so terrified. God only knew what hovered in the darkness, but I could feel its eyes burning into me.

CHAPTER SIXTEEN

After a few minutes I calmed down enough to scrabble through my sleeves and pockets until I found a hanky so that I could blow my nose and wipe away my tears. I had to approach this sensibly; getting myself in a tizzy wasn't going to help one little bit. I was just going to make myself see and hear things that weren't there if I let my imagination run away with me.

What had happened, after all? So, Brendan had locked me in a room I didn't particularly like the atmosphere of, but it was hardly the end of the world. It must be after midnight by now, so it was only five or six hours to daylight – Oh God! Five or six hours!

I wondered if I could hammer on the floor and wake Lil, but decided that far from waking her and bringing her to my rescue, I was more likely to frighten the life out of her.

I reached up and felt about until my hand fell on the doorknob, which I then gave an experimental twist. No, it was no good; Brendan really had locked me in – no escape there, then. I stared into the darkness, just about able to make out the shape of the bed and chairs, and the dim outline of the window. It was black as pitch outside. If Brendan intended to scare me witless, he had chosen a good night to do it. Not a hint of moonlight in the sky, and grey clouds hid any stars. That was the trouble with the country-side – no street lamps. In London it was never entirely dark, an eternal dusk fell over the city at night, so that even some birds were fooled and sang on. Of course it seemed to be dark compared to daytime, but it wasn't really – and it certainly didn't compare to this all-encompassing murk. I could barely see my hand in front of my face.

I was just debating whether to struggle across the room and get back onto the bed as I was getting cold and cramped, when I thought I smelled some-thing in the room that hadn't been there before. Even as I noticed it, my heart began to pound in the base of my throat and I strained my eyes in the dimness to try and see what it was that was with me.

They say not being able to see heightens your other senses – but being terrified heightens them more.

The first tantalising whiff was so elusive that at first I thought it was merely my imagination playing cruel tricks, but gradually over the space of perhaps five minutes, it grew steadily stronger so that it changed from being speculation to certainty.

The first hint of the dank and mouldy smell could quite easily have been the aroma associated with any room left empty for months on end, but it became stronger and stronger until I was swept, with horrified certainty, into that long dark passageway that led me in my dreams to the foot of the gallows.

I started to pray, quietly but with intensive passion, "Please God, don't let me go there again! Don't let me fall…"

The smell grew so strong that I almost gagged on the strength of it. Now it wasn't just the moisture-ridden passageway, it was the filthy cells, the scent of human misery of every sort, then it was the smell of wet earth and an open grave, the blast of evil air that pours from a newly excavated tomb, the stench of the charnel house…

I pressed myself as tight against the back of the door as hard as I could. Trying to make myself as small as possibly, trying to make myself invisible, as I had when as a child I'd played hide and seek with my sister, but knew that there would be no fun and laughter when she found me, for she was going to push me through the broken, peeling garden gate of the strange old woman who terrified us all with her mad ranting, filthy clothes and horrible smell.

My eyes were fixed on the window. If she came, that would be where she would stand. Somehow I knew that was where she had always stood.

All I could see was the vague outline of the frame. It was slightly less dark outside than it was inside, but only barely. Was that something? Was there a patch of deeper blackness, or were my exhausted eyes inventing the writhing shape, the hint of undulating whiteness that might almost be a face.

Nothing moved, my breathing was almost wholly suspended, the only sound was the pounding of my own heart – or was it? Was that the sound of footsteps in the hallway? Was it Brendan returning, having had second thoughts about doing this dreadful thing to me? Or was it Decima coming to face me, to punish me for having dared to doubt her?

With a shudder I closed my eyes and stuffed my fingers in my ears, repeating over and over again, "Oh God! Oh dear Lord! Please, please protect me from whatever it is out there!"

Barely able to hear through my plugged up ears, I could hardly believe that it was Lil's voice I heard outside the door, "Libby? Libby? Are you in there? What's going on?"

Almost fainting with relief I leapt to my feet and began banging on the door,

"Lil! Lil! Let me out! Brendan locked the door and smashed the light."

"Alright, alright! Calm down. He's taken the key so I'll have to get a spare, just a minute."

It seemed like an eternity waiting for her to return. I faced the door and did not dare to turn round. She was there. I could feel her staring at me – and she wasn't looking kindly, I knew that. I wanted to turn and assure her that I was now a convert, that I believed in her innocence and was appalled that she had been sent to die so barbarously and so young, but I dared not. I was afraid of what I might see. If Decima appeared to me now, it would not be as a pretty young girl, full of love and life, it would be as a half-decomposed corpse, swinging in a gibbet, lumps of rotting flesh falling to the floor with every eerie, creaking swing of the metal cage. I knew that because I could smell the corruption, and hear the tiny metallic squeak of the gruesome pendulum.

"For God's sake Lil, hurry with that key!"

❦   ❦   ❦   ❦   ❦

How she got me downstairs I'll never know. My trembling knees could barely support me and tears were streaming down my face, though oddly I wasn't really crying in the accepted sense of the word. I wasn't sobbing, there was no heaving chest and gasping breaths, just a steady stream of tears which trickled down my cheeks and left icy streaks in their wake. I felt so sad for Decima. She had terrified the bloody life out of me – and still I felt unbearably sorry for her. She was all alone out there – wherever 'there' might be, vilified for eternity for a crime she hadn't committed. No wonder she was angry. But more than anger, I felt her overwhelming despair. She couldn't let up on me. She couldn't risk me getting bored or blasé about her story, because that might lead to me simply packing up and going away. Lil was probably the last person on earth who knew and cared about her – and Lil was dying. Soon there would be no one left on earth who wanted Decima Watkins to be cleared of murder. No one except me. And as Decima had seemed to intuitively know right from the start, I hadn't been that bothered about her either. I had done this thing for Lil and the moment she had been too ill to care any more, I would have dropped it like a hot brick. Of course Decima was taking a risk of another sort, for if she scared me enough, her methods might just back fire on her and I would bugger off anyway. She'd come close to it tonight, but still I couldn't blame her. Sometimes you need a huge shock, an almighty kick up the backside, to bring home the depth of feeling, the desperate importance of something like this. It was all too easy to forget what others had suffered when one was warm and safe and cosy. How many kids today give a second thought to the men who perished in the trenches? How many football thugs stop to think how different their lives might have been if Hitler had won the war? For them the past is something to be ignored – a bore to be endured just to be able to say they have one more GCSE to their names.

But I was now with Decima on this one. Why the hell should the bastard who really did kill her sisters get off Scot-free while Decima carried the can? Maybe they were burning in Hell, if there really is a just God who had punished them, but in the meantime Decima couldn't rest in peace either. I had to do the right thing. I had to send her into the light to join Richard.

I could hardly believe I was thinking these thoughts. I sounded like a bad-taste American cable show – but in that moment I believed every word.

The reason? The expression on Lil's face when she looked over my shoulder and into that attic room. She looked older and more shocked than I had ever seen her. The harsh light of the bare bulb on the landing made her look as white as a sheet and she could scarcely drag her eyes away from whatever it was she had seen in the room behind me when she had finally managed to unlock the door and allow the light to flood in. I didn't turn around and I never asked her what she saw. I didn't dare to know.

She finally got me to the kitchen and proceeded to poke some life into the fire so we could have a cup of tea. I sat on a stool and watched her in silence, hugging myself into the crocheted throw she had grabbed from the back of the sofa on our way past the sitting room.

As she bustled about getting a mug from the sink side and putting tea in the pot, she asked, "What on earth has been going on? Why did you let Brendan into the house, you silly girl. And how did he get you to go up to the attics?"

"I didn't let him in – he broke in. And he told me you had collapsed up there and he had found you and was giving you heart massage. Funnily enough it did not seem quite the moment to double check his story."

"Well, no, perhaps not," she conceded thoughtfully, "He really is a

126

resourceful little man, isn't he? It's a pity I didn't use the gun on him when I had the chance. Maybe we need David to come and help us make this place a bit more secure."

At the mention of his name, everything Brendan had told me came flooding back and my voice was harsh when I retorted back, "I rather think the police will be rather more helpful than a market gardener. And just for the record, I don't think it would help matters at all to have you arrested for murder. It's bad enough having one skeleton in the family closet, thanks very much."

She ignored the latter comment and looked mildly surprised at the former, "Very well. I'll ring them in the morning. Have you and David had another quarrel?"

"Not exactly. Listen Lil, I wasn't going to say anything, because I was given information that I should never have had, but I can't sit here with you and not ask. What exactly did you mean when you said you had spiked Mum and Maddie's guns for them?"

She had the grace to look shamefaced, and then her expression changed to one that was slightly belligerent, "I suppose that means you know about the Trust. But I must say, I can't believe David discussed this with you."

"David didn't. Don't worry Lil, he has been your obedient lap-dog from the word go. He's treated me like a kid – just as you have. What the hell is all this about? Did you think I would throw you out on the street if I suddenly found I owned your house? And why me, anyway? The rest of the family are going to bloody love this, aren't they? I'm not the eldest child of the family, nor was dad. If you are going to hark back to things like trusts and entails, you should have gone the whole hog and picked Uncle Lionel."

"Now calm down, Libby. You are angry and you have every right to be, but I had to leave the house to someone – so why not my favourite?"

That wasn't going to wash – and she might as well know it.

"Don't give me all that old tat, Lillian. You know very well it's not the bequest I object to, but the fact that you didn't tell me before. How the hell do you think this looks now? The family are going to have a field day, saying we cooked this all up between us – and making out that you've lost your marbles and I took advantage of the fact. You don't seriously think they are going to take this lying down do you? We are going to be in Court from now until doomsday."

"No, I don't think so. You really are over-reacting now, Libby. Why should they bother about this old place? As you've pointed out on numerous occasions, there is no gas, highly unreliable electricity, the heating system is archaic – and there is not even a drive to the door. I should think they'll all be delighted to leave the house in your hands."

"Even with all those faults, Lil, this house is worth a bundle. It's huge, it's in good repair and it is isolated. Do you have any idea how much people would be willing to pay for a place like this, away from the rat-race, but near enough to hop back in when the appeal of the countryside begins to wear thin?"

"Really?" she ventured, hesitantly, "Oh dear! I really have dropped you in it, haven't I, sweetheart? I'm so sorry. But there really is nothing I can do about it now."

"Can't this trust, or whatever it is, be undone?"

"Not a hope. I tied it up tighter than – well, a hangman's noose. I didn't want your mother to be able to get her grasping hands on it after I was gone."

I wished she hadn't used that particular analogy, but apart from that, there didn't seem much point in labouring the point. What was done was done and I would have to face the consequences when the time came.

"Right, that seems to be that, then! Shall we go to bed? I'm whacked." Actually I had never been more awake in my life, but she was clearly flagging.

"What are we going to do about securing the house so Brendan can't come strolling back in when the mood takes him?"

"We'll just have to lock up as best we can, but if you don't mind, I'd like to sleep in your room – with the shotgun on hand."

"Of course, love. Do you want another drink before we go?"

"No, I'm fine."

I felt really bad when I saw how slowly she climbed the stairs, hoisting herself on the banister rail with every step. Obviously she was really in pain and it seemed a miracle that she still rose every morning and forced herself through the business of the day.Only at times like these did she let the façade slip and the true depth of her illness peep through. I was very afraid I might be explaining myself to the family much sooner than I anticipated.

That thought made me glance back down the stairs. This was going to be my house – and how the hell did I feel about that?

Lil wanted me to make my home here, to marry and bear children in a home that had been in our family for generations. I wanted to pack my cases and run away as fast as my legs would carry me – or at least a huge part of me wanted to. There was a little corner left that loved these bricks and mortar, that adored every stone lintel, worshipped each windowpane with a passion which stunned me. I had never felt this overwhelming sense of belonging before, never known such contentment in any home I had ever made. It was as though I had merely existed until this moment, had been content to simply have a roof over my head and a bed in which to lay my weary bones.

Suddenly I had a home – a real, warm home, that was all mine. The only thing lacking was a husband to share my hearth – and the man I had chosen to feel safe with had turned out to be as big a rat as the bastard who had locked me in a room I firmly believed was haunted.

Oh, David! How could you do this to me?

❦

CHAPTER SEVENTEEN

Lil slipped off back to sleep straight away, but I lay staring into the darkness for hours. I wasn't afraid, with her lying beside me. She seemed to be immune from Decima's ire – probably because she had been the one who had always believed in the girl's innocence – and I knew I was always safe with Lil beside me.

The trouble was, Lil wasn't always going to be beside me, was she? Most of the time it was hard to believe she was ill at all. She seemed the same old Lil of years ago, when I was a kid, lugging buckets of coal into the house, chopping her own kindling with the sort of hatchet I had been prone to scare myself witless with by imagining it in the hands of Lizzie Borden. Nothing had stopped her then, and it seemed incredible that anything should stop her now – but it was going to. I had to face that fact.

For once my thoughts were not taken up by Decima Watkins, but my Aunt Lil, and I'm not ashamed to say I shed a few tears when I thought of myself in this house without her.

Once again I watched the dawn rise over the hills, then staggered downstairs to make tea.

I might have stayed in bed if I'd known what sort of a day it was going to be.

Mother and Maddie arrived at the ungodly hour of nine, with an impossibly posh and incredibly dense social worker in tow.

I don't like to label people and I hate stereotypes, but this girl really was the epitome of all that is bad about Social Services. For a start when she spoke to Lil, her voice took on an entirely different tone, slow, high-pitched and patronising, as though terminal illness equated in her mind with loss of all faculties, including the normal thought processes.

To be fair, Lil dealt with her perfectly by speaking in a normal voice to all of us then switching to the same squeaky, 'for the benefit of the brain-dead' tone when she spoke to Ms. Hines.

Mother hadn't wasted her time. Brendan had obviously provided her with everything she needed and she used it with a ruthlessness which startled even me, who knew only too well how capable and determined she could be.

"Still in a dressing gown, Libby? Tut, tut. Hardly the picture of efficiency are you my love? Make some tea, there's a good girl. Ms. Hines wants to speak to your Aunt in private."

"I'll bet she does," I spluttered, too angry to even bother trying to emulate my mother's coolness, "Make your own tea if you want it – or send your little lap dog to do it for you. Go on Maddie. I'm sure you make it just the way mummy likes it. We have no Earl Grey, I'm afraid – Aunt Lil prefers Ringtons."

Mother threw a telling glance towards Ms. Hines, "You see what I'm up against, my dear? What could be more reasonable than that perfectly polite request? But no, Elizabeth and her aunt are determined to see me as the enemy, when all I really want is to see them both safe and comfortable."

Ms. Hines smiled in clear admiration for my dear mother, "I do see, Mrs. Richmond, but there really is no need for any of us to become fraught. As you quite rightly say, the care of Mrs. Farrell is our primary concern."

"My dear Ms. Hines, much as I cherish your intentions, I can assure you that my care is in perfectly adequate hands and your intervention is not required," said Lil, with deceptive sweetness.

"I'm afraid we must disagree, Auntie," inserted my mother swiftly, "Your care is in extremely undesirable hands and it is high time this state of affairs is brought to an end."

I suppose I must have been damn near puce by this time, for I caught Maddie grinning unkindly – that same smug, triumphant grin which had adorned her features years ago when she managed to get me in trouble for something she had done. I was grateful for it because it stopped me blowing up. I swallowed – with great difficulty – the bile that had risen in my throat, and wisely kept my mouth shut.

"If you are referring to Libby, I find your comments extremely offensive – she is, after all, the only member of the family who was willing to put aside her own affairs and come here to assist me when I asked her to."

"Yes, and we all know why, don't we?" interjected Maddie with bitterness dripping from every syllable, "She knew she was going to get a house and a pile of money in exchange for her dedication."

Aunt Lil looked at her as though she was something nasty the cat had dragged in, "It would seem you were misinformed, Madeleine. Libby will inherit this house whether she stays and helps or walks away right now. What matters to me is that she came knowing nothing of my plans for the house or my money."

"Yeah, right!" muttered Maddie, almost beaten but not quite, "She was on a pretty safe bet, though, wasn't she?"

"I really don't see what interest all this is to Ms. Hines," I interrupted, beginning to blush at the idea that this complete stranger should see us all exposed so meanly.

"It is every interest, Elizabeth, when your mental state is called into question. You have already attempted suicide whilst supposedly caring for your sick Aunt. There is a host of prescription medications in this house. What is to stop you using them for nefarious purposes – either on yourself or your charge? The temptation to come into your inheritance a little early must be overwhelming for someone as unbalanced as you have proved yourself to be."

It was only Lil catching hold of my arm that stopped me from launching myself at her. I could think of nothing but raking my nails down her carefully made-up face. I've often heard of people talking of the 'red-mist' coming down over their eyes, but I never really expected it to happen to me. I couldn't believe my own mother was doing this to me. By God, she had pulled some rotten stunts in her time, but I had always known deep down that she loved me. Suddenly my whole life with her turned into a filthy lie. It was like cutting into a beautiful piecrust, all golden brown and flaky, and finding a seething, writhing mass of maggots crawling out. Was a few quid really this important to her, that she would sell me down the river for it?

"I told you before, and I will tell you again," said Lil, firmly, coldly and calmly, "There have been no suicide attempts in this house. Libby had an unfortunate injury, but she did not inflict it upon herself."

My mother smiled, and the triumph and utter chill in it froze me for a moment, "If that is the case, then Libby will not mind showing her throat to Ms. Hines, will she?"

I didn't have much choice. To refuse would be to give credence to her words, but I dreaded the expression of shock and horror I would see on the woman's face when she saw the mess my neck was in. I took a deep breath then slowly drew aside the collar of my dressing gown. Mother and Maddie gasped with shock, but Ms. Hines was unmoved. I was stunned by the reactions. Surely it should have been the other way around? After all Mother and Maddie had seen the scars before, the newcomer had not. What the hell was going on?

"How the devil have you managed that?" whispered Maddie, managing to sound intensely savage and stunned in the same breath.

"What? What's wrong?" I asked, turning to Lil for an explanation.

"Nothing my love," she said softly, "There's not a mark on you." She smiled at me as I stared at her, completely mystified.

I put my hand to my throat. It still felt as tender as ever. I went to the mirror that hung above the fireplace and stared at my reflection. She was right. There wasn't a thing to be seen. The long column of my throat was as pale and unblemished as it had been on the day I arrived. Not a rope burn, not a bruise nor a graze, nothing.

With their evidence gone, there wasn't much Mother or Maddie could do. Ms. Hines was now looking askance at mother and it was fairly obvious she felt she was quite out of her depth. I hadn't convinced her that I was sane, but on the other hand, my mother hadn't done herself any favours either. She had evidently gone to town in describing the awful mess on my neck – injuries which could not possibly have healed themselves so completely in the couple of days since their last visit. They didn't hang around to explain themselves any further. My mother threw one last comment at me as she left, but essentially, she knew she was beaten – for the moment at least. "I don't know how you managed to disguise those bruises, Libby, but let me tell you, this is far from over. If you think the family will stand idly by and watch you inherit this house, you are sadly mistaken."

"From what I understand of the situation, mother, I don't have to wait to inherit – the house is already mine. See you around."

Lil and I followed them into the kitchen, as if to make sure they actually left the building, which I know annoyed the hell out of my mother. As they left, David arrived, a box of groceries in his arms.

Now I really was in an awkward situation. My heart gave a little leap when I saw him, his big frame filling the doorway, and my stomach tied itself into knots of anticipation and desire, but at the same time I now knew he had his own agenda where I was concerned. What did he really want – Hill Farm or me? Or neither of us?

Part of me wanted to be angry with him, after all, he had lied to me. Well, perhaps not actually lied, but he had omitted to tell me what he knew and that amounted to the same thing. And the reason behind his silence was almost as important as the silence itself. Had he stayed quiet because Lil had asked him to, or so that he would have time to make me fall in love with him before I knew the truth?

On the other hand, I couldn't afford to fall out with him just now. I needed an ally more than I had ever needed one. And he had promised to help me with my research. I hated the idea of being two-faced and stringing him along, but he had done the same to me, so why not?

I made my smile welcoming, but not too bright, "Hello, David. I wasn't expecting to see you today." That would do – friendly, but faintly casual, almost, one might say, disinterested.

"Lil rang me and asked me to drop in these few bits and anyway, I thought I told you I was going to take you to the local 'Black Museum'," he countered, absentmindedly opening up a packet of biscuits he had just brought and picking one out.

"Oh, was that today?" I said coolly, though I could barely contain my excitement.

Lil chipped in, "What was that?" and David explained what the day's mission was going to be.

"Do you think I might come too?" she asked diffidently and David grinned and swept her into a great bear hug, making me wish, for one foolish second, that I was her, "Of course you can, sweetheart! We'd be delighted to have you along. It'll do you good to get out. I don't believe you've set foot outdoors for days."

"Haven't really felt up to it until today," she admitted, smiling up at him in obvious adoration. Oh, God, I thought, he's the son she was denied so many years ago. And I'm going to break her heart by telling him to sling his hook – when I've finished using him for my own purposes.

We had a quick cup of tea, more of the biscuits, then we set off.

The articles were housed in the no longer used Victorian 'lock up' – not, thank the Lord, the same prison which had held the condemned Decima. I certainly wasn't ready mentally or emotionally, to walk down that self-same passageway I knew so well from my dreams. This had merely been the overnight holding place for brawling drunks or over-pushy prostitutes. The real gaol was some miles away, but still there, David assured me, and I had only to say the word and he would take me there too. I was too full of various emotions to speak on the subject and merely shook my head. My face must have told of a deeper feeling, because he took my hand and gave it that brief warm squeeze which I found both comforting and – now – totally alien.

Fortunately his friend arrived at that moment and he released me swiftly. Introductions were exchanged then Dan Gordon, the curator of this curious collection, showed us around.

It was an odd experience, I have to admit. Even the most bizarre and cruel weapons of death look clinical and harmless when contained in glass cases. Here was a dagger, mercifully cleaned of the lifesblood of the victim, there a hammer, similarly shiny. Bottles empty now of poison, a tin of "Eureka" weed killer, looking as pristine as if it had just come off the shelf of the shop. Macabre and fascinating. Though I swiftly averted my eyes when he showed us a hangman's noose – I'd seen one of those too closely ever to want to look upon one ever again.

"That wasn't Decima's?" I whispered in anguish to David and he promised me that it was not. Somehow I knew he was telling the truth – I felt I should have instinctively known if it had been the cause of her death.

Dan was a mine of information. He seemed to know the method and motive for every murder in the place and it was with some reluctance that I finally asked him about Decima. Suddenly it all seemed a bit too real for comfort. Until now it had all been a bit academic – just stories either written or imagined. But here I was in the presence of the actual instruments of so many deaths, probably including my ancestor. I suddenly wasn't sure I was ready for any of it.

"David must have told you we are interested in Decima Watkins. I must say it seems odd that nothing to do with her is on display. I would have thought poisoning three of your own family members must warrant a place in any Black Museum." I tried to keep my tone light, partly to keep my own distress at bay, but mostly to convince him and the others that I was not so deeply involved in all this that it might affect my judgement. The last thing I needed now was to have anyone else joining my mother and sister in thinking I had lost my mind.

"You'd think so, wouldn't you?" He smiled warmly and I found myself liking him. He might have a strange job and a possibly unhealthy interest in it, but he seemed pretty normal to me, "But I'm afraid, then, as now, the Allinghams are a powerful family around here! Decima is kept in the vaults at their request – and, I might add, at the earnest request of her own family too."

"Can people do that? Tell you what to display and what to hide away? It hardly seems democratic."

"Well, at the end of the day, the exhibits in these museums are very personal things. We have to be aware that we can easily cause offence and distress."

"Even after a hundred and fifty years?" I was slightly incredulous.

"For as long as there are family members who can be bothered to protest.

135

You see, we don't have the right to display these objects, not if it means upsetting the family of the victim or the perpetrator."

"I suppose so. But I can't believe anyone would care after all these years."

"But evidently they do."

"So it would seem. But you do have the objects relating to Decima's crimes?"

"Oh, yes. She's there in the basement with quite a few others. Do you want to see what she left in our care?"

"I certainly do."

"Then follow me."

CHAPTER EIGHTEEN

The basement was as anonymous as the rest of the building. Eggshell paint and modern furniture had done its job well. There was little trace left of the original use of the rooms we entered. The cell doors had been removed and each room was lined with functional metal shelves and cupboards. Dan led us to the far end and began consulting a clipboard list to help locate the Decima Watkins file.

It didn't take long and within a few minutes he was taking a bunch of keys from a hook by the doorway and unlocking a metal cabinet, "Here you go," he said, hoisting a smallish leather bag from the interior. I stared at it with, I must admit, extremely mixed feelings. Part of me was frightened, the rest agog to know what it contained.

On the face of it, there could be no less interesting article. An old, deep leather bag – the sort that looks like the ones used by old-fashioned doctors in the movies. Carpetbag shaped, but made instead of scuffed brown leather, with a well-worn handle. It must have been old when Decima used it, but I suppose that was only to be expected. You would hardly send one of your best valises into prison with a murderer, would you?

"Is that all there is?" I asked breathlessly.

"Yep – no murder weapons in this case. I looked up our notes when I knew you were coming and was quite surprised to find that the source of the poison was never discovered. There were no containers in the house and Decima was never found to have purchased any – well, she never seemed to have signed a poisons register anyway. She had bought many other things – she seemed to have been used as a general dogsbody who was sent on errands when the servants weren't available, but it never appears to have been proved that she ever bought or had access to poison."

I was shocked. I knew by now, with strange certainty, that Decima had been innocent, but I assumed she must have been foolish enough to run her head into the noose by buying or handling poisons. From what Dan was saying, she had been found guilty without even the most basic of circumstantial evidence.

"Pardon me? How the hell could she be hanged if they couldn't prove she'd had access to the means of death?"

"Unfortunately for her she had requested to travel to her grandmother's house after the deaths of her sisters. The Prosecution claimed she could have disposed of the evidence at any point during her journey, or afterwards in the hills surrounding Hill Farm. It seemed there was a canister of rat poison which mysteriously disappeared from the cellar of her own home. It had been there, all but forgotten, for years and was, as a consequence, of the sort which had never been stained with soot to prevent its accidental use."

"But that does not mean Decima used it. Any member of the family or staff would have been able to get to it."

"Ah, yes, but none had Decima's motive. She had supposedly been unhinged by the loss of her lover."

"Sounds like a put-up job to me," said Aunt Lil with a disgusted sniff, "What say you, Libby?"

"Couldn't agree more, Lil," I said decisively, "Well, let's see what's in the bag."

"Not here," said Lil swiftly, placing her hand over mine and stopping me from touching the leather handle, "Let's take it home and do this in private."

Dan looked suitably appalled, "You can't take it away – I mean, I'd be for the high jump if I let the exhibits leave the building."

"But this isn't an exhibit, is it, my dear?" said Lil reasonably, "And I think you'll find this actually belongs to us. We are, after all, Decima's surviving next of kin – and I'm certainly the oldest."

That stumped him and stunned me. I hadn't quite thought of the situation in this light, and I certainly hadn't imagined taking Decima's belongings home with me. My breath was almost suspended as I watched the emotions flit across Dan's face. He had absolutely no idea how to deal with this unprecedented event and I had to feel sorry for him as he struggled with his conscience. Evidently he felt Lil had a pretty strong case for her contention, but he also knew he would be in big trouble with his superiors if he let us walk out with one of their precious – and extremely old – possessions.

David – Mr. Reasonable – as usual came through with a solution which suited us all, "How would it be if we merely borrow the stuff, Dan? You can make an inventory of what is in the bag, we will sign it, and return it to you in – say, one week?"

Dan looked doubtful, but one glance at the stubborn expressions on mine and Lil's faces convinced him he was going to have to comply, "Very well," he muttered, "But you will have to sign a receipt."

"No problem. Shall we go, ladies?"

"Just a second," I said, having had a sudden thought, "Dan, I don't suppose there is a picture of Decima anywhere, is there?"

"There is. I can't remember if it is a daguerreotype or a photograph, as that rather depends on the year it was taken, but there definitely is one. The authorities had more or less taken to keeping records of everyone who passed through their hands by this time – victim or criminal. The photos of Jack the Ripper's victims are particularly harrowing," he said this with a slight relish that I didn't really want to know about.

"Do you think I could see it?" I asked hastily.

"Sure – but I really can't let you have that."

"No, but you could photocopy it for me," I hinted sweetly, with my most appealing smile. He grinned ruefully, "I could do that, I suppose. Come on then. Bring your Gladstone bag with you."

Gladstone bag. Of course. That's what they were called – possibly not by Decima though. My history was extremely sketchy and I had no idea if Gladstone had been around in 1859. It had been enough of a shock when I had found the Duke of Wellington was still alive – just about – in the period leading up to the Crimea. I thought everyone who had anything to do with Waterloo was long dead by then – but apparently not.

We arrived at Dan's office and he searched a filing cabinet until he found the file he was looking for, "Here she is," he announced, pulling out a pale green folder and opening it up on the desk. The likeness of Decima Watkins lay on the table before me and I was afraid, for a moment, to pick it up. I knew exactly what was terrifying me. I was dreading her being the exact image of myself. It would have been much too spooky to have looked upon a long dead face and seen my own reflected there. Fortunately I did not have this hurdle to leap. The visage which gazed up at me was vaguely familiar – but only as might be expected in a family member. For a start, despite the solemn expression, she was much prettier than me. She looked tired and unbearably sad – not unexpected in the circumstances. But her face was her own and not mine. As I looked at her I wondered how her family had been able to dismiss her as 'plain' – she was far from it. Today she would have been an actress or even a model, but on second thoughts, no. Her face had character. It was not at all the blank canvas that the faces of the very young can sometimes be, before life leaves its mark. Decima's face showed every moment of the anguish she had suffered, but it was certainly not plain. But then, dysfunctional families work like that, don't they? Pick on the vulnerable one and put him or her constantly down, so that the rest never actually have to face up to the fact that one might have more advantages than all the others. If I can't be rich, beautiful, successful, talented, then I'll make damn sure you never are either. Sibling rivalry gone mad. And in Decima's case it had gone more than mad, it had ended in tragedy. I was more convinced than ever that Decima had not murdered her sisters, but had been used as a convenient scapegoat – kill two birds with one stone, that would have been the unspoken plan. Protect the real killer and get rid of the thorn in our sides in the same action.

Lil saw tears glistening in my eyes and gently took the photo away from me, handing it back to Dan, "We'd like a copy, please, but put it in an envelope for now, would you?"

"Can we also have a copy of the museum's notes on her case too?" I asked hurriedly, surreptitiously wiping away a tear.

He shrugged, not bothering to argue. His body language seemed to be saying 'in for a penny, in for a pound'.

I was stumbling when we walked out, the bag, wrapped in polythene, clutched in my arms like a baby. I could hardly believe my good fortune. To actually have something which belonged to Decima in my hands. I had thought my luck would end with the discovery of Richard Allingham's diaries, but this was beyond anything I could have hoped for. David's part in all this was rewarded with a smile which apparently had a stunning impact on him, because he went all tongue-tied for a brief moment, but swiftly recovered himself and became his usual 'Joe Cool'.

Lil and I both sat in the back seat of the car on the way back home, the precious bundle on the seat between us. We kept exchanging excited little smiles and I knew she was as eager as I was to get home and open up the bag. We knew it did not contain anything particularly amazing, because Dan had shown us the inventory of its contents, but the value of the items meant nothing to us at all. It was the very fact of holding things which had been touched by Decima. That was all that mattered to either of us.

❧   ❧   ❧   ❧   ❧

Spread out on the dining room table it was not a spectacular sight. One black dress, creased, but not faded – no crinoline. That was an unnecessary

140

encumberment in prison. Life, I knew now, was hard in Victorian gaols. Punishments ranged from picking oakum; not being allowed to look at or speak to other prisoners and the treadmill. Voluminous skirts would only have been in the way. It seemed she had been permitted to wear her stays, for here they were, white cotton, stiffened with whalebone and showing that her waist must have been twenty-two inches at the very most. Having said that, judging from the size of her dress, she could not have stood much taller than five feet.

Fine lawn underwear and knitted silk stockings, then from the bottom of the bag, her little leather boots. These I stared at in horrified fascination, for I felt I had seen them before. In fact I knew I had, adorning my own feet, peeping from beneath the hem of that same black dress. I could not restrain a shudder of horror as the nightmare came back to me with all its usual reality. The smell which assailed my nostrils was the dank passageway, but strangely enough that quickly gave way to the sweet scent of some flower or other, faint but most definitely present.

It took David, the horticulturist, to recognise it, "Good God, even after all these years you can still smell her perfume. Parma violets if I am not mistaken."

"Quite right," said Lil, "Very popular until overtaken by Lavender."

I laid the boots quickly aside, "Is there anything else?"

"A black velvet drawstring bag," answered David, peering in.

"I think you'll find that is a reticule, my dear," said Lil, picking it out, "The Victorian equivalent of a Gucci handbag."

I could see her fingers were trembling slightly as she pulled it open. The cord which held it closed must have perished for some reason and it snapped with a tiny puff of dust. It was most odd, because nothing else showed the least sign of age. Decima might have had these clothes stripped from her dead body only yesterday. Whatever the secret of the storage conditions at the museum, they certainly worked well.

Lil tipped up the bag and carefully shook out the contents onto the white tablecloth. Three heads all leaned closer to see what was there. Once again it was not much. The poor girl had left this world with scarcely more than she had entered it.

A small silver watch on a chain, a narrow gold ring, a handkerchief, a tiny bottle of perfume and the dusty remains of some long-dead flower, which David confidently identified as a rose, but which frankly could have been anything. I was vaguely disappointed. Not only were there no letters or diaries, but what was there was almost too predictable – just the sort of romantic nonsense any young girl would carry in her bag, even today. I had thought better of Decima than to fall for all that old tat. But then, what else would she have had with her in jail? If she had any love letters from Richard Allingham, she certainly wouldn't have allowed her horrific family to get hold of them. I could imagine there would have been no worse torture for her than to think of them going through her things after she was dead. No, Decima would never have left anything for her relations to find and gloat over. She either burned her private stuff, or she hid it – so well that it would probably never be found.

David picked up the watch and flipped open the front cover, "This is engraved," he said, "D.W. with love and admiration, R. A. A."

"Oh, my God," I breathed in awe, "He bought it for her. It's from Richard."

"It would seem so," said Aunt Lil, "And what a charming gift it is. I suppose they were both counting the hours until they were together again – unfortunately that day never came. How sad life can be sometimes."

None of us felt we could deny that.

I took the watch from David and held it in my palm, staring down at it. It was warm, warmer than it would have been just from the heat of his hand. The time stood at three minutes past eight. The time she had died, I felt sure of it. The watch from Richard had stopped at the moment of her death. No, it couldn't be. Now I really was letting my imagination run riot. Inanimate objects would not and could not be influenced by outside events. I would check the museum notes later and then I could laugh at my own melodramatic stupidity when I found that Decima had died at any time other than three minutes past eight.

David broke my reverie by speaking, albeit reluctantly, "Dammit! Look at the time. I really have to go. I'll ring you later, Libby, if that is alright."

"Feel free," I muttered, still examining the contents of the bag.

"See our guest to the door," chided Lil, pushing my arm to attract my attention.

I was loath to be distracted, but he had been good enough to take us to the museum, introduce us to his friend and to ensure we were given access to this treasure, so I did not have much choice but to put down the watch and drag myself away from the table.

At the back door, he took my hand and drew me outside, carefully shutting the door behind us, "Are you okay, Libby?"

"Fine. Why shouldn't I be?" I withdrew my fingers from his clasp and pressed my back against the door, trying to put a little space between us without being too obvious about it.

"You don't seem to be your usual self, that's all. I wondered if there was something worrying you." He looked so hangdog that I nearly melted. Damn Brendan to hell's flames for putting doubts in my mind. Most of me was sure David was a perfectly nice guy, but always now there was going to be that niggling little worry that he was stringing me along with clever acting and a black soul.

"I'm alright. I suppose all this stuff about Decima is getting to me a bit. I never expected to actually handle things that had belonged to her. You've got to admit it's a bit macabre and spooky."

"They're just things, Libby. Don't get too freaked out. Practically every house in the world must have something in it that was once owned by a dead person. Furniture, jewellery, even clothes. Museums are packed with 'em."

"Yes, but this is a bit more personal than that, isn't it?"

"Only if you let it be."

"I'll try to bear that in mind," I assured him dryly.

"Make sure you do."

He leaned forward, obviously intending to kiss me, but I was ready for him and immediately offered my cheek. He flinched slightly at the insult, but to give him his due, he merely gave me a peck, then walked off down the path.

I watched him go, feeling as though I wanted to run after him and fling myself into his arms. Of course I did no such thing. A romantic fool who carried a dead rose in her bag might have done – but not me.

❦

CHAPTER NINETEEN

When I went back into the house, I heard Aunt Lil on the phone and I could hardly believe my ears; her tone was clipped and decisive and her words astounding,

"Dan? This is Mrs. Farrell. I was there earlier with David Wright – you remember, good. Then listen and listen carefully. I don't care how you do it. See your superiors, consult your solicitors, but take note. You can have everything back from the Gladstone bag except the reticule and its contents. We have found them deeply personal to our family and we are not returning them to the museum."

Evidently he tried to argue, but she cut him short, "Don't give me all that, Dan. You said yourself that they are only with the museum because they were granted by the families of the victims and culprits – well this family is claiming something back. I'm Decima's oldest surviving relative and I want my inheritance in my hands."

She caught sight of me as she put the phone down and smiled with a slightly shame-faced triumph, "I don't know how I had the courage to do that, but once I had held Decima and Richard's love token, I knew I couldn't bear to part with it."

I simply crossed the room and hugged her.

After a bite to eat I went back to Richard's diaries. I sat in the old chair, suddenly not afraid any more that I might drop off and have my nightmare. The watch, ring and, in a tiny china dish, the disintegrated rose, lay on the coffee table in front of me. From time to time I glanced up from the books to smile softly at them as they glinted dully in the late afternoon sun as it grew slowly redder on its journey towards the horizon.

"Of course I wasted no time in following Decima to her grandmother's home in Derbyshire. I could scarcely believe the good fortune that my own

home at Havering was just a few moments ride away, across country. Decima took to watching for me from the attic window and I would see her waiting there as I crested the hill."

Oh my God, I thought, swallowing deeply. I was right about the attic window. She did spend most of her time there, waiting for him to come to her when he could get away from his own family. It had seemed odd from the first that a member of the family should have spent any time at all in what would then have been the servants' quarters, but this explained it all.

"Her grandmother, who is a fine old lady with a heart of gold, is deeply sympathetic to our plight. She has no affection at all for her son-in-law, Decima's father, and feels that her daughter is weak in the extreme for not standing up to her bullying husband. She can think of no reasonable explanation as to why Decima should not be married to me and has encouraged me to at last take my courage in my hands and bring Decima home to meet my parents. She – and I own, myself too! – feel that they could not meet Decima and not love her, and so the meeting has been arranged."

"Evening – By God! I have never been angrier! The meeting was an unmitigated disaster! My parents could not possibly have been ruder or more unkind. Decima was devastated! Nothing I could do could stem her tears. She sobbed and sobbed in the carriage home. It wrenched my heart to see her so. I kissed her and told her that I would always love her, but nothing could comfort her. I swear I could not recognise my father when he told Decima that she had dared to raise her eyes too high and that he would never countenance our marriage. She has no fear, though, my little firebrand! She told him, with eyes that blazed as furiously as his own, that she cared nothing for him or his money and he could cut me off without a penny if he wished, but it would never alter her feelings for me!

"That's easy enough to say, Miss, when you have food in your belly and a roof over your head! Come back to me in five years when you have known hunger and destitution – see how far your love carries you then!" I have never heard him so bitter – I might almost say evil! I answered him civilly, as his position as my father commands respect, but I too was firm, "Decima is my choice, papa, and nothing you can say or threaten will sway me. We will be married, with or without your blessing! Naturally I would rather it was with, but that decision must lie with you!"

"You've had your head turned, boy, by a pretty face. Take my advice – bed her and get the fever for her out of your blood, but don't make the

mistake of marrying the wench. You'll live to regret that folly, believe me! Her father is an upstart, her brothers a scandal, her sisters well known for marrying money and position! You are a half-wit if you think she loves anything about you other than your riches and your status!"

I had no chance to argue further for the butler, obviously on some pre-arranged signal, came to the door of the salon and announced that my father's carriage was at the door. He made it quite evident that he expected us to leave so we followed him across the hall. When he reached the door, he turned and spoke to Decima in a tone of pure hatred that I had never thought to issue from the lips of my father, "You, young woman, should go home to your father and do your duty by him! If I catch you in the company of my son again, I will have you whipped at the cart-tail for the whore you are!"

Decima went white and gasped with shock, but before I could stop him and take him to task for the insult to my betrothed, he had heaved himself into the carriage and cracked his whip so that the horses almost bolted so startled were they. Decima turned to me with a bitter little smile, "Oh look, Richard, I never knew it before, but I know it now – the Devil drives a curricle!" I could not in all honesty disagree with her."

I laid the book down on my lap, whew! They certainly didn't pull their punches, these Victorian worthies. Fancy telling your son to bed a girl and not marry her, then call her a whore.

"The Devil drives a curricle" what an evocative comment. Of course, in my case "the Devil drives a Jaguar" – for that was Brendan's preferred vehicle.

I wished I hadn't thought of Brendan just then, for he was probably still wandering about the countryside – and it was getting dark. I thought I had better make sure Lil locked up good and solid tonight.

ఌ   ఌ   ఌ   ఌ   ఌ

It was the same old story in the morning. Just as I had finished breakfast and was about to ensconce myself in the chair and bury myself in the past, the telephone rang. Lil answered, then called to me.

"It's Tom's wife Alison Hills, for you."

I was mystified and mouthed, "Who is Tom?"

"The vicar," hissed Lil back, covering the mouthpiece with her hand.

"Oh! Right." It all came flooding back – but what did his wife want with me? There was only one way to find out. I took the phone from Lil and exchanged the usual pleasantries before Alison came to the point, "I hope I'm not disturbing you?" she asked politely. With a glance of longing towards my piles of books and papers I replied equally courteously, "Of course not. What can I do for you?"

"Well, Tom was telling me a little something about you – nothing personal, you understand, he would never do that. But I realized you must be feeling pretty cut off up there at Hill Farm. I know you can't get out much because of Lillian and it must be a trial, since you are used to living in town, so I wondered if you would like to join me for coffee," she sounded so hopeful that I didn't have the heart to refuse. Perhaps it wasn't me that was feeling lonely and cut off?

"That would be lovely." I was proud of myself, I even sounded enthusiastic to my own ears, "When would you like me to come?"

"This morning – about ten thirty – would that be convenient?"

"Of course. Where are you?"

"In the vicarage, next to the church." She managed to speak this piece of obvious information as though my asking was perfectly justified and I laughed, "What an idiot I am. Where else would one find a vicar's wife?"

"Not at all. Quite a lot of Rectories have been sold off and the vicars given smaller houses. Some of these old places are huge – this one isn't so bad, as it's only a little village. I'll see you later, then?"

"Certainly. I'm looking forward to it."

"If your Aunt feels up to it, of course she is welcome too."

"Just a minute I'll ask her," I said, and relayed the invitation to Lil, who shook her head vigorously.

"No, I'm afraid she's not feeling a hundred percent this morning. I'll see you at ten thirty. Bye."

When she rang off, I asked Lil about her desertion, "I hope she's not a boring prig and you've dropped me right in it, Lil," I said warningly.

"Not at all. She's perfectly amiable," said Lil, with dignity, "I just don't feel like going out, that's all."

"It better had be. If I have to spend a tedious morning being roped into various village events and onto boring committees, I'll be pretty annoyed, to say the least."

She laughed, "I'm sure you'll have a very nice time indeed. Now get back to your studies. You've got another half an hour or so before you have to set off."

Half an hour didn't seem very much time for Richard Allingham. I didn't want to get thoroughly engrossed, then have to drag myself away, so I picked up the notes from the museum instead.

They were not the usual badly typed leaflets from small independent museums, but well laid out and clear. However, as a non-exhibit, Decima's story was merely a few lines at the bottom of the last page. It told me nothing I did not know already, except for one thing. It mentioned her defence lawyer, Mr – later Sir Horton Brooks. Apparently he had been vociferous in defence of his young client – so much so that he had earned the sobriquet "Babbling Brookes". Society at the time put his continuing carping on the subject of Decima down to his having fallen under her bewitching spell. Strangely enough, this rather tended to convince people of her guilt rather than her innocence. If even a middle-aged man of Horton Brookes' standing could be swayed from the path of righteousness by her enchantments, what chance had the poor beleaguered Allingham? No wonder he had tried to defy his parents on her behalf.

It said very little else, except that Horton Brookes, had, in his later years, written an autobiography in which he touched briefly on the subject of Decima Watkins and her trial. A copy of this book, due to its local connections, was available in the local library.

Just as I gained this piece of information, Lil called me and told me I ought to be getting off to Alison Hill's fund raising coffee morning. She said this to tease me a little, but I had the sudden horrid feeling she might be right. Alison hadn't actually said I would be the only person there. What if I was walking into a lion's den of Young Wives and Women's Institute members?

I drove all the way into the village imagining all sorts of horrors that might be waiting for me in the vicarage, but I really ought not to have troubled myself. Of course Alison was alone – not even Tom was with her.

She was a lovely person – just right for Tom. She was tall and slender – the sort of figure for which I usually automatically hate a woman, being shortish and dumpyish myself. But since she had absolutely no idea how to dress her model's frame with style or panache, she was instantly forgiven. She was one of those women who are terribly self-conscious about being tall and spend the rest of their lives silently apologising for it, by stooping, wearing flat shoes and calf-covering flowery skirts. For God's sake, tall women. Be proud of it. All us shorties are only jealous, you know, that's why we ask how the weather is up there, and if your parents put manure in your shoes. Not that I could ever be accused of that sort of thing myself. Being bullied at school for your own particular bugbear tends to swerve you away from taunting others for the rest of your life. Mine was glasses and spots. Thank God for contact lens and witch-hazel. Not that my dear sister has ever let me forget the ugly duckling years – in fact she refuses to accept they are gone forever. She merely awaits the day when I fall into depression and let things slip back, so she can feel superior again.

Alison made the coffee – fresh, thankfully, and I stayed with her in the big, stone-flagged kitchen while it brewed. I sat at the huge oak table, covered, comfortingly, with magazines, papers, notebooks, pens, children's drawings and crayons. All the usual paraphernalia which accompanies normal family living, but which certain women are expert at hiding, in order to tacitly chide those of us who are less organized and perfect.

I felt immediately at home. I didn't have children myself, but I was pretty sure that this mess was how my future home would look. It was bad enough now, with just myself to untidy it.

"So," I began, when she handed my cup to me and joined me at the table, "what has Tom been telling you about me?"

"Just that you've come to look after Lillian and that you had had a few odd happenings in the house which you felt might benefit from a clerical visit."

"Oh. I had sort of hoped he wouldn't put any of that about. It makes me look something of a loony – or mildly hysterical at the very least."

She hastened to set my mind at rest, "I'm terribly sorry if Tom has done wrong, but I do assure you, he has mentioned this to no one but myself and I wouldn't dream of gossiping. And I do promise you that neither Tom nor I think you are in the least odd or hysterical. You would be surprised how many perfectly stoical, ordinary people find strange things happening in their houses at times like these."

"Times like what?" I asked, forgetting my slight annoyance in my intrigue at what exactly she was talking about.

"Well, when there is someone dying, to put it bluntly. These old tales of pictures falling off the wall, and clocks stopping persist because they sometimes have a root in truth."

"Are you seriously telling me that you believe stuff like that really happens?"I was incredulous. Weren't modern vicars and their wives supposed to be above all that after-life mumbo-jumbo? I seemed to recall someone actually saying that they were getting to the stage where they wouldn't be believing in God for much longer.

"There are stranger things in Heaven and Earth, you know," she said placidly.

149

Know it? I had been living it. But I wasn't sure I was quite ready to tell her that. I wanted to know what her point was first. She hadn't invited me here out of the blue, I knew that now, and whilst I was sure she was far too nice to have any sinister motives, I had learnt enough over the past few days to understand that everyone in the world has their own ideas and wants, and they could be fairly ruthless in getting them.

"Look, I don't have any hard feelings that Tom confided my troubles in you. You are his wife after all, and most partners tell each other everything, but I really would like to know what you are driving at. Sorry to be blunt, but I don't like pussyfooting around. Out with it Alison. What do you want from me?"

She looked a bit shocked that I had been so direct, then, taking a sip of her coffee, she seemed to come to a decision, "Can I trust you, Libby? This is all a bit frowned upon by the Church. I can't risk upsetting the powers that be because of Tom. I love him to bits, but I'm the first to admit that I'm not ideal vicar's wife material."

"You can trust me," I said, "Now spit it out."

CHAPTER TWENTY

I looked at her blankly for a few seconds, "Am I being completely obtuse here? I'm afraid I don't know what you are talking about."

She glanced behind her, as if to make sure her husband hadn't walked in on us, "It's quite simple, Libby. I want to hold a séance at your house. This is almost too good to be true. And certainly too good an opportunity to miss. There is a very real possibility we could get in touch with Decima and speak to her, to find out exactly what it is she wants from you. Don't you see? Instead of all this silly running around, tiring yourself out with your investigations and finding tempting little snippets here and there, we could just ask straight out what happened."

In her enthusiasm she was almost tripping over her words, such was her hurry to get them out – and to convince me that it was a brilliant idea. My face must have shown my horror and distrust, because she began to babble even more, "Oh, I know it is a difficult thing for the cynical to believe, but I have a very dear friend – and trust me, she is marvellous, just marvellous! I know it sounds odd to those who don't believe..."

I felt it was time to stop her gallop. "Alison! I may have been a cynic at the start of all this, but I'm certainly not one now. Take my word for it, my misgivings come, not from a lack of belief, but rather the opposite."

"Then what is the problem?"

"The problem is I would be utterly terrified to have anything to do with a séance. I'm sorry, but it is entirely out of the question. I don't approve of meddling with things we don't really understand. My sister and her school friends once messed around with a Ouija board and they got hold of a horrid man who said the most appalling things. They all swore they were not pushing the glass. I learned my lesson then, and I've never forgotten it. Behaviour like that opens doors and lets things in. Things that have no business here. I wouldn't dream of letting you hold a séance in my house."

She looked terribly disappointed, but then visibly brightened, "But Sophia is a professional. She would never let anything bad happen – and it is fairly obvious that Decima is trying to contact you, isn't it?"

"Decima is doing just fine on her own, thank you. She's been getting her point across very well so far."

"Well, at least would you allow Sophia to come to your house and look around? I suppose I can see that you might be nervous about calling up the dead – it is difficult for those with a closed mind to contemplate," I resented the 'closed mind' crack, but allowed it to pass and she plunged on, "Perhaps Decima might to able to communicate with Sophia directly."

I thought about it for a moment, then nodded slightly reluctantly, "I can't see any harm in that. If Decima can talk to someone with a psychic gift, I see no objection, but don't think I'm going to allow any of that 'bell, book and candle' nonsense, because I won't change my mind."

She looked delighted, "Thank you, Libby. I'm so grateful. I'm sure this will be a valuable step in our journey towards a greater understanding of the afterlife. Sophia will be ecstatic. I will ring her right this very moment. Will this evening be alright for you?"

Now I started to panic a little. I know that in theory I owned Hill Farm now, but it was a bit rich bringing home these people without consulting Lil first, "Steady on, Alison! I'll have to ask my Aunt if she minds. It is her home, after all."

"Of course. Forgive me. I'm letting my excitement run away with me. By all means speak to Lillian, but I think you will find she is very open-minded. We have had many a discussion on this subject."

I had a feeling that Alison had probably done the discussing and Lil had merely listened politely, but I didn't disabuse her, "Very well, but I'm warning you now, if Lil says no, then that is the final word on the subject. I will not have her upset at this time."

"Naturally, that is understood."

We finished the coffee and she offered me home made biscuits. To give her due credit, she immediately changed the topic of conversation. She asked me about living in London and my job – anything, in fact, other than Decima.

"Are you planning on going back to London when – when this is all over?" she asked, stumbling delicately over the reference to Lil's ultimate demise. I must say I found that rather curious from someone who professed to believe that death is merely passing into another room, but the hesitation was definitely there.

It was a question which made me pause, for though I had assured Brendan several times that I had no intention of going back, that had only been for his benefit, in the hope that he might take himself off, knowing that I was going to be out of his reach. Now, however, things had changed radically. I owned Hill Farm – and I would be unable to sell it. Weighing things logically, it seemed rather ludicrous to stay in a place I hated, paying vast sums in rent and other expenses, when I had a lovely home here – for free. All right, there had been mentions of money, but I had no idea how much – or little – that might amount to, so I would still need to earn a living, but I had been promising myself for years that I would have a go at making a career out of writing – this was my chance. If I failed at first, I could always take in lodgers to pay the bills.

"No, I'm not going back. Lil has made sure I can stay at Hill Farm for as long as I want to, even after she has gone, so that is what I intend to do. You had better get used to me as a neighbour, Alison. I think I may be here quite some time."

"Won't you miss London? I know I do."

"Do you really? That surprises me, I must say. I had you marked down as a country girl, through and through."

She smiled, "I suppose I am. I didn't come from the centre of London, but the very edge. But countryside here and there are two very different things. Everything here is so very..." she stopped as she struggled to find the correct descriptive word, "Emphatic!" she finished, at last, with a wry grin, "That sounds very silly, but if you know this part of the country, you must know what I mean."

"I wasn't born here, but I did spend a lot of my childhood here, and I know exactly what you mean. The weather, the people, the terrain – all of them rugged, uncompromising, unforgiving – and yet beautiful. It's not a county you could pass through and not notice, is it?"

"Hardly."

I looked at my watch. It was a polite nothing, for no matter what time it said, I fully intended to take my leave, "Well, I really must be off." I had a sudden moment of inspiration to make my leave-taking less obvious, "I promised Lil I would call at the library and take her some books. She's finding enforced inactivity rather a trial, as you can imagine. Where is the library from here? I seem to have lost my bearings somewhat."

She gave me directions and after bidding me goodbye, and arranging to ring me later that evening, she went back indoors, presumably to telephone the mysterious Sophia with her good news.

153

Within ten minutes I was entering the incredibly tall doors of the village library. It was an old building, but since the words "Braxton Public Library, 1880" were carved into the stone lintel, it evidently had never been used for any other purpose. It seemed to be rather an imposing erection for so small a place, but if rich landowners such as the Allinghams lived in the vicinity, it was perhaps no surprise that such a gift should have been presented.

The inside was filled with that familiar odour of books old and new, dust and overlaying it all, polish. I approached the desk, behind which sat a woman of about my own age, who smiled at me and asked, in a normal tone of voice, which rather shocked me – I was expecting the librarian menacing whisper, "Can I help you?"

"I hope so. I went to the Braxton Police museum the other day and in the leaflet I was given, it said you might have a copy of the biography of Sir Horton Brookes."

"I don't suppose you know the author?"

"Actually, I think it may have been Brookes himself – an autobiography in other words. Just a minute, I think I have it in my bag." Luckily I had remembered to bring my notes and within a few minutes she was going through her microfiche for me. Horton was soon found, though he was put away in the basement and not on the shelves. She went off to fetch him and I looked around. Apart from a metal rack containing the latest paperbacks, the place looked much as it must have done in 1880, with dark wooden shelving, parquet floors and high arched windows, which had to be opened and closed with the aid of immensely long mahogany poles with brass hooks on the end. I breathed deep. I love the smell of books. Books and old churches – I could breathe it in all day.

She came back and handed me the leather-bound, gilt edged tome, "I gather it is a somewhat heavy read, so good luck with it," she said with a grin.

I thanked her, gave her Lillian's library card – then decided to join on my own behalf. After all, I was a resident now, wasn't I? We filled out the form and I felt a little leap of pride in my breast when I wrote down my new address for the first time ever. I think that was the moment when I realized it was really true, that I owned a house of my own, that I would live there for the rest of my days and, most importantly, that I was going to make a life for myself here. I suppose I ought to have been scared. I certainly had been when I moved to London, but somehow this just felt right.

On the way back to the car I saw an advert pinned to a post, "Wright's Garden Centre – bedding plants now in". It gave the location and though I hadn't been here for several years, I found I knew exactly where it was, so, quickly, before I could change my mind, I took the road that led to it, and not the one that led home.

❦ ❦ ❦ ❦ ❦

It was something of a relief to realize that it was a large and obviously bustling concern. Nothing about the place gave any indication that David Wright might be short of money – and though I refused to accept that had been the main reason for my visit, it certainly didn't disappoint me.

I wandered around for about half an hour, amazed that I was able to kill that amount of time in a garden centre. I had never been an earthy sort of person. At home we had one of those gardens which are so beloved of the suburban middle-class. A large, neatly trimmed lawn for the children to play sedate ball games on – anything rough and we were banished to the park – surrounded by flower beds with lilac bushes, flowering raspberry and forsythia – with a mock orange at the bottom next to the Bramley apple tree, so old and gnarled that you were lucky to get one pie from it in October. My dad took care of the lawn every Sunday, and weeded the beds three times a year, when he had absolutely no choice but to protect his little girls from the sneakily encroaching brambles and nettles. As long as my mother didn't spot a dandelion he was safe.

Once in London, of course, I had lived in flats and managed to kill every house plant I had been prevailed upon to buy or accept as a house-warming present.

This was a revelation. Suddenly there were rank upon rank of gorgeous plants that I could have in my newly acquired garden at Hill Farm. Luscious colours, exotic shapes, fabulous scents. I was swept away by a myriad of possibilities. In my head my garden was transformed into a picture-book cottage garden, lush with growth, bursting with eatable delicacies. It did not occur to me until much later that Lil would have had such a garden if she had been able and the chances were that the soil and climate would preclude any of it. Just in that moment it didn't matter, I was in a fantasy world and I was loving it.

"Hello, what are you doing here?" said a voice behind me. I was so engrossed that I nearly jumped out of my skin. My hand flew to my heart, "Dear God! Do you have to creep up on me like that?"

David, for it was him of course, laughed and took hold of my hand, "Sorry. I thought you had heard me. Can I interest you in a coffee?"

155

I was about to decline when I realized that it was now very nearly two hours since my last cup, so I nodded.

Instead of whisking me off to his office, he took me to the tea-room in the centre and when I began sniffing appreciatively at the aroma of the 'soup of the day', he politely asked if I would like to join him for lunch. I suppose I ought to have said no, but I was starving and past being coy. I knew he was watching with subdued amusement when I tucked into a three-course lunch, but I didn't care. I've always been a great believer in listening to my body and my body was saying 'feed me!' and saying it loudly.

"One of the things I like about you, Libby, is the way you never say you're on a diet. God, I'm tired of women on a bloody diet."

I stopped mid-stuffing my face, "Are you trying to say you think I'm fat?"

That made him really laugh, "For crying out loud. Will I never learn? First rule of being a man – never mention weight to a woman. She'll think she's too fat, too thin, too busty, too flat chested. No, I don't think you are fat – and before you start, not too thin, either. I'm not a chubby chaser, but I don't like stick-insects either."

"Chubby-chaser? What a dreadful expression. You ought to be ashamed of yourself."

"I am, thoroughly. Would you like another coffee?"

"Yes, I would, thank-you."

I watched him as he walked across to the counter to fetch it, admiring his rear view almost without noticing that I was doing it. He stayed for a minute there, chatting to the girl and smiling amiably at her. She gazed adoringly back and when he walked away, she threw a mildly poisonous glance in my direction. Oops! Treading on someone's toes. Well, I thought grimly, tough luck, lady. You can have your chance when – and if – I dump him.

"So, to what do I owe the pleasure of your company?" he asked as he sat down.

"I was in Braxton at the library, so I thought I would come and see your business for myself. I must say it is very nice. Do you do well with it?" I could have bitten out my tongue! How obvious was that? Why not just ask to audit his accounts?

He raised a quizzical brow, "What a leading question. I don't quite know how to answer that. Modesty prevents me from boasting, but on the other hand, to be too deprecating might kill all my hopes with you."

I don't think I could have gone any redder – and of course embarrassment made me snappy, "Oh, fuck off! I don't know how you

156

always manage to put me in the wrong, but you do. I don't know why I came here, but I'm sorry I did." I scrabbled in my handbag and threw a twenty pound note onto the table, "That should pay for my lunch. Good bye."

He was evidently mad too, for he grasped my wrist, "A tenner will take care of it, let me get your change."

"Give it to your little friend over there in the short skirt," I said bitterly.

"Has she a short skirt? I hadn't noticed, but I shall certainly have a look now that you've mentioned it."

Heads were beginning to turn to observe the fun, but he completely ignored the stir he was causing. He still had my arm and I twisted and writhed in his grip to free myself, "Let go!" I hissed, "You are embarrassing me."

"Oh, I don't think you need any help from me on that score."

"Bastard!" Tears were near and I think he knew it.

Suddenly he was contrite, "I apologise. That was uncalled for. Sit down, I want to talk to you…"

"Well, I don't want to talk to you."

"Yes, you do. And I think we need a bit more privacy. Come up to my office."

"No!"

"Don't be childish. I'm not in the mood." He sounded as though he meant it.

I followed him up to his office.

❦

CHAPTER TWENTY-ONE

He held the door open for me then closed it behind us. I suppose I should be able to describe his office, I'm usually quite observant and, dare I admit it, nosy, but I was acutely aware of him behind me and the slight tension I felt drove all other thoughts out of my mind. I heard the key click in the lock and turned to confront him, not that I got very far. Before I could say a word he was across the room. He took me in his arms and began to kiss me, and I found I couldn't – or didn't want to – resist.

"You do know you are the most awkward, contrary bitch, don't you?" he whispered hoarsely as his lips travelled across my cheek and down to my throat. My head went back so he could reach the spot he wanted more easily, "I have been told so," I said, lowering myself onto his desk, because my legs suddenly refused to support me, "But I have to say it's not the most romantic of pick-up lines."

He laughed, but it was low and throaty and I felt it rumble through my flesh, raising goose bumps. It doesn't sound too hot, I know, but God! I could have flung myself down there and then. I tried to bring us both back to our senses, "I thought you said you wanted to talk to me..."

"I lied," he said bluntly, "I've never wanted to talk less in my life."

Oh, you know what happened next. I'm not going into details. Suffice it to say his calls were held for quite a while and I drove home much later with a stupid grin on my face and it wasn't because I had eaten a particularly good strawberry cheesecake.

Lil was lying down when I went in the house, so I didn't disturb her. Alison and her request for contact with the 'other side' could wait until later. I mooned about for a bit, unable to settle to anything, then recalled the book I'd brought from the library and suddenly David was banished to the background for a bit whilst I read what Horton Brookes had to say about Decima. Well, the moment at the garden centre was over.

The librarian wasn't far wrong about it being a fusty, boring read. Brookes was a man who had been very much in love with himself. He evidently couldn't imagine anyone not being fascinated by his every utterance, so he uttered a lot. It took me ages to find Decima, until I had the bright idea of looking for her name in the index. Bloody David Wright. He had managed to remove my brain, I think, along with my inhibitions and several items of clothing.

Brookes, writing some years after the event, still hadn't lost his very obvious affection for his erstwhile, and ultimately doomed, client.

"For every man there must be some regrets in life and mine was undoubtedly my defence of Decima Watkins. I cannot regret that I met her, for a more remarkable woman I have never known, but I do regret, very bitterly indeed, that I was the man chosen to defend her. I know now, though I failed to recognise the fact as a much younger man, that she was fated to die. Powers stronger than my talent had decreed her demise and I might not have bothered wasting my time! I can say no more for those who wished her dead are still in a position to damage myself and my family. Suffice it to say that I swear to this day that I firmly believed Decima to be innocent of the heinous crimes for which she was hanged, and I can only pray that those responsible will pay for her death in the next life if not in this.

The girl herself was a creature of rare beauty. When one first saw her, this was not immediately obvious, for she was shy and reticent. Until she knew and trusted one, her eyes were downcast and her voice quiet. When she finally raised those magnificent green eyes the impact was remarkable! It is a little known fact that she had been mildly deaf from childhood and this gave her face, when listening, a curious intensity which made a man feel he was the most fascinating, riveting orator even born. I cannot begin to describe the emotions this raised in the breast of any man in her vicinity. I suspect all any man really wants is to be a little god in his own household, to be the final arbitrator in every dispute. Decima gave one that feeling.

I tried, by God, I tried, to cut through the mesh of circumstance which bound her, but her own misery prevented her from being much help. I have known many women who have lost a loved one, but I have never known one who suffered agony of loss that Decima suffered. I could only envy the man who had raised such passion in her – yea, even though he was a dead man! I would have given much to have inspired such devotion in a woman of Decima's calibre!

159

You may ask, dear reader, if such a paragon had no flaws, no unpleasant traits of character that might account for her rousing such hatred in her enemies that they should have brought about her death with such viciousness. Of course she did! But her flaws made her human! It would be hard indeed to love a goddess, but Decima was no marble idol to be set upon a pedestal. She was very much a woman of warmth and sensuality. Indeed the only moment of disappointment I knew in her was when I read the post mortem after her death. The doctor certified that she had given birth to a child. She never told me this and I never knew what happened to her baby – I suspect it died at birth, for no one else seemed to have knowledge of its whereabouts none that they would admit, in any event. But the very fact of it must tell one that Decima failed in the one, vital ingredient which must go towards creating the perfect woman. She was unchaste. I can only hope that it was her lover who had stolen her virginity for one could perhaps forgive her this fall from grace if it was in the cause of true love. But one must then question the character of a man who would deflower a maiden for his own gratification without benefit of wedlock.

I make no judgement, I merely state the facts."

Make no judgements. God almighty! The man was a pompous ass. I think I hated him. He must be wrong. Decima could not have had an illegitimate baby. She wouldn't have been so stupid as to make love to Richard knowing what the consequences might be. Victorian girls were under no illusions as to how harsh the world was to unmarried mothers. And Richard would not have taken advantage of his loved one. He was a gentleman through and through. I knew it. I sensed it.

But here it was in black and white.

I've often heard the expression 'I was gutted', but it had never been so graphic as it was in those few stomach-wrenching seconds of disappointment. I literally felt as though I had had my abdomen ripped open with a blunt knife. How could she do this to me? It had all been so romantic until now. It was all very well for me to be swept away by passion. I was a modern woman, with birth control and nothing to lose. Making love on a man's desk in his office was a bit of harmless fun. For Decima to fall from grace after Richard's father had called her a whore and told his son to make her his mistress. That was just playing into the old bastard's hands. Why had she done it? Why had she been so bloody stupid? And most important of all, what had happened to her baby? Was it even Richard's? She might have met someone else after he died. It was possible. He had been killed in

1855; she hadn't died until 1859.

Suddenly the idea of a séance didn't seem quite so ridiculous. If this baby had been kept so close a secret that even her own defence lawyer hadn't known about it, then it was hardly likely I would find out about it from other sources. It certainly wasn't going to be mentioned in the Allingham diaries. The time between Richard's meeting Decima and being sent back to the front was too short for him to have known about the baby if it was his – and if it was not, she either had it before she met him – and she would hardly confide that. Or it was after his death. Whatever the truth, Richard wasn't going to know it. But where else could I look? Damn Decima's family. They would have made quite sure none of her private papers survived. I would never read her own words, of that I was perfectly aware.

And as for Brookes' assertion that he was fighting against unseen powers and had no chance of ever saving her – well, he would say that, wouldn't he? He was hardly going to admit he was an untalented, inept fool who failed to do his job properly and cost a young woman her life.

In frustration I laid all my papers aside. There did not seem much point in pursuing the matter any further. I had come to a dead end and unless the mysterious Sophia really could break through the veil of death, I would never know what really happened in the Watkins family home after Richard was sent to his death in the Crimea.

I went slowly up the stairs, feeling suddenly weary. Lil was awake and bade me enter when I tapped on her bedroom door. I went in and sat on the side of the bed, "Feeling any better?" I asked.

"Not really – but what is wrong with you? You seem very down. Did you have another quarrel with David?"

"How did you know I had seen David?"

"I'm not completely senile yet, you know. I can see what is going on between you two. You could cut the atmosphere with a knife when you are together."

I tried to laugh it off, but I found myself blushing, partly at the memory of our time together that afternoon, but mostly because I was being so bloody obvious. So much for holding him at arm's length and playing it cool.

"No, we haven't had a row. We nearly did, but he managed to defuse the situation – as usual."

"You'll do him good – he's had it too easy with all his other girl-friends. They've let him get away with murder."

"All? Just exactly how many have there been?"

"A few. He is a single man, after all."

"He is now. Why did his marriage split up, Lil?"

"I think you should be asking him that, don't you?"

"Easier said than done. We never seem to get any time alone together, and when we do, we argue."

"And whose fault is that?"

"Certainly not mine," I snapped, then joined her laughter, "Ok, I get the message. I'm a little snippy at the moment – but I do have rather a lot on my mind."

"Speaking of which, how are you getting along with Decima?"

"Not too well. I've just found out she had a baby, but I don't know what happened to it."

"So that was true, then?" she asked, completely unfazed by this astounding revelation.

"You mean you knew about it?" I said, aghast, "Why the heck didn't you tell me?"

"I wasn't sure it was the case. This was years ago, when I was asking one of my aunts about the story. Don't forget Decima was a taboo subject in the family. I wasn't exactly encouraged to ask questions."

"I'll bet you weren't. Well, do you know what happened to it?"

She looked thoughtful, "I have my own theory, but no proof – I must stress that most strongly, Libby, because what I am about to tell you will set you off on one of your flights of fancy."

"Go on," I said, carefully negative. I refused to let her get me excited again. It was all going to end with a tantalizing story, but no conclusion, as Decima's tale always did, and I wasn't about to get worked up about it.

"Well, I've looked at our family tree and I've noticed that Decima's eldest sister, though married for many years, remained childless until 1855, whereupon she suddenly produced a son. There were never any siblings. It's not impossible that such a thing could happen, but curious, just the same."

"You think Decima had an illegitimate baby and her family covered the fact by giving it to her married sister to raise?"

"It has happened before," she said calmly.

I supposed it had, but it didn't make it any easier to accept. Poor Decima! Everything I had read about her so far had mentioned how fond she was of children, and how much all her nephews and nieces adored her. How painful it must have been for her to have to hand her child over to another woman to raise – even if that woman was her sister.

Unfortunately, it also put a whole new complexion on the murders.

Suddenly Decima was not without a motive for poisoning her sisters. She now had revenge in mind, as well as distress at losing her lover. I know I would want to kill anyone who took my baby away from me.

Perhaps that was why she waited so long after Richard's death before she began her campaign of terror. She wasn't killing her siblings because she was unbalanced by the loss of her man, she was completely enraged and distraught at being forced to watch her baby lie in the arms of another woman.

It was almost worse than having your baby adopted by a stranger and never seeing it again. To hear your little boy speak the word 'mama' to your sister instead of yourself must have been the most exquisite torture.

Decima's father was worse than a miserable old fool; he was a calculatingly cruel bastard. I hated him. And I hated his weak and stupid wife, and his smug, self-satisfied bitchy daughters. It was a pity Decima didn't manage to poison the lot of them.

Lil saw the expression on my face and laid a bony hand on my arm, "I knew I shouldn't have told you. Libby, you have to remember this all happened a very long time ago and nothing we can do will change the past. And I may be wrong. Decima's baby probably died at birth – she must have been miserable enough to miscarry, when she heard the news of Richard's death and knew that he could never come home and make an honest woman of her. And it was probably that misery that made her kill her sisters, if indeed it was she who did it."

"But you told me she didn't do it. It was you who convinced me to start this stupid investigation in the first place."

"I know, and I'm beginning to be sorry. You have to admit that nothing we have found really clears her name, does it? We just seem to find more reasons why she might have committed the crimes. At first we thought that her affection for Richard Allingham couldn't possibly have been strong enough to prompt so extreme a reaction, but now we find they were soul mates and that when he died she lost the love of her life. To add to that, we now find she really did have a baby which must have been his, and had it taken away from her. I'm sad to have to admit this, but Decima looks to me like one very angry, but seemingly powerless young woman. In those circumstances, a jaunt to the 'dark-side' not only seems likely, but frankly, positively necessary. Decima desperately needed to vent her frustrations somewhere, and the only power she wielded was in the form of some forgotten white powder, lying at the back of a dusty shelf."

163

I was stunned, utterly and completely speechless with amazement and fury.

"Lil, you can't believe she did it. You must know she did not."

"I don't know anything of the sort – and you don't either."

I wanted to cry back, like a three year old, "I do so!", but of course I did no such thing. Instead I refused to let her influence my thoughts. I instantly changed the subject – but without telling the whole truth.

"Are you getting up this evening?"

"No, I think I'll stay here. I'm really not feeling well today."

"I'm sorry to hear that, because I've invited Alison over for wine and girl talk. Will we disturb you? Do you want me to ring and cancel?"

She smiled – a forced one, but warm, "I wouldn't hear of it. I'm glad you've started to make friends here. You need friends when you live somewhere as isolated as this."

"Well, we won't be staying up too late, but you can always knock on the floor if we disturb you."

"I'm sure it will be fine. Now, any chance of a cup of tea?"

"Of course."

Whilst I was waiting for the kettle to boil, I rang Alison and told her to bring Sophia and a bottle of wine when she came over that evening.

CHAPTER TWENTY-TWO

I knew I needed to look at the family tree Lil had been talking about. I wondered where she would have put it – somewhere safe, that's for sure.

I don't know why I didn't just ask her when I went upstairs to take her tea, but something prevented me. She looked really ill, to be honest. White, exhausted and somehow drained. For the first time in my memory, she looked as though she didn't have a scrap of strength in her bones. It was at moments like these that I had to realize that she really was dying and that I would soon have to say my final farewells. Most of the time she fought to stay normal, to go about pretending nothing was happening, then she would be hit by a thunderbolt. I know I had seen it all before, but still it shocked me when it happened. I'm only human, after all, and burying your head in the sand comes naturally. It was far easier for me to imagine that the whole cancer thing had been a complete mistake by the hospital. Any day now we were going to get a letter, saying that they had fired the idiot who had misdiagnosed her and that they hoped she hadn't been too inconvenienced by the thought that she was going to die, when really she wasn't. I knew it was stupid, but Lil simply didn't act as though she was ill. Of course everyone reacts differently to bad news, but Lil had just seemed to rise above it. She treated her illness with the disdain it deserved and it seemed the only way it was going to get her was to sneak up on her when she was least expecting it.

Quite apart from all that, I felt she wouldn't approve of my interest just at the moment. I had been too emphatic. I had the distinct impression that I had rather frightened her with my strong feelings on the matter. She felt I had become too emotionally involved, and she wasn't far wrong. Decima was beginning to dominate my every thought and action. I had to prove her innocent. I felt as deeply ashamed of her barbaric demise as she must have done.

Decima was important to me – Decima was me.

Oh God! Had I really thought that? Perhaps Lil wasn't wrong to be concerned that I had allowed Decima to become an unhealthy obsession – but how could I help it? She had been cheated of so much, had had so much heartache and misery. Who would not be moved to tears and anger by her story?

I found the family tree in the desk drawer.

Naturally before I could even unroll it and have a proper look, the telephone rang. I was tempted to ignore its shrill, demanding beckoning, but I'm afraid I'm one of those people who just can't ignore a phone. Alright, we've already established that I'm nosy. I admit it. But if I hadn't been inquisitive, I wouldn't have managed this far, would I? And in my defence, telephones are particularly insistent. It even drives me nuts when I hear one ringing on the television. I find myself shouting at the screen, "Will someone answer that bloody phone, please! Are you all deaf?" Sad, I know, but there it is. Anyway, I went to answer the phone, in spite of straining at the bit to read the family tree.

"Hi," It was David, as I secretly hoped and thought it might be.

"Hello," There fell an awkward silence. Well, what exactly did you say to a man whom you have just ravished on his desk at work? 'Thanks for this afternoon', 'The unexpected bonk was great, shall we do it again soon'? Your guess is as good as mine.

It seemed he was having similar problems and the silence grew from being awkward to being downright painful. As a result we both tried to break it in the same moment, then stopped again as we realized the other was speaking, "After you," he said at last, much to my dismay, "No, no, you first – after all, you must have rung me for something."

"Just to make sure you arrived home safely, that's all," his voice sounded curiously gruff, as though he was impatient with himself for all this stupid shilly-shallying.

"As you can hear, I did. Why, did you think euphoria might run me off the road and into a ditch?" I had to say something to lighten the mood. This was far too heavy for my still-present little buzz of happiness.

"Who's Euphoria?" he asked, almost innocently enough to fool me. We both laughed, "Idiot! You know exactly what I mean."

"I do – and I'm delighted you feel yourself to be euphoric. I know I do."

This was by far the most romantic thing he had ever said to me and I felt a broad grin stretch across my face, "Really?"

"You've had your compliment. Don't start trying to squeeze another one

166

out of me. Anyway, to hastily change the subject. Just as I was about to ring you, I had Rick Allingham on the phone. Bad news, I'm afraid."

"Oh dear. Nothing serious I hope?"

"I think it might be for you, Libby, and I'm sorry. He's had some ancient Great Aunt on the phone to him, absolutely tearing a strip off him for letting the Allingham diaries off the premises. Apparently one of the indoor staff let it slip to her and she went ballistic."

"I suppose I can understand that. They are pretty old and rare."

"It seems that wasn't the problem. It's not that they were lent, but who they were lent to."

"Oh! I know the Aristos are supposed to hate journalist and the gutter press in general, but that's a bit heavy-handed. After all, I can't publish anything without their permission..."

"You are not getting this, Libby," he interrupted impatiently, "I don't mean anything like that. She found out who you were. She's livid with Rick for associating with anyone from the Watkins clan. I don't know what trouble Decima caused them, but by God, even a hundred and fifty years hasn't been enough time to wipe it out. Rick has been told in no uncertain terms to get those diaries back – pronto."

I felt sort of sick and shocked by this development. All that poor Decima had done was fall in love, and she was still being hated for it. I could hardly believe what I was hearing, "But I haven't finished reading them, yet, David. Rick can't really mean to leave me in mid air as to what happened."

"I don't think he's got any choice, my dear. The Aristo is talking Police, robbery, solicitors, the full Monty. You are going to have to give them back, now."

I glanced longingly towards the table, "I suppose I have no choice. I'd better get in the car right now and take them over there."

"Look, I don't want to see you disappointed over this. How about if I tell Rick I'll pick up the books and bring them to him – we can say you don't really want to see him as you are so upset – then I'll nip here first and quickly photocopy the last few pages. If you don't tell, no one need ever know..."

I couldn't begin to describe the feeling of relief that swept over me. My voice was soft and grateful as I asked, "Would you really do that for me?"

"Of course,"

"Thank you, David,"

"No problem. I'll be there in about half an hour."

"It's a pity you can't stay for the séance."

"What?" I was surprised to hear him sounding shocked.

"It's not really a séance," I amended hastily, "I've just someone who claims to be psychic coming round,"

"Be careful, Libby. I don't approve of that mumbo-jumbo. I think it has the potential to be dangerous."

Because I agreed with him, but couldn't admit it, I naturally got a bit snippy, "I know what I'm doing. I'm not a half-wit. Just because you've taken liberties with my body, don't think you can run my life."

"Hey, hey! Remember me? I'm David, not Brendan. Do whatever you like. It's no skin off my nose – but don't say I didn't warn you if you suddenly get green slime running down the walls and blood bubbling up through the bath plug hole."

"You watch too many horror movies," I said lightly, but I was hardly comforted.

"Very probably. I'll be with you in a few minutes. Mark the pages you want me to copy and bundle everything else up in a bag or something, so I can run straight in with them and leave Rick to reflect on his weak nature and broken promises."

"Consider it done."

Once again the family tree could have to wait for a later date.

❦   ❦   ❦   ❦   ❦

I nipped upstairs to look in on Lil and found she was still asleep. This seemed a little odd, but I could see she was breathing rhythmically and her face was serene, so I left her alone.

I then spent an unhappy half-hour gathering all Rick Allingham's property together and putting place markers in the pages I wanted copying. Various words and phrases kept leaping up off the pages at me and the longing to ignore Rick Allingham and keep the notebooks was almost overwhelming. There was so much still I wanted to know. Before I had only been vaguely interested in the war journals, but now I was desperate to read them, to know more about the man for whom Decima had risked everything – even, I now knew, her reputation. What on earth had possessed the pair of them to risk pregnancy and ignominy just for the sake of a few rapturous minutes in the sack? And who was I to judge, after what I had done that afternoon? I had never really believed love could sweep you away so completely that you threw all caution to the winds, but isn't that what I had just experienced with David Wright?

It was the word 'love' that brought me up sharp. This was going too fast even for little old impetuous me. David was a nice man, who was fun to be with and had been spectacularly kind to my Aunt, but had I really fallen in love so quickly and so completely that I was prepared to forget the warnings I had been given about his ambition and his financial acumen? I really did have to slow things down from now on.

David was true to his promise and arrived promptly at seven and dashed straight off again on his errand of mercy. My heart gave a tiny leap when I saw him, then plunged into my stomach as he disappeared again. The tiny sick feeling of disappointment was such that I suddenly realized I hadn't eaten anything since lunch and though it had been an admittedly large lunch, I had worked most of the calories off in the afternoon. I made myself a couple of cheese and pickle sandwiches and tucked in. If this Sophia woman was half the psychic she claimed to be, I might stand in need of sustenance later in the evening. I think if your head is going to spin round and you are going to hurl pea soup, it probably helps to have your stomach lined first.

I was, of course, making these light-hearted comments to myself because I was scared witless by what might happen. I had already seen what Decima was capable of and I was really afraid of opening any portals that might give her more room for manoeuvre.

When I thought about this, I had to give a rueful grin – oh, how far I had come. In less than two weeks I had shaken off my natural cynicism and become a full blown believer in the after-life, ghosts, telekinesis – next I'd be seeing fairies and little green men.

Luckily my introspection was disturbed by the arrival of Alison and Sophia – who proved to be nothing like I had imagined. She was neither an ethereal, dreamy hippie, dressed in flowing coloured Indian silk and cotton, nor a homely Doris Stokes type. She was just a very ordinary, middle-aged woman, with grey hair, a rotund figure and rather startling orange lipstick. I suppose she must have thought it suited her, but it certainly didn't go well with the lilac eye shadow. I was immediately disappointed. She was no match for Decima. I couldn't imagine feisty, courageous, bitterly angry little Decima answering a call from this fully paid up member of the Braxton Mother's Union.

Introductions made and refreshments offered and refused, we began the session in earnest. She asked first if she might wander around the house, to 'get the feel of the place'.

"Certainly. The only room you can't go in is my aunt's room. She's

169

unwell and fast asleep at the moment. Her room is…"

"There's no need to tell me. I'll know which room it is when I get there."

Smart-arse, I thought.

"Fine. Shall I lead the way?"

"No, I will go first, if you don't mind – and don't tell me anything about the house, or your ghost. I like to see if I can feel it for myself first. If I'm at all confused, I'll ask you questions."

"Okay."

And off we went.

She did, as predicted, correctly identify Aunt Lil's room, but I have to say I wasn't particularly impressed by this feat as it is, (a) the Master bedroom and situated at the front of the house, over the main living room, and (b) the only room with the door fast shut. I let that go, though. No point in being unpleasant to people when they are sincere and well meaning. There would be time enough to get nasty if she started asking for money for her services.

It was very quiet as we wondered around. Apart from the occasional squeaky floorboard and Sophia's rather stertorous breathing (apparently she was asthmatic) no one said a word and the house was silent. I would almost say ominously silent, but perhaps that was with hindsight.

Even though I was, by now, utterly convinced Sophia was a charlatan – despite Alison plodding after her like a pet dog, with an expression of dreamy admiration on her face – I was decidedly relieved when she by-passed my bedroom without a second glance – no bogey-men in there, thank God.

She hesitated for a long time outside Lil's room, then walked on, making no comment.

At the attic stairs she exchanged a triumphant glance with Alison and said in a hushed, almost reverential tone, "Here we have the crux of the matter."

I felt a shiver run up my spine, but determinedly dismissed the tiny wave of terror that began to sweep over me. Of course she was going to pick on the attics. All attics were dark, neglected and spooky. It was traditionally the place where ghosts were banished. There was no room for them in the rest of the house.

The same pattern was repeated on the third floor. Sophia plodded heavily, but surprisingly quietly along the passageway, pausing at each doorway and peering into each room. Alison pattered after her like an obedient terrier and I brought up the rear, trying not to get the feeling that there was another party right on my tail, and strenuously resisting the temptation to turn and look behind me.

Why did it have to pop into my head right this moment that it was always the one at the back of the line that was grabbed and murdered in war and horror films? Something dark and nasty, be it a monster or a Japanese sniper, always appeared silently, menacingly as the last person passed and with a barely discernible breath of air, that isn't even noticed by those going on before, a hand goes over the mouth to stifle the startled scream, and one more victim lengthens the ever growing list.

By God, I didn't want to be at the back of that particular queue and there wasn't a thing I could say to change the situation.

My heart sank as she stopped by the back room where Brendan had locked me up a few days before – was it only days? It seemed like months ago. All my past seemed to have faded away since I arrived in Derbyshire. It was as though my life in London had never happened, as if it was the vague remnant of a dream or something that had happened when I was very young and had almost forgotten. I suddenly remembered that I had not even phoned any of my friends or work colleagues to let them know how I was doing. I had instructed them not to ring me in case Lil was in a really bad way and calls might have disturbed her – but, to be honest, I hadn't given any of them a second thought since I discovered Decima. How dreadful was that? What a terrible friend I was proving to be. Joanna and Laura must have been frantic by this time, wondering if I was alive or dead. Normally not a day went by when we didn't ring or meet up, though I had to admit things had cooled a little between us after I met Brendan. I understood now that they neither liked nor trusted him, but didn't know how to tell me without appearing to be either interfering or jealous. God, what a mess I had made of my life up until now.

I silently vowed I would ring them both first thing in the morning, then turned my attention back to Sophia, who was slowly walking towards the centre of the room.

She turned to face Alison and I, crammed in the doorway, reluctant to enter fully without her permission.

"Oh, yes!" she said, with a tight smile, "I can feel something here. There's misery in this room. Real, deep, unremitting unhappiness, but anger too. It's making my nerves tingle and my hair crackle with electricity. This young lady is one very irate spirit. No wonder you could feel her presence, Libby."

❦

CHAPTER TWENTY-THREE

Right on cue the door at the bottom of the attic stairs slammed shut with a bang that reverberated through the entire house, making me nearly jump out of my skin, likewise Alison. Sophie appeared to be entirely unmoved by this startling event, even smiling slightly and saying quietly, "I'll take that as a gesture of agreement. I think we can safely say we have a very angry young lady on our hands. Now let's see if she can tell us why."

I knew why, but I wasn't about to confide in Sophia. If she were genuine she wouldn't need or welcome any help from me. If she was a charlatan, the sooner I found out, and rid myself of her, the better.

It had started to go dark while we were touring the house and I now asked, trying desperately to keep my voice steady, "Do you mind if I switch on the light?" Thank heavens I had had the foresight to get David to put in a new bulb, on one of his visits. I didn't think I could stand darkness as well as tension.

She nodded briefly, then invited Alison and myself, with a crooked finger, to step fully into the room and I had to admit that as I approached her the hairs on the nape of my neck and on my arms did lift slightly, as though affected by static electricity or cold.

"Can you feel it?" she asked, "Can you feel the presence?" Was it my mind playing tricks or did the hundred-watt bulb dim slightly, then brighten again?

I wanted to say airily, with great unconcern, that I could not feel any presence but our own, but the oppressive silence of the house, after that last bang, and her own subdued excitement, coupled with the very definite existence of goose-pimples on my arms and legs, made me unsure of what I was feeling. I merely nodded as Alison breathed, "Oh, yes!" in an awed tone.

"Now, Libby, I am going to ask some questions. Answer only what I ask, don't elaborate when you answer. If you accidentally give me false information, or cloud the issue with your own theories, you will make it very difficult for me to contact our subject. Can you do that?"

"Yes," I said succinctly, starting already on her explicit instructions.

"Very well." She closed her eyes, "Does the letter 'D' have any relevance to you?"

"Yes."

"I'm a little confused here. I don't recognise the name I'm being given. It's almost as though it is a number, but in a foreign language – perhaps Italian?"

"I think it is originally Latin," I said. Italian was close enough. I was prepared to allow her a little information for that gem.

"Ten? Is it the number ten? Deci-something?"

"Decima," I said, but Alison could have told her that and all this skirting around the issue could simply have been window dressing to impress me. I couldn't, just at this moment, recall whether I had mentioned the name of my resident ghost to the vicar's wife.

"There were ten in the family, then?"

"Yes. She was the youngest." Sophia raised a finger in admonition. Too much information, apparently. I fell silent.

"Now I'm getting an 'R'. Is there an 'R' in the story?"

"Yes."

"Good. Now let me see, Robert? No, Richard. Is it Richard, Libby?"

"Yes." Still not impressed. This was all common knowledge. Children in Braxton probably learned about their local murderess at their grandmother's knee.

"My first thought, when we were led to the attics, was that Decima must have been a maid servant, possibly in love with her Master's son, but this room was not Decima's bedroom. It was important for another reason." She moved across to the window and as we followed her, I felt a chilly draught on my face and shoulders, though the casement appeared to be fully closed. Indeed, when I looked closely, I saw that it couldn't have been opened for years, for the edges were painted over and therefore sealed with layer after layer of thick gloss. I tried to repress a shudder.

"She waited here for him, didn't she? She could see him as he rode across the hill and fields towards her. He would always pause on the crest and give her one last wave when he rode away. Afterwards, when they had been forced apart, she would come up here and will him to appear on the hilltop. All through the long bitter months after he died, she would sit here,

173

sewing tiny clothes, and pray for him to come back to her. Eventually a comfortable chair was brought up here from downstairs."

If she was right and that same chair still existed, then I knew it was downstairs now and that I had fallen asleep in it more than once – with horrible consequences.

It seemed I was not expected to make any comment at this point, for she continued, "Did you know she had a baby?"

"I suspected it."

"She gave birth here, in this house, I think, but then it was taken away from her and given to one of her sisters to raise. I feel that her father must have been very angry with her. He felt she had brought shame on the family. There was an older woman living here then – an Aunt perhaps?"

I shook my head, "It's me who lives with an Aunt."

"A grandparent then. Her grandmother offered her a home here, with her baby son, but her father would not hear of it. She thought her heart would break when she left."

I looked at her. She seemed very sincere, but in the back of my mind, I had to admit that if I were piecing together the story of a girl who had an illegitimate baby in the nineteenth century, this was exactly the scenario I would come up with! It was pretty classic stuff, really. It could have been written by Dickens or Hardy.

"Can I ask something?" I said rather stiffly. This was all very well, but it wasn't helping me to find out exactly what I could do to help. I knew all this. I had read Richard's own account of the love affair, and for all I knew, Sophia was indeed a psychic – but not one in touch with the other side. She could be reading my thoughts and knowledge – unlikely, I know. But no more far-fetched than believing that Decima was here in this room with us and telling her story to this middle-aged woman.

"I can't promise I can answer you, but yes, ask away,"

"What does Decima want from me?"

Sophia closed her eyes and a tiny frown appeared on her brow, as though she was concentrating very hard. I had to admit, she was good. One might almost believe she really was trying to contact the dead, listening to try and hear that still, small voice from the other side.

The silence in the house became more profound. It was like being wrapped in a thick blanket. I knew there must be noises going on all around me. There must be birds singing outside, I had seen a lark soaring on one last spree before nightfall from where I stood. There would be aeroplanes going over, trains down in the valley. The house itself must be making its

174

usual tiny creaks and groans, like an old, arthritic man stretching his aching muscles and bones, but I could hear nothing. No radiator pipes clanging, no wind whistling in the eaves.

The stillness stretched my nerves to breaking point, but I had to stand and wait for her to speak, not screaming in frustration and fear, not running away and saying 'be damned to it all, I don't care anymore.' It was then that I thought I caught the faintest whiff of Decima's perfume. I tested the air, but it was gone. Imagination probably, but very convincing just for that one instant.

When Sophia finally spoke it was in a perfectly normal tone of voice, as though she were passing a message from someone on the other end of a telephone who I couldn't see or hear, "She wants her baby back."

To say I was taken aback was to vastly understate the matter. I was utterly astounded. I had been expecting her to say that Decima was reiterating her innocence of her crimes and that she wanted me to clear her name. To ask me to give her baby back to her was utterly ridiculous. She had been dead for a hundred and fifty years. If her baby hadn't died at birth, even if it had lived to be a hundred, it would still be long dead and beyond my reach. Surely she was in a better position to wander the afterlife and find her son than I was.

"I don't understand," I stuttered at last, "What does she mean?"

"The family tree. She knows it doesn't matter any longer, but she wants the family tree altered – and she wants the rest of the family to know about it."

"But I don't know how to do that. I don't know which sister had her child. They had dozens of descendants."

The attic door slammed again, with even more violence and noise than before – the only trouble was, it was already shut tight.

Sophia shivered and whispered, "There is someone else here, now. An older woman, in her forties, I think..."

Suddenly she was bundling me towards the door, her breath coming in short, agitated gasps, her voice teetering on the edge of panic "Get out of here, Libby. She means you harm..."

It was all so unexpected. I was shocked and stunned by the change in atmosphere, which now felt icy cold and oddly threatening, and the alteration of Sophia from a woman in control and supremely confident, to an agitated little old lady, guiding me hastily down the stairs. I wasn't sorry to go, but I found myself resisting her pushing hands. There was something incredibly irritating about being shoved around in my own house, "Don't be

175

stupid. What can she possibly do? She's dead for God's sake!"

My answer came in the form of a huge crash from the room behind us. It sounded as though the whole roof had collapsed. After that I needed no second bidding. I shot down the stairs like a bat out of hell.

As I walked into the living room, a glance at the window made me realize that the heavens had opened whilst we were upstairs and it was now raining steadily and very heavily. The noise we had heard upstairs was probably nothing more than a particularly loud crack of thunder. That was what I hoped, anyway.

"That's odd. I never heard rain on the roof when we were upstairs," I said conversationally, trying to sound ordinary, as though I was always being threatened by beings from the 'other side' and that it was a mere nothing.

Sophia sank into the nearest chair – which happened to be the chair – then she hastily rose and took a place on the sofa, "Do you think we might have a drink of something, Libby. I feel a bit drained now,"

"Certainly. Do you want tea or coffee, or shall I open a bottle of wine?"

"I don't usually imbibe except with a meal, but a glass of wine would be most welcome, my dear."

"Make yourselves comfortable. I won't be long."

They had obviously been discussing things whilst I was in the kitchen getting the wine and glasses, because they both turned guiltily and looked at me when I came back into the room.

"Well, what's the verdict?" I asked. There was no point in being coy. We all knew something odd was happening in the house and it would be insulting to Sophia not to admit that she had been uncannily accurate with her story.

"You have a problem, Libby," said Sophia softly, "And I'm not about to hide the fact from you."

"You couldn't hide it if you tried. I think I have been aware of that for a while. But what is the solution?"

"I don't think Decima is going to be satisfied until you grant her wish. She wants final acknowledgement that she gave birth to a son and that all those in your family who are descended from him are also descended from her."

"I suppose that is easy enough to do. I don't quite know how to go about it, but I can find out…"

"That isn't really the difficulty here, Libby. There is another spirit who is equally determined to stop Decima from having her way. I suspect it is the

176

sister who raised the boy, but I'm not sure."

"You are joking," I protested. Wasn't it bad enough to have one haunting? I certainly didn't want two.

"I'm afraid not. I can't be sure, my dear, but I think the other woman is the one who has been causing your injuries. Decima does not seem to be particularly vengeful, more frustrated. Anything she has done has been to attract your attention."

Strangely enough that made sense. I had felt a definite affinity with Decima and had been rather hurt when she had appeared to be showing a lack of trust in me.

"What do you suggest we do about this? I put myself entirely in your hands. I don't know if you are aware of this, but Lil has given the house over to me, which means that I shall be living here for the foreseeable future – but I would like it to be alone. I could probably just about cope with Decima as a house guest, but this other one has definitely got to go."

"Well, I suppose if you free Decima from her earthly shackles, there won't be much point in her sister hanging about, will there?"

"And how do you suggest I do that? I hope you are not going to suggest an exorcism. I'm afraid I really can't be a party to anything like that."

"I was going to suggest we use a Ouija board, to see if we can find out the name of the foster mother," she spoke diffidently, and with every good reason. The expression on my face must have told her just exactly how I felt about that particular idea.

"Do you have a better solution?" she asked, not unnaturally irritated by my hesitation.

"Oh God!" I ejaculated, "I can't believe I'm even contemplating this. Do you have any notion how appalling I think this tinkering is?"

She patted my arm comfortingly, "I know. I do understand, but I assure you, I know what I'm doing. Shall we have a glass of wine and relax a little before we begin?"

As we sipped wine and listened to the steady rainfall outside, Alison busied herself folding and cutting pieces of paper into little squares and writing the letters of the alphabet onto them. On the final two she wrote the words 'yes' and 'no', then took them over to the table and arranged them in a circle. Once that was done, Sophie took one last deep gulp of wine and asked for a glass tumbler to be our pointer. I brought one from the kitchen, giving a nervous glance about me as I left the room to rejoin them. I felt I was being watched, and as always when I sensed observation, it was a menacing, unfriendly entity. I could not repress a shudder and wished with

177

all my heart that I had not agreed to any of this. We were straying into forbidden territory now and I was frightened. Really, really frightened. Not watching a scary movie with eyes hidden in hands frightened, but deep, unrelenting, stomach churning terror that I could barely contain.

I had a really bad feeling about this.

It grew even worse when I entered the sitting room and found that Decima's silver watch was lying on the table beside the black felt-penned letters.

"Where did you find that?" I asked hoarsely, pointing to it. I knew I had put it away earlier in Aunt Lil's desk and had turned the key upon it.

Neither Alison nor Sophia were near the table. They were still on the sofa waiting for my return. When I spoke they both turned and looked to where I was indicating, "What is it?" asked Sophia, "We haven't put anything on the table except the letters. I'm afraid we were both sneaking another half-glass of wine whilst we waited for you."

I could see by their faces that they were telling the truth. They had no idea I had any possessions of Decima and they certainly wouldn't have known where to find the watch, even supposing I had been gone long enough for them to open the desk and bring it out of its little drawer.

I swallowed deeply, "It doesn't matter," I said, "Shall we begin?"

CHAPTER TWENTY-FOUR

I swear to God, if she had begun by saying, "Is there anybody there?" I would have fallen into strong hysterics – and I wouldn't have known if I was laughing or crying. Thankfully she did no such thing. She invited us all to take a seat around the table, then we all placed a finger lightly on the base of the up-turned glass. It began to slide across the smooth surface of the polished table almost immediately, almost as though it couldn't wait to begin. It reminded me of those frisky horses at the beginning of races that can't wait to kick up their heels and be off while the jockey struggles manfully to keep behind the line. I could feel it thrumming and vibrating beneath my finger and I found myself pressing down hard to try and control it until Sophia whispered, "Don't try to press or push it, let it go its own way." At once I relaxed and it began to slide experimentally towards the letters, without touching any or stopping. Sophia took a deep breath, "Are we ready?" Alison and I nodded and she asked aloud, "Are you with us, Decima?"

The glass slid and hovered beside the 'yes'.

"Do you want to speak to us?"

Again, 'yes' .

"Did you give birth to a baby boy?"

'Yes'

"Did one of your sisters raise him for you?"

The glass rattled against the table as though in anger or agitation and shot across the table at high speed towards the, 'no'.

"Did your father give your baby to one of your sisters?"

'Yes'

"Which sister was it?"

The watch, which had remained on the table because I was too afraid to move it, suddenly began to spin wildly on its concave back then shot across the room. We all watched its trajectory in stupefaction. It looked for all the world as though some impatient hand had swept it away, but no one had gone within inches of it. It fell to the floor some feet away, thankfully unbroken. We exchanged a glance, but soon our attention was brought back to the table for the glass beneath our fingers was rocking wildly. It felt as though two hands had grasped it and were now fighting for possession.

It managed to slither towards the 'A' but before it could tell us anything more, it grew almost unbearably hot beneath our fingers – it was not a gradual climbing of temperature, but a sudden heat. We had all just reached the point where we were going to have to pull our hands away when it suddenly shattered into a thousand pieces, bits of glass flew in every direction and we all instinctively turned our faces away and threw our hands up in a protective fashion, fearful of the consequences of the flying debris.

It took a few moments for us all to calm down enough to think of examining ourselves and each other to make sure none had sustained an injury. There was glass everywhere, over the table, on the floor, and the paper letters had been blown asunder by the force of the miniature explosion, so that the area around the table looked like a little snowstorm, but not one of us showed even a speck of blood. I found I was shaking uncontrollably, frightened, angry, distressed – you name it, I felt it.

"Jesus Christ Almighty! That's it!" I yelled, "One of us could have lost an eye. I'm not playing these games any longer. I've had enough. Thank you for trying to help, ladies, but I suspect you've probably made things a damn sight worse."

I don't honestly think either of them was in the least bit sorry to be so rudely ejected from my house. They both hastily gathered up their coats and handbags, and I felt sure it was not because they were afraid of me.

As she walked out of the door, Sophia turned back to ask one last question, ignoring the fact that the rain was pouring down on her, "I know it was all a mess and incredibly unsatisfactory, Libby, and I'm sorry, but tell me one thing..."

"What?" I said shortly.

"Was there a sister whose name began with 'A'?"

"Yes, there was. Goodbye, Sophia."

Why didn't I tell her that 'A' was the sister from whom I was descended? I didn't even want to admit it to myself.

With an odd look at me, she was gone, and I went back into the house and upstairs to make sure Lil was undisturbed by the events of the past few hours.

She was sitting up in bed when I looked around the door, having apparently just woken.

"Have we had visitors? I thought I heard voices."

"You did. They've just gone. You've slept a long time – and through some dreadful noises."

"Have I?" she said, smoothing the coverlet with a slightly shaky hand, "I thought I heard thunder a little while back, but I was so tired, I just ignored it."

Perhaps it was for the best that she thought the banging in the attic had been thunder. It was what I wanted to believe, but if I really thought it was true, why didn't I go up there and see if there had been any damage done? I didn't bloody well want to, that's why – and there was no need to furnish her with the full details.

I sat on the edge of the bed, "Lil, I want to talk to you,"

"Go ahead, my dear. You can say anything to me, you know that,"

"I've had an odd sort of day, Lil, and I want your advice on what I ought to do next."

"Go on, I'm listening," she said, tilting her head slightly sideways, giving her the look of an intrigued sparrow.

I told her about Sophia's visit and her conclusions. She heard me in silence, then appeared to think deeply for a moment before looking directly at me and saying firmly, "This has to be put to the family, Libby. I really ought to see them all and explain about the house anyway – and I suppose I should be saying my goodbyes. Yes, that's it. We must call a family conference. You will find all the names and numbers in my address book downstairs in my desk. Ring them all tonight and see if they can get here for Sunday."

I looked blankly at her, "What?"

"Don't say what, dear, say pardon."

"All right. Pardon? You really are expecting me to ring around the family and invite them here so that they can personally hear from you that I have stolen their inheritance from under their noses? You do jest."

"Don't be silly. Not one of them can possibly have been expecting to inherit Hill Farm. I've made it obvious for years that its fate lay entirely in my hands and that I would decide when and if to part with it."

"If you say so, Auntie, but I think you are in for a rude awakening. Mother and Maddie's attitude must have alerted you to which way the wind was blowing."

"Oh, I think Marjorie and Maddie are the exception, not the rule. Don't worry so much, Libby. I'm sure the rest will be perfectly fine with us both, but I really don't think we can take it upon ourselves to change something as fundamental as a family tree without at least consulting them."

There did not seem much else I could say, so I went downstairs to make her something to eat. While the soup heated on the stove I set about vacuuming up the broken glass. It made the most appalling rattling, grinding noises as it was sucked up, but I wasn't about to try and sweep it. I'm sure I would have been cut to shreds. It really was everywhere.

I took Lil her supper on a tray, rather concerned to notice how white she was looking in the light of the bedside lamp. She was scarcely visible against the pillows as she lay propped up, with her eyes closed and her mouth falling partly open. I shuddered as I had the sudden thought that she was never going to leave her bed again and I could scarcely bear it, "You will be getting up tomorrow, won't you, Lil?" I asked diffidently.

She opened her eyes and smiled cheerfully at me, "Of course I will, love. I'm just having a bit of a bad day today, that's all."

We both knew she was lying.

"I'm going to start making the phone calls, now. You haven't changed your mind?"

"No, invite them all for high tea on Sunday - I suppose we'll have to at least feed them. Do you think you can manage to shop for that, and to make a few sandwiches?"

"Of course I can," I said, with a sinking heart. Bad enough that I was going to have to face all those various Aunts, Uncles and cousins, but to watch them despising my ability in the kitchen was the ultimate trial. And I was going to have to clean the house, too. It would suit their purposes beautifully if they could accuse me of not looking after Aunt Lil properly.

I spent the next two hours ringing around my relatives and inviting them for tea on Sunday. Unfortunately they all wanted to chat, not having heard from me for several months – not since my cousin Monica's wedding, to be precise – another event of refined torture, when Brendan had been at his most charming and everyone had been planning my own nuptials to the gallant Irishman I had so surprisingly managed to hook.

It was nearly ten before I had finished and I had just flopped onto the sofa to try and recover from the intolerable strain of being nice to my family when the phone rang. It made me jump violently, as I had grown so used to the calls going out, I wasn't really expecting any to come back in.

Obviously I was still suffering from a reaction to the events of earlier, because my hand was trembling as I reached to pick up the receiver, "Hello?"

"Hello, it's David. What's been going on? I've been trying to get through to you for hours."

"Sorry. I've been rather busy. Aunt Lil has decided on a family conference and I had to make the calls."

"Oh," he said slowly. There was a short silence, then he added quietly, "Does that mean what I think it means?"

"That she wants to say goodbye?" I asked.

"Yes,"

"Well, sort of, but there are other things too. I'll tell you everything when I see you. Did you manage to do the photocopying?"

"I did, but that's why I rang. I won't be able to get them to you for a couple of days. I have a problem at another garden centre. I'm going to have to go to Lincolnshire for a while."

"You have another garden centre?" I asked incredulously.

"I have two more, actually."

"Oh. I see. How long will you be away?"

"Three or four days. Will you be okay without me?"

"Of course. I'm perfectly capable of looking after myself."

"I meant with Lil. From what you've just told me, this does not seem to be the best time for me to be called away."

"We'll be fine. Don't worry about Lil and me. We have a family party to look forward to."

"And are you looking forward to it?"

'Not in the least."

'Never mind. Chin up. Oh, I nearly forgot, you have something else too."

"What?"

"I managed to make Rick feel so guilty about his betrayal, that he's sent you a little gift."

"What is it?" I asked suspiciously. I wasn't sure I wanted a present from the turncoat Allingham.

"It's the first Richard's trunk – a sort of small travelling desk and vanity case combined. A bit battered on the outside, but perfectly preserved inside. His batman brought it back from the Crimea for his family. Rick inherited it, but says he's never used it beyond looking inside the lid when he got it at eighteen."

"Oh yeah," I said sarcastically, "And how long will it be mine before some old crone in the family tells him to take it back?"

"That won't happen. He assures me that it is entirely his own property and no one can tell him what to do with it – unlike the family papers, which form part of an archive. I'll bring it with the photocopying when I come next week – okay?"

"Yes, fine. Thanks." I didn't sound particularly grateful, but I was feeling pretty bereft as I realized I wasn't going to see either him or Richard's papers for days. To be honest, I wasn't quite sure which event was upsetting me more. Don't get me wrong, I was, by now, pretty well smitten by Mr. Wright – as my mother had always predicted I would be – but I also really wanted to read the next installment of the Decima and Richard saga.

This longing, however, was swept from my mind as I put the phone back in its cradle because I suddenly recalled whom it was I had so far neglected to ring. My mother. Oh dear God above, I would have to telephone my mother and invite her to Lil's little soiree.

With the utmost reluctance I dialled the number and nearly dropped the phone when Brendan answered. For one stunned moment I thought I had mistakenly dialled his number, but deep down I knew I had not. I swallowed deeply and asked icily,

"What the hell are you doing there?"

"Libby? What a pleasant surprise. Do you want to speak to your mother? Just a moment I'll hand you over to her." There was a brief pause then my mother's sleepy tones came across the wires, "Hello, Libby? What time of night is this to be ringing anyone?"

"It's only just gone ten, mother," I said reasonably. She giggled, "Sorry, I've been in bed for hours."

Oh, my God! She was in bed with my ex-boyfriend. Please tell me it's not true, Lord, I prayed silently. I pulled myself together with difficulty. I simply wouldn't think about it, that was all.

"Lil asked me to ring and invite you and the rest of the family over on Sunday," I said, in as businesslike manner as possible.

"Mighty gracious of her. What is this for – a damage limitation exercise?"

"I think she wants to say goodbye," I answered tersely. Let her be the one to feel guilty for a change. She bloody well ought to.

"Very well, I'll be there and so will Maddie. What time?"

I told her, then added, "Do me a favour, mother, don't bring that arsehole you are currently sleeping with."

"That's no way to speak of your future step-father, sweetheart."

"Very funny," I said, determined not to be rattled.

"And for the record," she added silkily, ignoring my interruption, "We're not doing that much sleeping."

184

I heard Brendan laugh in the background.
And I wasn't entirely sure how I felt about it.

CHAPTER TWENTY-FIVE

It wasn't until I put the phone down for the last time that I suddenly realized I was alone. Of course Lil was in the house, but she was so far gone with her painkillers that she might just as well not be there.

I don't think I've ever wanted company so much in my entire life. The way I was feeling, even Brendan would have been welcome. On second thoughts, I wasn't that desperate.

I made myself a coffee that I didn't particularly want and wondered whether I was tired enough to drop straight off to sleep if I went to bed. The trouble was, the answer to that was an emphatic no. Speaking to my mother on the phone had been like a douche of ice cold water. I had never felt more awake. I was so full of emotions of every description that I think I could have run the London Marathon and not drawn breath.

What the hell was going on with my life? I had come to visit my aged aunt less than two weeks ago and since then I had gained a stalker, a new boyfriend, a house, a family who were deadly enemies and a huge case of paranoia. I had turned from a cynic with a healthy disregard for all things paranormal to a passionate believer in ghosts, apports, telepathy and mediums who can hear voices from the 'other side'. I was a mess and I had no idea how to sort myself out.

I paced about a bit, trying to stop my mind from whirring like an annoying battery-powered toy. There were so many things to think about and I couldn't stop them all crowding into my head at once. Frankly it was starting to make me feel ever so slightly unwell. I knew I had to do something or I might just be found in the morning, a gibbering, insane wreck.

One glance about me told me exactly what tasks I could use to tire myself and blot out the world. The cottage was badly in need of a spring clean. I had been seeing to the bare essentials since my arrival, shopping, cooking and washing up, but dusting and hoovering had been sadly neglected. There was a faint, but definitely discernible layer of dust over everything. If the family were going to be gathering at the weekend, then I needed to put everything in order. Bad enough that I was going to have to admit that they were all being cut out of Lil's will, without showing them how very undeserving of the inheritance I evidently was.

I realized I couldn't really get the vacuum cleaner out without disturbing Lil, but I could make a good start on the dusting. I was a bit daunted when I remembered that all the cleaning equipment was kept at the 'cellar head' as we always called it – that's the row of shelves cunningly fitted at the top of the cellar steps, making full use of every available inch of space in the house. I didn't particularly want to open the cellar door. After the attic, the cellar is always the next spookiest place in the filmmakers' haunted house. It is, when all is said and done, the place where the bodies are buried. Whether ancient graveyards upon which the house has been constructed, or the last resting place of the unfortunate – and now furiously angry – murder victim, the cold, dark, scary cellar is going to be the place where evil, smelly decaying things crawl out.

I hovered uncertainly for a moment, then shook myself angrily. Get real, Libby. No one was buried in the cellar. If Decima was haunting this house, she had no interest in the basement. She probably never even went down there in life. This part of the house would have been the stamping ground of the servants in the eighteen hundreds.

Setting my shoulders determinedly, I reached for the door and pulled it open, refusing to acknowledge the slight shaking of my hand. I nearly jumped out of my skin as a broom, apparently dislodged by the opening of the door, fell forward. In a split second I changed from cringing away thinking that something horrible was attacking me, to catching the stupid thing before it hit the floor with a clatter and woke Lil. I managed to force a little laugh at myself, more to instil confidence than because I was genuinely amused by my own jumpiness. This was getting beyond a joke. When something as simple as a brush handle could scare me, I really was going beyond what was reasonable behaviour.

I searched my huge handbag – you know the sort; everything a woman would need to survive on a desert island, from a sewing kit, through mobile phone, walkman, tampons and a pearl-handled penknife. Don't ask, I just always wanted one – until I found my walkman and an Oasis tape, turned it on, donned the earphones and spent the next hour or so studiously avoiding thinking or doing anything but doing my Mrs. Mop impression and singing along with Noel and Liam.

It must have been after midnight by the time I was satisfied all the woodwork in the house would survive the critical scrutiny of Aunts Polly and Ethel. I took off my earphones and was just by the kitchen sink, virtuously rinsing out the now filthy dusters, when someone tapped on the window – or at least, I thought someone had. Either way, I must have jumped back three feet, my heart pounding and my breath coming in laboured gasps. I peered out into the dark and the rain, but could see nothing, only my own white face reflected back to me. The longer I stared, the more frightened I became. There was nothing to account for the noise, but I knew, beyond any shadow of doubt, that I had heard a knocking sound. Suddenly I was aware of the feeling that someone was standing behind me and my eyes travelled across the glass until I thought I saw another face reflected there, as though a woman was waiting in the doorway of the sitting room. I whirled round, hoping against hope to see Aunt Lillian standing there, but there was nothing, no one.

I stared in disbelief at the empty doorway until the tapping dragged my attention back to the window. I could have cried with relief when I saw that a broken branch of wisteria, hanging off the main stem, was blowing occasionally against the glass.

No chance of sleep now. My heart was still beating like the bass on a bad CD player. I thought that if I didn't sit down, my knees would fail me, so wobbly were they. I perched on a high kitchen stool, made myself another coffee, and then carried it through to the sitting room. It looked like it was going to be a very long night. There was no way I could brave the stairs, traverse the dim landing, with its portrait of the stern-faced Jacob Watkins who had so brutally betrayed his youngest daughter; I didn't want to pass the attic door with its association with the poor, heartbroken, pregnant girl, and then go on to my bedroom, which I now, after all that had happened, was convinced had been Decima's bedroom too.

I sat on the settee – no way was I risking the comfy old chair, just in case I should happen to drop off to sleep. I switched on the television, which Lil and I had hardly watched since my arrival, and flicked through the channels until I found an old movie – a nineteen thirties comedy, thank God. I think I would have turned into a screaming wreck if it had been a horror film. I tried to concentrate on the flimsy plot, sipping my coffee and determinedly keeping all thoughts of my family out of my mind. Gradually I began to calm down and even feel a little sleepy. All my fears were receding slowly until the film ended, whereupon I put down my cup on the table and decided that I could probably sleep if I were to go upstairs.

As I reached the door, a noise behind me attracted my attention and when I looked around, Decima's watch was slowly spinning on the table next to my coffee cup. I watched it in horrified fascination for a few seconds, then started violently as it suddenly shot across the room towards me. I wrenched open the door and legged it for the stairs as though the hounds of hell were on my tail. Halfway up the lights flickered and went out.

It was then I heard the baby crying. Faint, but unmistakable, the wail of a newly born baby. With a terrified sob I threw myself towards Lillian's door. For five gut-wrenching seconds I couldn't find the handle and I was flailing about in the pitch dark, whimpering like a frightened child until the knob came under my grasping hands and I plunged into the room, the door hitting the wall next to it with a reverberating crash, fit to wake the dead. It didn't wake Lil though, and I had another few tense seconds whilst I felt my way across the room, stubbing my toes against the unseen furniture, my hands spread before me to protect me from walking into anything that might smack me in the face, until I reached the bedside and felt about for her to convince myself she was still breathing. She was. I got into bed beside her, not bothering to get undressed, merely slipping my shoes off my frozen feet. Then I slid under the blankets so that my head was covered, my ears stopped with shaking fingers, so that I couldn't hear any other unearthly sounds that Decima might send my way. There I stayed, taking comfort from the sensation of my companion's regular, though rather laboured breathing, until the dawn broke and drove away the shadows and noises that had so terrified me.

❦   ❦   ❦   ❦   ❦

By seven the following morning I was back in the kitchen, making myself yet another coffee. I felt dreadful. Only someone who has done it can understand how indescribably grimy one feels after doing hard physical labour, then sleeping in the same clothes, without the benefit of even a wash. I felt disgusting and could hardly wait for the heater to work so that I could have a bath. It took about ten minutes for me to recall that the electricity had gone off again last night. I was so desperate to get clean that I thought I might just boil a few pans of water, along with the kettle, just to get enough water for a tepid few inches. I had put them all on the Aga to heat when the telephone rang.

It was Dan, from the museum.

"Hello, I didn't expect to hear from you again, I must say," I remarked in a friendly way. I was so relieved to be hearing another human voice, I think I would even have been chatty to my mother, had she rung me.

"Hi, Libby. I hope this isn't too early for you? I wanted to be sure I would catch you before I went off out for the day."

"No, it's fine. I've been up for hours. Are you going anywhere nice?" I was desperate to keep him talking; he was so ordinary, so pleasant. Just hearing his voice on the other end of the line reminded me that there was a real life out there, away from this house, with living people, who had normal lives; nothing weird happening, no darkness, no feeling of impending doom, no aura of evil and despair.

"Just tramping in the hills with a gang of friends, but we're taking tents and if the weather improves, we'll probably stay away the whole weekend," he said enthusiastically. I had been thinking that I might ask to tag along if he were going somewhere exciting, but my own enthusiasm quickly faded. It might be his idea of fun wading ankle deep in boggy terrain, with the prospect of a damp sleeping bag on even damper ground, but it certainly wasn't mine. Now, if he'd said he was planning a day of shopping in Buxton or Chesterfield, followed by a pub lunch and the pictures, he might have had himself a date.

"Oh, that sound nice," I said dully, "What did you want with me?"

"I thought you might be interested in something which has just been donated to the museum,"

I regained my zest for life in a second. A dozen exciting possibilities rushed to mind and I picked on the one that appealed to me the most, "Not Richard Allingham's diaries?" I asked breathlessly. It would be typical of the snotty aristocrats to deny me access to the diaries, but then donate them to posterity.

"No. I didn't know he had written any. But they are diaries of a sort, though not exactly. No, these are the case notes of dozens of arrests made by Inspector Lazarus. He shouldn't really have kept copies, and that is why it has taken his family so long to admit to their existence and give them to us."

"Inspector Lazarus?" The name rang a bell, but for the moment I couldn't quite place it.

"He's the man who arrested Decima Watkins."

It all came flooding back, "Of course. He came here to get her."

"He did indeed. It was his beat, so to speak, so that even though the murders were supposedly committed in Manchester, he was the man who was sent to arrest the suspect."

"And do these notes you have mention her?"

"They do. He tells the full tale of her arrest, her subsequent imprisonment whilst she awaited trial, and his own removal from the case when he expressed doubts as to her guilt."

"And you are prepared to let me have them?" I was incredulous.

"I have the photocopies of the relevant portions in my hands as we speak. I thought I might drop them off with you on my way past. Would half an hour be convenient?"

"Half an hour would be wonderful," I said warmly, "Thank you, Dan. You don't know what this means to me."

"Oh, I think I do, that's why I have forgiven your Aunt for dropping me in it over the watch and the ring."

I had the grace to blush slightly, though of course he would never know it.

"Yes, sorry about that. I hope it didn't cause you too much trouble."

"Not really. My employers have to accept that families can always change their minds about donations. Frankly they're use to it – as my Granny always used to say, 'there's nowt so queer as folk'."

"She was a wise woman."

"She was indeed. Right, see you presently then."

With that he was gone. I put the phone back in its cradle and stared thoughtfully at it for a moment. I could scarcely believe the odd coincidence of these papers coming to light at this precise moment – or was it a coincidence? I turned my attention once more to Inspector Lazarus. Now there was a name to conjure with. What a pity he couldn't have lived up to it and brought poor Decima back from the brink of death. Evidently he tried. I was warming to him already.

I warmed to him even more thirty-five minutes later when Dan had given me the papers and gone off back to the waiting land rover to join his woolly-hatted, stout-booted friends.

The housework was forgotten as I settled myself on the sofa and prepared to find out what Inspector Lazarus had to say on the guilt or innocence of Decima Watkins.

"The case of Decima Watkins was probably one of the most baffling and frustrating of my career. The long and the short of it was that I found no evidence whatsoever to support the fact that any crime had ever been committed. We were sent to arrest the young woman on the strength of an

anonymous tip-off and once she was in custody it seemed to me that someone, somewhere, was determined to make away with her. I never found out who – I was never given the chance, for as soon as I made my doubts known, I was taken off the case and it was handed to some young fellow who had been in the Force but a few months. He wanted promotion and did as he was told. When I began to stir the waters I was called into my superior's office and warned that I was annoying some very important people. It was intimated to me that I had better keep my opinions to myself or I would find myself without a career or a pension to look forward to! I regret now that I wasn't braver, but a man has to feed his family and I can only hope that Decima Watkins can find it in her heart to forgive me, wherever she is now!"

WHAT? I couldn't believe what I was reading. Inspector Lazarus had actually gone on record to say that not only was Decima innocent, but that he didn't even believe her sisters had been murdered – AND NO ONE LISTENED TO HIM.

After that the housework could go to the devil. I had to read on.

❦

CHAPTER TWENTY-SIX

"I was sent to Hill Farm, Near Braxton, in the County of Derbyshire, to arrest a young woman who was suspected of poisoning her sisters. This was the sort of task I always hated. Women are such emotional creatures. When you arrest a man, you can take a gun. If he resists, you can hit him, even shoot him if he is violent. But women! Women cry! What the devil is a man supposed to do when faced with a weeping woman? And the worse their crime, the more they weep! Prostitutes weep a little, peering all the time at you between their fingers, to gauge whether you might be open to a little of what they offer in exchange for their freedom. Baby farmers weep loud and protest their love of their little charges, even the ones that are dead from malnutrition and ill treatment. Thieves weep and look you in the eye, affronted at your vicious accusations, all the while hiding their latest acquisition in their petticoats. But murderesses weep the best. They are utterly convincing. They weep for their lost loved ones, heartbroken, appalled, bereft. How can you be so cruel to a poor widow? A poor orphan?

Yes, I hate arresting murderesses!

Decima Watkins was different. She did not weep. Nor did she look defiant, cock-sure, or unfeeling. She was just shocked. Plain and simple. It had never crossed her mind for a single moment that this thing might happen to her – because she did not know her sisters had died of anything other than natural causes! I swear that was the case. She just seemed utterly stunned that anything else could be imagined.

Her grandmother wept and begged, but Decima simply laid a calming hand upon her arm, "Grandmama! Please don't distress yourself. The Inspector is just doing his duty. I'm happy to go with him as he requests. It will not be long before I am back here, safe and sound. How could it be otherwise, when I have done nothing wrong?"

She looked me straight in the eye, "Is it necessary for you to shackle me, sir?" she asked, her voice faintly musical. I don't think I have ever heard a sweeter tone. It was this that made me look at her properly for the first time. Prior to that I had stolen glances, but had maintained a fairly constant scrutiny of the hat I held in my hands. It was never easy making an arrest in any circumstances, but when it had been borne upon me that I was in the home and company of a gently reared young lady, embarrassment had been my over-riding emotion. But don't for one moment think that it was this that coloured my view of the situation! It might not happen as often that I was called upon to charge a person of the upper classes with a crime than those of a lower degree – but it does happen, and I see no difference then! A criminal loses his or her right to class in my eyes! Prison is the same, rich or poor! And a hangman's noose knows no difference between a clean neck and a dirty one!

I think she must have been the loveliest creature I have ever set eyes upon. It was not obvious at first, for she tended to keep her eyes downcast, so that her face was not fully visible. When she lifted her chin and met my gaze, I was stunned. I have never seen greener eyes, nor clearer. Her skin was white as chalk, her features perfectly proportioned. A mouth made for kissing, I found myself thinking as my glance passed over those cherry lips, just parted enough to show a glimpse of tiny white teeth. Her figure was full enough to make a man forget his wife, albeit briefly! She was dressed in deepest black, relieved only by a small white lace collar. A silver watch hung on a chain about her neck and shone against the material of her dress, rising and falling with her breathing, showing that though she had a calm demeanour, she too was labouring under a great strain. I thought she was trying to hide her fear and distress from her grandmother, for the old lady looked fit to collapse, so agitated had she become.

"No, Miss, there's no need for shackles," I answered her quietly.

She cupped a long-fingered hand behind her ear, "I beg your pardon?" I had forgotten that I had been warned she was a little deaf. I repeated my answer a little more loudly and she nodded as though to acknowledge her acceptance of my response.

"Then we can go." She kissed her grandmother's wrinkled, tear-streaked cheek and preceded me out of the door. She took a shawl from a bench by the door and allowed me to lead her out to the waiting carriage.

She said very little on the journey. I did likewise. It would not have been appropriate for me to make small talk, the circumstances of her arrest being so very grave. And I had no wish to make a friend of her, to exchange pleasantries, only to have to send her to her doom at a later date. Even so, I felt my heart swelling with pity for her. She gazed out of the window, and the tears that had been so far avoided, fell then, but silently, secretly. She raised her hand occasionally to brush them away, surreptitiously, hoping, I think, that I had not witnessed her weakness. There was something very lost and lonely about her. My instincts told me that she had experienced much grief in her young life. There was an aura of sadness about her that spoke of a lack of hope for the future. If ever I have met someone who had really lost the will to live, it was Decima Watkins.

I had the young constable bring her a cup of tea before I began my interrogation. Bad enough that she should have to be locked in a cell, without denying her the small comfort of a warm drink.

She sat at the table opposite me, her eyes never leaving my face. Nothing in her behaviour either then or later, spoke guilt to me. Before God, I swear the girl had done nothing to disturb her own conscience. Of course I was accused of partiality, of having fallen for a pretty face, and these words will have to wait until after my death to be read again, but I state now, on my honour, I was not in love with her. After that first moment of shock at her very attractive appearance, I thought of her more in the light of a daughter than a lover. In truth she was young enough to be my daughter and perhaps it was her very youth, coupled with those clear, green eyes, which convinced me she could never have committed the crimes of which she was accused.

"Do you understand why you have been brought here, Miss Watkins?" I asked gently. Again the cupped hand behind the ear. I had to remember to speak more loudly and clearly for her.

When I repeated the question, she shook her head, "Not really," she answered firmly, "You say my sisters Charity, Phyllida and Jemima have been murdered, poisoned perhaps, but I had no notion that anything of the kind was being considered – and certainly not laid at my door!"

"Nevertheless, that is what has happened."

"How? And why? I simply cannot believe this!"

"It is, perhaps, for you to tell me those things, Miss Watkins," I sounded more angry than I felt. It was frustration, I suppose. How could I question her over matters of which I felt sure she knew nothing?

"I wish I could help you, sir. If I could think how to refute these accusations, I could go home."

"Perhaps if you just tell me what happened when each of your sisters died, then we could find some proof of your claims of innocence?"

195

She nodded again, "It is painful to go back to those times, but I will do my best," she said.

"According to witnesses in the household, the first bout of illness occurred when you and your sisters had taken tea together. The maid states that, very unusually, you asked for lemon in your tea, but the others had milk, as always. Why was that?"

She blushed to the roots of her hair, "I was feeling unwell. The thought of milk turned my stomach."

For the first time I knew a moment of real doubt. I looked into her eyes, "Was it perhaps the thought of the arsenic in the milk that turned your stomach?" I asked harshly, hardly able to believe that I had been so taken in by her.

"No!" She was genuinely anguished, "I was just feeling unwell!"

"But this was not an isolated incident. According to the maids, you avoided milk for several weeks – during which time your sisters frequently fell ill!"

"I was ill myself!" she shot back.

"But not so ill as your sisters, who were sick unto death, as the saying goes! You had better give me a plausible explanation for your avoiding milk during that time, Miss, or I shall begin to think the worst!"

"Very well, I will tell you the truth, but my papa will not like it! He wanted this matter kept quiet at all costs. But I cannot say anything with another person in the room." Her eyes looked sideways at the grey-garbed wardress who stood immobile and apparently indifferent by the door. I knew I should not dismiss the woman, but I also appreciated that the girl before me had something to say which she wanted and expected to be for my ears alone. In a split second I had taken the decision, "You may go and get yourself a cup of tea, Mrs. Bolt. The prisoner will be safe enough in my care." Her eyes widened slightly with the shock of this dismissal, but she said nothing, merely nodded and took herself off. Decima waited until the door had closed behind her before she said quietly, "I was with child! That is why I could not tolerate milk, nor cheese, nor several other things which I would normally eat with no thought. The feeling lasted only a few weeks, then passed away."

That, I must admit, I had not been expecting, but I did not show any emotion as I pursued, "What happened to the child?"

"It is in the care of one of my sisters," she answered, seemingly indifferent. I did not ask which sister, for I felt she would not answer – and it was in no way related to the case. I had my answer as to the avoidance of

milk. I continued presently on a different course.

"Would you say that you are a close family?"

"Our homes are very near to each other," she said. I felt she was being evasive and decided to be more straightforward, so that she should have no opportunity to misunderstand me.

"Do you love your sisters, Miss Watkins?"

"They are my flesh and blood,"

"That does not answer my question, Miss! Do you love your sisters and brothers? Do you hold them in affection, esteem, respect? Do they love and honour you?"

She held my glance for a long time with those magnificent eyes, "No," she said simply.

I was suddenly aware that I had led her into making an admission that could stretch her neck! Thankful that I had dismissed Mrs. Bolt, I added hastily, "You must have had good reason for saying such a thing. Tell me about your childhood."

"Childhood? What childhood?" She gave a small, mirthless laugh, "I was never a child, sir! From the moment I was old enough to lift my sisters' babies, I was a little nursemaid. I was more competent than many a trained nanny. And I did it all with a good heart, because I thought the love I was demonstrating was returned a hundredfold! I thought my assistance was appreciated, my sacrifices worthy of admiration. Imagine my horror, my utter desolation, when I was made to see that I was considered of no consequence in the family except as an unpaid servant. I had thought that my every action was being observed and valued. I could not have been more mistaken! All that I did was simply accepted as my duty, my role in life. Servitude what was I had been born for and I had no other hope or right!"

She sounded so bitter, so angry, that I knew I needed to understand how she could have come to so disheartening a conclusion.

"You say you were 'made to see' the error of your assumptions – what exactly do you mean by that?"

"I fell in love, Inspector Lazarus. Only that! It sounds perfectly natural and innocuous enough, does it not? You would not have thought so if you had seen the reaction within the family to the idea that they might lose their little servant to a rich man! My sisters were mortified that I might make a better match than they. My brothers indifferent to my suffering. My father roared and stormed that he would never allow me to leave the shelter of his roof, that he had not lavished food and clothing upon me merely to lose the comfort of his old age to the upstart son of a man who had cheated him in

197

*business. I was instantly a pariah! A traitor! My sisters wept that they could
not be expected to care for their own children when they had been led to
suppose that I would be there to run their nurseries. My mother took to her
bed, saying that I was a viper in her bosom and that she felt death was
hovering near to her. Not one voice was raised in my defence. Only my
grandmother stood by me, but even she was powerless in the face of her
dependence upon my father's bounty! All that she could do was offer to take
me into her home in the hills, knowing that Richard could visit me secretly
there."*

The result of that misplaced generosity had been pregnancy. I could not
say I blamed the girl for taking her small pleasures where she might. She
stood little chance of withstanding these overwhelming objections to her
marriage.

Unfortunately such subdued fury and the subsequent misery when she
was forced to give birth alone, pass the child to one of her sisters, then lose
the man she loved to the war, made the notion that she might have sought
revenge only too plausible. And yet I still thought her innocent. I do not
know why, for everything she had told me spelt guilt and her father cannot
have taken the decision to risk losing yet another of his children lightly.

I wanted to beg her, "Tell me something that will save you, Decima, for
God's sake!" But I could say nothing.

She looked at me for a long time before she said softly, "Even though you
have a kind face, sir, I can see that you now despise me. You think I killed
my sisters because I was angry, bitter and frustrated. I cannot deny I had
those feelings, for I did! But above all I was sad. Simply sad that those
people who ought to have loved me most could not find it in their selfish
hearts to spare one spark of compassion for my misery. I did not even
manage to tell Richard that he was to be a father before I heard news of his
death. I was not even accorded the honour of receiving official notification.
I had to read his name in a casualty list in a newspaper. To this day I have
not had one word of condolence for my loss – for the loss of the only man I
will ever love, and the father of my child. I had my baby wrenched from my
arms and I have to watch, each and every day, another woman taking the
smiles that should be bestowed upon me. Her arms are full, but mine are
empty, as is my heart. I did not murder my sisters and I do not want to die in
ignominy, but I really have nothing left to live for, no hope, only despair."

I knew I should not do it, but I ignored every instinct which screamed at
me not to touch her when we were alone in the room. I reached across the
table and took her hand, "My dear child, please don't think that your life

might just as well end! You must fight this, to the end! I know it seems now that nothing will ever make you happy again, but I am much older than you and I know that things are never as black as they appear."

She smiled softly, turning her hand in mine so that she could grip my fingers, "I told you that you had a kind face. I want you to know how much your faith has moved me, but believe me, things could not possibly be blacker. You try to comfort a dead woman! Would to God that you lived up to your name, Inspector Lazarus."

CHAPTER TWENTY-SEVEN

I found I had tears rolling down my cheeks when I finally laid aside the papers of Inspector Lazarus. Poor little Decima seemed to have developed a death wish and I couldn't honestly say I blamed her. Not a single member of her family gave a toss for her misery or for the trouble she was in – or if they did, they were too damned cowardly to do anything about it. Where had I heard all that before?

When the hammering on the ceiling began, I nearly jumped out of my skin, my heart pounded like a piston and I thought for a moment that I might faint, until a wave of relief swept over me like a warm blanket on a cold night. Of course there was nothing ghostly about that noise. It was Aunt Lil, banging on her bedroom floor with an old walking stick of Uncle Frank's – her signal to tell me she was ready for a drink and something to eat.

When I took up her tray, I also took the notes I had already read. She greeted me with a smile, but I could see by her pale face and the dark rings around her eyes that she was in pain. I thought my news would cheer her.

"I've brought you something to read, Lil. Dan at the museum came good in the end. He's given us the diary of the arresting officer. Even he didn't think Decima had committed the murders."

I was surprised at her reaction. She sank back on her pillows with a sigh of relief, "Thank God! Now I can die in peace."

Her words upset me more than I wanted to admit, "Bloody hell, Lil! Don't talk like that. Surely this wasn't all that important to you?"

"Yes it was, love. It still is. I've suspected for years that this house should never have come to me. I want to put that right. I know Maddie is older than you are and by rights she ought to have been first, but I have a feeling that you are the one Decima has chosen as her successor. If she had lived, her grandmother would have left this house to her, and her children after her." Her eyes were bright, with fever I supposed, though she didn't feel particularly warm when I laid a hand on her forehead.

"So you really think Adelaide was the sister who took Decima's baby?"

"I do, and I intend to tell the family so when they all gather here on Sunday."

"It won't be easy to convince them, Lil. We have no proof."

"Proof be damned. They'll just have to take my word."

"Good luck," I said wryly. I had a feeling that mother was going to be very busy on the telephone between now and Sunday.

I went back downstairs and ate my own lunch before picking up Inspector Lazarus' notes where I had left off. It seemed that he was now utterly convinced of Decima's innocence and spent the next few days trying his hardest to prove it – I knew how he felt.

"I had no choice but to send her to the prison, for I had not the authority to release her as I would have preferred. Frankly nothing she had told me pointed to her innocence, but still I believed in it as surely as I believe in God above! The girl would no more kill her sisters than I would.

I went to see her parents. Surely they, having had a day or more to consider the consequences of their defection, would now admit that they did not think the child was guilty.

The mother, perhaps unsurprisingly, refused to attend the interview, saying that she was prostrate with grief and fear. Bed seemed the best place for her, so I bade her think no more about my presence in the house and rest herself in readiness for the trial. That sent her off in high dudgeon!

Jacob Watkins grudgingly invited me into his study and I took a seat opposite him at his large oak desk. He helped himself to a large cigar from the humidor in front of him, snipped the end with a silver cutter and lit it, blowing out huge clouds of smoke. He did not offer me one, for which I was quietly grateful, for it was as much as I could do to sit under the same roof as him, without having to accept his hospitality in any other way. I noticed his hand shook slightly and deduced that he was not feeling quite as relaxed as he wished to appear. I took the opportunity to examine his face whilst he was engrossed in his cigar. He would not have been unhandsome had it not been for the florid countenance and hanging jowls. Evidently he was a man who enjoyed the pleasures of the flesh to the full, overeating, excessive drinking and, for all I knew, debauchery too!

"I'm a busy man, Lazarus. State your business quickly, will you, and let me get on," he said suddenly, catching my none-too-friendly eye upon him.

"Very well, sir. I will not beat about the bush. I have done as my

superiors bade me and arrested your daughter on, may I say, the flimsiest of evidence. Now I wish to investigate the alleged crime further. I want your permission to apply to have your deceased daughters exhumed and their bodies examined for traces of poison."

He sat up in his seat, almost choking on his cigar smoke, his face nigh-on purple, "Dear God! Have you people no compassion? Do you really expect me to agree to that preposterous, heartless request?"

"Sir, I have every sympathy for your loss, believe me. But I cannot, in all conscience, pursue your daughter for a crime that might never have been committed! There was, after all, no question of post mortems at the time of the deaths. Had there been any hint of foul play, surely you would have reported it then, not so many months later."

Several tense seconds passed before he answered, "Naturally I was unwilling to believe anything untoward had occurred, but Decima's continuing defiance of my wishes and my growing fears for the rest of the family forced me to acknowledge my deeply hidden suspicions. You may take my oath that no man will be happier than I if you find my fears are unfounded, but I cannot possibly allow the desecration of my other daughters' graves."

I lost my temper then, "How the devil am I supposed to investigate a crime that may not even have taken place? What evidence do you expect me to lay before a jury that will clear Decima's name?"

"She is in God's hands," he said simply, leaning back in his chair and looking at me with eyes as cold as a dead fish.

"I suspect she is in the hands of the Devil himself!" I snapped.

Within two days I had been called to the office of my superior and removed from the case. Before God, I swear I tried to investigate further in my own time, but every avenue was blocked and I was presently warned that if I did not mind myself, I would not only be disciplined, I would find myself without a job or a pension. Sorry as I was for the unfortunate child, I had a family of my own to consider.

I went to Court to see her travesty of a trial, but I could not face the execution. Decima Watkins died an innocent. I don't know why, or how anyone could wield such power that they could manipulate the course of a trial in an English Court, but I saw it happen and there was nothing I could do to prevent it."

I wasn't crying this time. I was angry. Dear God! That poor kid was surrounded by bastards. She didn't stand a chance. But why? What the hell had she done that she deserved to die for it? Not murder, of that I was wholly convinced.

I could understand that her father and mother would be mortified to have the world know that she had produced an illegitimate baby, but surely not enough to see her hang? And did her father really have that much power? I'd have thought that sort of influence was the province of Richard Allingham's father – but why should he continue to be interested once his son was dead? Decima might have been the mother of his grandson, but it meant nothing in Victorian times, when legitimacy was everything. Nowadays the law see's no difference between a child born in wedlock or one born on the wrong side of the blanket, as the saying goes, but then it meant the difference between being allowed to inherit and being ignored. The Allingham family could not have been worried that Decima's child would try to claim anything from them. Their son was dead. Any embarrassment would belong to the Watkins' not the Allinghams.

There was a missing clue. I just knew it.

Then I noticed that there was another page I hadn't read. Apparently Inspector Lazarus had something more to add.

"One curious thing did happen later, after the execution. Hill Farm, the house where I had gone to arrest Decima, and where her grandmother still lived, was the subject of a burglary. As soon as I saw the address on the crime sheet, I took over the case. This time no one tried to stop me. I went hotfoot to the house. The grandmother, Mrs. Threlfall, had a strange tale to tell. The house had been broken into one night when she was absent. Every room was turned upside down, thoroughly ransacked, with the contents of every drawer and cupboard strewn about, but not a single thing had been stolen! Not a penny piece of money, of which there had been a considerable amount, not an item of silver or jewellery taken. Evidently the thieves had been looking for something, or they would not have been so thorough, but it was not money or goods. The old lady had no idea what they might have been after and was as puzzled as I. Coming, as it did, so soon after Decima's death, I could not help wondering if the break-in had anything to do with her, but with no notion as to what might have been stolen, I had no choice but to leave the entire incident as an unsolved mystery. Decima was an enigma in life and in death!"

Now, that was weird. What had they been after? And did they find it? I would probably never know.

Sunday afternoon came all too quickly.

Almost as if it had been planned with military precision, the entire family arrived at the same moment. I wouldn't have been at all surprised to learn that my mother had ordered them all to meet at a pre-arranged point so that they could travel the rest of the way in convoy. They were showing Lil and I a united front right from the word go, and let us be in no doubt of it.

I was chilled, to say the least, to find myself confronted by stiff faces and cold eyes. These were my aunts, uncles and cousins, for goodness sake, but I felt vaguely threatened by the atmosphere they brought into the house with them. I couldn't quite accept that Uncle Lionel, who used to dandle me on his knee, was now looking at me with tight lips and undisguised contempt. Aunts Polly and Sally I could understand. They had always been a pair of frosty-faced old harridans, but Cousin Monica? We had exchanged Barbie dolls. As for Peter and Scott, how could you hate someone who had helped you build a tree house in the woods?

Twelve of them – all ranged on one side of the room, girding their loins for battle – with Lil and me on the other.

Lil prevented the outbreak of hostilities by announcing that tea would be served before any discussions would take place. I could see they were all rather deflated, but had no choice but to comply. We ate a desultory meal, drank tea from the best china and generally talked about the weather and our health for half an hour until the plates were cleared away. Sally and Polly insisted upon washing up – but then they were always to be found in the kitchen at weddings, christenings and funerals, up to their elbows in suds. In the blink of an eye all the pots were washed, dried and put away and we rejoined the others in the sitting room.

My mother, naturally, fired the opening sally, "Well, there they are. The co-conspirators."

"Stop it, Marjorie," said Lil wearily, "I'm not in the mood for your histrionics. There has been no conspiracy and you know it. Libby had no idea what I was planning – and there was no reason why she should have known. It was nobody's affair but mine. In case you have all forgotten, this house is mine, to do with what I wish."

"It's not quite that simple, Lillian, and you are fully aware of that fact. This house has been in our family for generations. We all had a right to say what was to become of it." Evidently Lionel, as the eldest present, had either been elected spokesperson or had so decided himself.

"It's still in the family," said Lil, "Who the devil do you think Libby is? One of the Kennedy Clan?"

"It should have gone to one of the older generation first," said Lionel sniffily, not very happy that Lil was daring to stand up to him, and to be facetious to boot.

"You, you mean." said Lil, not pulling her punches, "Well, let me tell you, Lionel. I don't like you and I never have. You are a pompous, tight-fisted old ass. You've got half a million in the bank, gathered from the deaths of relations to whom you barely spoke in life. You're nothing but a skinny old vulture and you had about as much chance of inheriting this place as being knighted."

"There's no call to be insulting," interjected Aunt Polly, "You've always been a hard woman, Lillian, and I see approaching your judgement day hasn't softened you."

"Thanks for reminding me that I'm dying, Polly – and by the way, I don't like you either." I nearly laughed out loud at Polly's stunned expression.

My mother decided it was time to offer her own little fan for the flames, "This is not quite so straightforward as you like to hint, though, is it Lillian. Elizabeth has one or two little secrets of her own."

"What are you talking about?" asked Lil, in a bored tone of voice, as though she had heard all mother's protests before and found them unutterably tedious.

"This fellow Wright whom she has been seeing. I understand his business is rapidly expanding and he wants more land. Hill Farm is not going to stand for very much longer if he gets his hands on it. The house will be knocked down and one of his dreadful, common little garden centres will be built before you are cold in your grave. Libby's are not quite the safe hands you are trying to imagine, are they?"

I was livid. First that she should so malign David and his business, but mostly that she really believed that I would be weak-minded enough to stand by like a compliant little wifey whilst he tore down my inheritance.

"That is not true," I said breathlessly, struggling to control my ridiculous desire to cry. This was just horrible. All these people were supposed to love me best in the world, and they all hated me. Oh, God! Where had I heard that expression before?

"Oh, come now, Libby, don't get all tearful on the man's behalf. His agenda has been clear from the onset. He tried to woo Lillian with his rather obvious charm and penchant for flattery and she fell for it hook, line and sinker. Then he found he was too late and she had already made the house over to you. It didn't take a genius to work out what his next move would be. And you, poor fool, fell straight into his arms. It would be laughable if it wasn't so pathetic."

I thought it safer not to try and answer her. Lillian quietly took my hand and squeezed it comfortingly, "I think you have said enough, Marjorie. I'm not a complete idiot, and neither is Libby. David Wright is a perfectly nice young man, but I made these plans many years ago, before I even knew of his existence. If you think I would be dense enough not to protect myself and my property from unforeseen events, then you are a bigger fool than I took you for. Hill Farm will still be standing long after we're all dead and gone, you may take my word upon that. Now, whilst we are still all feeling heated, I might as well broach the other reason for this meeting. Libby and I have been investigating the family history and have discovered that there is an error in the family tree. We intend to put it right."

A babble of protest arose at this and Lillian was forced to explain in full detail about Decima's baby and Adelaide's role in its upbringing.

The younger members of the family were mainly indifferent to this bombshell news, but Lionel, Polly and Sally were almost apoplectic, "You are seriously suggesting that we agree to the taint of illegitimacy be admitted in our family? You really have taken leave of your senses. You have no proof that Decima had a baby, apart from a few scraps of paper from highly unreliable sources. And absolutely no evidence at all that Adelaide took the baby from her."

"I know it is true," said Lil firmly.

"You take one step in that direction, lady, and I will fight you every step of the way," said Lionel aggressively.

"I will help him." said my mother. She was rather white and I could see she had been shocked by the revelation. I don't think she could have been more upset if she had found out that my father was illegitimate rather than his great, great grandfather. It certainly did not fit in with her scheme of things, that's for sure.

"I'll do what I have to do," said Lil, "Now, if you would like to listen for just a few more moments, I have something else to say. I realize you all feel very badly about what has happened, so I have an offer to make. This is goodbye, so I would like you all to feel free to take some small memento of me from the house. The only things that are not included are those articles which have always been here, like the old chair in the sitting room and the bookcases, the bureau, the pictures and anything else of that nature. My personal property is at your disposal."

They needed no further bidding. Like a swarm of locusts they descended, picked their own particular favourite items, then left.

When they had all gone Lil looked around the sadly depleted rooms and gave a tiny laugh, "Dear God! I feel as though I've been robbed. Thank heavens I had Decima's watch and ring safely in my pocket. At one point I thought Lionel was going to ask for the pennies that will be used to hold my eyes shut."

"Never mind, Lil," I said comfortingly, "It's only stuff."

"I'm sorry, my love. I suppose it should have been your 'stuff'. I never imagined they would take my words so literally and with such glee."

"Don't worry about it. You've given me enough. And if it's enough of a sop to keep them happy, it will be worth it."

"Only time will tell on that one."

❧

CHAPTER TWENTY-EIGHT

Lil went straight to bed after the family left; I could see she was upset, but she didn't say anything – what was there to say? They had all proved themselves to be money-grubbing vultures, with no compassion for her situation or interest in mine.

I watched a bit of television, to try and take my mind off the events of the past few hours, then as soon as it was sufficiently late for me not to look ridiculous, I followed her up.

I peeped around her door and was relieved to see that she was fast asleep. I had rather thought that her distress would have kept her awake, but apparently not.

I climbed into my own bed and switched off the light. The house was very quiet and I was just beginning to get to that stupid stage of actually listening for noises instead of hearing them when they happened, when I fell asleep myself. I must have been more drained than I was allowing myself to admit.

Birds bickering on the roof woke me about seven and I thought I might just as well get up as lie there wide-awake. I made my usual visit to Lil's room and she still seemed asleep so I was about to quietly withdraw when something stopped me.

She was more than unusually silent and motionless. With my heart in my mouth I tiptoed across the room and lightly touched her cheek. It was stone cold. I needn't have bothered being quiet. Some time during the night, Lil had breathed her last, and I had not been there to bear her company. I drew up a chair next to her bed, held her frozen hand for a few minutes and said my farewells.

Dear old Lil. I was going to miss her. We had been through a lot together these past few days, but I was remembering the Lil of my childhood more than that. She had always been grey-haired, though she could only have been in her fifties when I was born. Women had aged much faster in the old days. A woman of fifty now would consider herself to still be in the prime of life and would think nothing of using little tricks to make sure she stayed that way. I was entirely sure Lil had never used a bottle of hair dye in her life, nor gone to the gym to keep her tummy flat, but resorted to a huge rubber girdle to keep her figure in trim. It was hard to imagine my own mother must now be the same age as Lil had been when I had my earliest memories of her.

This thought prompted another. Oh, God! I would have to ring round all the relations again to tell them the news – plus the doctor, I supposed, and the undertaker. No time to sit around remembering the good old days. I had tons to do.

With a heartfelt sigh, I kissed Lil on the brow, said goodbye out loud and went downstairs.

It wasn't until I reached the kitchen and put the kettle on that reality struck home. I was alone in the house – and it was now my house. Suddenly the enormity of what Lil had done for me became really clear. Now I wouldn't have to go back to that god-awful job that I had grown to hate, I could move my stuff out of that poky little flat and I could write, as I had always wanted to – and I could have a dog. I hadn't owned a dog since I was a kid and even then it had been one of those mad mongrels which owed allegiance to all and yet to no one. It's memory only stretched as far as the last person who had fed it and it hadn't even had the sense not to run into the road and get itself killed within a year of its arrival. No, I'd have a proper dog. A sane, friendly, intelligent beast, with glossy fur and a sense of fun that could be curtailed when the mood was not right for 'fetch'. David would know someone who sold lovely, doe-eyed puppies.

David. Oh no. I had no contact number for him. He hated mobile phones and refused to have one, and the agreement was that he would ring me every couple of days to keep in touch. Heaven only knew when the next call would come. I supposed I could ring the garden centre and ask the staff there to give me the number of his other concern, but I was reluctant to do it. That smacked of desperation – they wouldn't know why I needed to speak to him, they would just assume I was one of his more smitten kittens who couldn't bear to be apart from him. They would also think he hadn't given me the number on purpose, so that he could escape my cloying attentions.

I gave myself a mental shake and pulled this train of thought to a swift halt. Bordering on hysteria, Libby, I told myself. What the hell do you care if his staff gossips about you? Tell them to ring and inform David of Lil's death. No gossip, no problem.

Suiting action to thought, I picked up my cup of coffee and headed for the sitting room, where I could make my calls in comfort – it was, after all, going to be a very long, drawn-out affair.

I dialled my mother first, hoping and praying that Brendan wouldn't answer again. He didn't, and she took my news quite calmly.

"Well, I can't say I'm surprised. She looked ghastly yesterday."

"After the mauling you lot gave her, I should think she did," I said, an edge of bitterness creeping into my voice. Her words had reminded me of just how lonely and distressing Lil's last hours must have been.

"She got off lightly," said my mother, in a coarse tone I had never heard her use before, "Her behaviour has been appalling from beginning to end. She should never have been allowed to get away with her sneaking and conniving."

I decided I wasn't in the mood for a quarrel, "Well, never mind that now. You have all the rest of your life to make me suffer for Lil's sins. Now, will you do me the favour of ringing the rest of the family and telling them?"

"Certainly not. This is your little mess now, Libby. You wanted the inheritance – well, take everything else that goes with it."

I bit my tongue. Stuff her. I would do everything myself. I didn't need her, or anyone else.

"Fine. Then at least tell me if you know how I can get hold of Dad. He ought to be told that Lil is gone."

She gave an unkind laugh, "Dear God! You don't think he told me where he was intending to take his fancy piece, do you? You are incredibly naïve sometimes, Libby."

I made my goodbyes hastily and put the phone down. Next I rang the doctor's number and left a message with the receptionist, telling them of Lil's passing. Maddie was third on the list. She sounded unfriendly, but not downright malicious, even offering to ring the hotel where she thought Dad might be staying. Apparently it was a favourite of his and Elaine's. I came off the phone feeling ever so slightly hurt and rebuffed. Why should Maddie know these things about Dad, when I knew nothing? I thought we had a special relationship, but evidently he confided more in my sister than he did in me, even though she had made it very clear that she sided with Mum in their divorce. It seemed that the old advice for keeping men, "treat 'em mean, keep 'em keen" worked for fathers as well as for boyfriends and husbands.

210

It took me about another hour to work steadily through the list of family and friends. I would really have preferred to drop my bombshell and hang up, but of course they all wanted to talk, to condole and to relate their own particular memory or anecdote of Lil. I was near to tears and badly in need of a drink by the time I had finished.

I was almost relieved when I heard the knock at the door which I thought heralded the arrival of the doctor. I was half-right. The doctor was there, but he had company. I didn't have to wonder for long whom the slight, greying man and his black, taller, heavier, younger companion were.

A warrant card – or what I assumed was a warrant card, never having seen one before – was flashed before my startled eyes, "Miss Elizabeth Roberta Richmond?"

"Yes,"

"I am Detective Inspector Goodenough, this is my colleague Sergeant Bristow. I understand you reported the death of one Lillian Farrell this morning?"

Ironic name for a policeman, I thought, then, "Yes," I said, again, wondering where this was all leading.

"Then I must ask you to accompany me to the station, Miss. I have some questions to put to you,"

I was flustered by this unexpected turn of events and barely noticed that the doctor brushed past me and went up the stairs, "Why can't you ask me here?" I asked.

"Are you refusing to accompany me?"

"Yes – no! I don't know. I just want to know what this is all about. I rang the doctor as soon as I realized Lil was dead. I haven't done anything wrong, have I?"

"That's for you to tell us, Miss. We have had an anonymous tip-off that your aunt was – shall we say – helped on her way. Naturally we have to investigate that possibility."

"I beg your pardon?" I had heard him perfectly plainly, but the hearing of his accusation didn't help me understand the meaning of his words at all.

"If you'll just come along with us, Miss. I'm sure the whole thing will be very swiftly explained."

"Are you arresting me?" I was incredulous, utterly stunned, and yet the whole thing had an odd feeling of déjà vu. And suddenly I knew why. Decima Watkins had been standing on this very spot when Inspector Lazarus came for her – with a charge of murder – just like me now. Because that was precisely what they were suggesting, without being too crude about it. Someone had told them that I had killed Lillian.

Sweet Jesus! I was within a hair's breadth of a murder charge and the trouble was, I could not be sure that Lillian had not died of an overdose. Hadn't she said yesterday, "Now I can die in peace"? What if she had taken too much of her medication? How the hell was I going to prove that I didn't give her the fatal dose? There was only me here.

I started to shake uncontrollably and the Inspector noticed it. Oddly enough he was very kind, speaking quietly to me, "Come on, love, get in the car. They don't come down too hard on mercy killings, you know,"

"Can I get my handbag and my house keys?" I asked, trying to pull myself together. This panic was just making me look guilty.

"Sergeant Bristow will get those for you – and the doctor will take care of Mrs. Farrell."

I burst into tears then, with the realization that Lil was going to be autopsied. They were going to cut her open. All she had wanted was to die in her own bed, then be buried in the local churchyard, next to Uncle Frank. And now they were going to lie her on a slab and butcher her poor old body.

He held onto my arm as we walked down the path and down the lane to the lay-by, but after that everything became a bit of a blank. I don't even recall getting into the car – though I did notice that thankfully it was a plain one. I don't think I could have stood the shame of being carted off in a paddy wagon, with handcuffs and a blanket over my head to hide me from the press. There went that fertile imagination again. Calm down, Libby, you silly cow. You haven't been arrested; they don't even know that Lil didn't die of natural causes yet. She was terminally ill, as the doctor will testify, should things get that bad. This is just a very bad taste jape by one of the family. A couple of hours at the police station and all will be sorted out. I told myself all this sternly as we drove down the familiar lanes towards the police station.

I had never been in a police station before in my life. Not even to present my driving documents for a minor traffic offence or report a lost item. The shaking began again when they sat me in a little room, bare but for an empty desk and two chairs. A plump policewoman brought me a cup of tea, which I sipped gratefully, then I was left alone for ages. I say ages – it certainly felt like a long time, but I doubt it was more than half an hour at the very most. I wasn't wearing my watch and there was no clock in the room.

The Inspector returned presently and smiled at me in a friendly manner, "All right?" he asked kindly.

"I think so," I replied, "I'm still a bit stunned, to be honest. I've never been in a police station before,"

"Lucky you. I'm in one every day. Have you finished your tea?"

I nodded.

"Good, then shall we go and get this over and done with? It shouldn't take very long."

I nodded again and followed him out of the room, down seemingly endless corridors and into another similar room, but one which contained all the paraphernalia for recording evidence. This seemed a bit over the top for an informal chat, but I didn't have much choice but to comply with his request to sit. We were joined by the policewoman who stood by the door, silent, staring straight ahead and not even attempting to catch my eye.

The whole situation was beginning to look like a television cop show and it was with great difficulty that I kept my face straight and didn't ask when we could expect John Thaw lookalike to walk in and start banging on the desk and shouting at me.

He started up the recording machine, introduced himself, then asked me for my name and address and if I understood why I was there.

"No, not really."

He looked a bit taken aback, "I did explain that your Aunt's death was to be investigated?" he asked.

"Yes, but I don't see what it has to do with me – and for the record, I don't think she could strictly be referred to as my aunt. I called her aunt because she was so much older, but I think she was more properly some sort of distant cousin."

"Does it matter?" he asked, somewhat wearily.

"I don't suppose so, but I wouldn't wish to be caught out in a lie. Lil wasn't my aunt, okay?"

"Fine. Now that we have that straight, may we continue?"

"Certainly," I was beginning to relax. I knew I hadn't killed Lil, so why should I be afraid? Having said that, Decima knew she hadn't murdered her sisters, but the small fact of being innocent hadn't saved her. Thank God we had done away with the death sentence.

"I understand from our source that you stood to inherit your … Mrs. Farrell's house and a very considerable amount of money."

"I don't know about any money, Lil never mentioned that. And the house was already mine. She made it over to me several years ago on the understanding that she could continue living there."

"So, you could only claim the house upon the death of Mrs. Farrell?"

"Yes, but I would happily have lived there with her. Lil and I were very close."

"So close that you couldn't bear to see her in pain?"

"Naturally I didn't like to think of her suffering, but she never seemed to be all that uncomfortable, to be honest. She managed her illness very well."

"I'm sure she was very good at hiding her pain, but I have it on the doctor's authority that she must have been in agony on occasions."

"If she was, she never let me see it. Lil was a very special and precious woman."

"I'm sure she was – and I'm sure it was hard for you to think of her lingering on in this horrible manner."

"If you are trying to make me say that I killed my aunt, you are wasting your time. I don't know who put this malicious accusation to you, but it isn't true. I could no more kill Lil than I could kill myself."

"I've been told that there is a suspicion you attempted that very thing only a few days ago."

Bloody Brendan! Or Mother or Maddie. One of the bastards had landed me right in it.

"You were misinformed," I told him, as calmly as I was able.

"Do you have any proof of that?"

"Do you have any proof that I attempted suicide, except the word of a mischievous, anonymous caller? Someone who evidently did not have the courage to leave their name?"

"No," he admitted shortly.

"Well then, you'll just have to take my word for it, won't you?"

"It would seem so," he said dryly. He shuffled the papers he had brought in with him, apparently checking on his notes. I knew he was only doing it to gain a little time, to unnerve me before the next question.

"Are you categorically stating that you deny any involvement in the death of Mrs. Farrell?"

"Absolutely. Can I go now?"

"Presently. I have some paperwork to complete. We will have the result of Mrs. Farrell's autopsy later this afternoon, and if that is clear, so are you. In the meantime, we have taken away the various medications from the house, plus a letter we found. We'll need your finger-prints for comparisons."

It was then that I recalled the shot gun that Lil had pulled on Brendan. I hoped to God she really did have it properly licensed, or I was in big trouble. As for the fingerprints, I couldn't honestly remember any occasions when I had handled the medicines or pills – Lil had basically looked after herself in that department, so I should be in the clear even if Lil had taken an overdose.

I wondered what the letter said. It was rather distressing to know that Lil had left me a last message and now the world and his wife would be allowed to read it before me. What can't be cured must be endured, I could almost hear Lil saying.

I smiled a little smile, "Can I have another cup of tea?" I asked the Inspector.

❧

FAMILY TREE

Jacob Watkins m Maryanne Trent

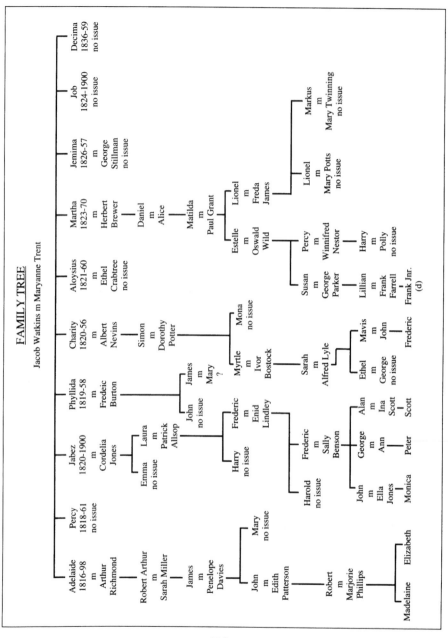

Chapter Twenty-Nine

It was early evening before they released me. The autopsy on Lil had been inconclusive. She certainly had a lot of morphine in her bloodstream, but that was hardly surprising considering how far-gone her cancer was, and how much pain she must have been in.

Her note didn't tell them much either. No admittance of suicide, but plenty of references to her affection for me and how glad she had been to spend these last weeks together. It seemed she had known death was imminent, but that in itself proved nothing, neither suicide nor a request for mercy killing. As I had suspected, my fingerprints were not on any of the bottles, only Lil's and the pharmacist's. I was not completely off the hook, but it was unlikely that they were going to be able to proceed on the evidence they had.

It seemed Lil did have a license for the shot gun and I was warned by Inspector Goodenough that if I intended to keep it, then I would need to renew the license in my own name and that he would be along to check that it was adequately secured, as stuffed under my aunt's bed was not an acceptable place to keep it. He added that the only reason why he hadn't taken it away was because I was now a woman alone in a remote cottage. That made me feel tons better, I don't think.

With a sigh of relief I assured him that the gun would be presently in his care permanently, as I had no use or inclination towards the keeping of a firearm.

It was then that he informed me that there was a young man waiting for me in reception, who had been waiting for several hours to take me home.

David. Thank God, he must have arrived back early from his trip and been told where I was by the officers who had been swarming all over Hill Farm all afternoon.

I flew out of the secure door and into the reception area, a huge smile on my face. It was wiped off immediately when I realized that it was not David who waited for me, but Brendan.

I turned back to ask the Inspector to give me a ride home in a police car, but he was gone, the thick door, only opened by the keying in of a pass-number, clicking heavily shut behind him. The policeman behind the glass partition was busy on the telephone.

I looked at Brendan and he grinned broadly at me, "Hello sweetheart, all ready to go?"

"I'll make my own way, thanks," I said shortly.

"Oh come on, Libby. Don't be childish. Your mother asked me to come over and help. She's given Lionel an almighty bollocking for ringing in with the anonymous tip-off and is now engaged in arranging the funeral. She was sorry to be so nasty to you this morning. All this has made her realize how stupid this quarrelling is."

Only one thing he said sank in, "It was Lionel?" I asked incredulously, "The rotten old sod."

"Yes, well, he saw everything slipping between his fingers. You can't really blame him."

"Not blame him? I've been treated like a criminal all day. I'll kill the old buzzard when I see him."

"I'd save threats like that for when we get out of here, if I were you, love," he said, laughingly taking my arm.

He seemed so warm, so natural and friendly, that I let him lead me out. I was tired, upset and rather depressed by the events of the day. What was the harm in accepting a lift back to Hill Farm? He was evidently over our little romance – well over, I would have said, since he was now sleeping with my mother. So he had been a bit odd when we had first split – well, he wasn't the first person in the world to be led into strange behaviour by a soured relationship – and I doubted he would be the last.

His Jaguar was parked in front of the old-fashioned police station and I couldn't help but smile as I walked down the wide, sandstone steps towards it. I had been over-reacting more than somewhat when I had paraphrased Decima and thought that in my case the devil didn't drive a curricle, but a Jaguar.

Brendan was harmless. He had a bad temper and he was capable of doing stupid things when he lost it, but really he was okay. It had been nice of my mother to send him to see I got home safely, and very nice indeed of her to start the funeral arrangements. She knew I had never done anything like that before and I was probably daunted by the responsibility.

218

The Jag purred away from the kerb and I relaxed back in my seat, "Thank God today is over. What a nightmare that was."

"We'll soon have you home, sweetheart. A brandy and bed, that's what you need."

"That sounds good. Thanks for coming for me, Brendan. I hope this means we can be friends from now on. I never wanted to hurt you, you know. We were just wrong for each other…"

"Forget it, Libby. I don't even want to remember what a wanker I've been. Let's just go on as though nothing had happened, shall we?"

"Suits me."

It was so warm and comfy in the car that I fell asleep and I didn't wake until we were drawing into the lay-by just below the house. He went around the car to the passenger door and tried to lift me out. I protested mildly, "Don't be daft, Brendan, I can walk. I'm awake now."

He stood aside and let me clamber out, making no attempt to touch me again, for which I was truly grateful. Friendly chat was one thing, being touched by him, even in a helpful way, was quite another. I hadn't quite forgotten myself that much.

As we approached the door, I was gripped by a sudden feeling of deep unease. Something told me that I ought not to trust him inside the house, but when I turned and tried to politely dismiss him on the doorstep, he pretended not to notice my reluctance, "Not come in? Get real, girl. You don't think I'm leaving you here alone until I've checked the place over and made sure the plods haven't done something stupid like breaking the locks and leaving you vulnerable to burglars. Anyway, I think we both need that brandy, don't you?"

To tell the truth, I was glad, just for that moment, not to be in the house alone. I wasn't afraid, exactly, just a bit dubious. Lil had died there that morning, and my entire stay had been plagued by odd occurrences. Brendan was infinitely better than no one.

He pressed me into a comfy seat in the sitting room while he fetched us a tot each of Lil's medicinal brandy. It certainly hit the spot. I began to feel warm and relaxed the moment it soothed its way into my stomach. Actually, a bit too relaxed. I realized something was wrong the moment I took the second sip. My hand was too heavy to lift. As I gazed at it in genuine puzzlement, it looked and felt as though it didn't belong to me. Startled I transferred my gaze to Brendan, who was sitting opposite me, a grin on his face – at least I thought he looked as though he might be grinning. I blinked and tried to focus on his face. It was a blur.

219

"What…" I felt as though my tongue were too large for my mouth, and it also appeared to be covered with fur, "What have you given me?" I managed to say, but my voice sounded odd and far away.

"Rohypnol, sweetie. You know, the one they call the 'date-rape' drug. You'll soon be completely relaxed – well, helpless, I suppose you'd say. But cognisant, at least for now. Of course, if you were to wake up in the morning, you'd probably have forgotten everything, but that needn't worry us. Drink the rest of your brandy like a good girl, and then you can leave everything to me. There's not another thing for you to worry about."

My brain was fuddled, but not so fogged that I didn't understand what he had done to me – so far. What really worried me was what he intended to do next.

He came across and took the glass in his hand, "Drink up," he urged softly, smiling kindly into my eyes. I wanted to resist him, but I simply couldn't. Not a muscle would move to my command. He pressed the glass to my lips and tipped it. I managed to block my lips with my tongue so that most of the liquid dripped and dribbled out of the corner of my mouth, but some went down my reluctant throat and I felt myself gagging and choking as it burned its way down.

He watched me dispassionately for a few minutes, until he judged I was helpless enough to be carried without a fight, then he swept me up into his arms and headed towards the stairs, "You know, Libby, it needn't have ended this way. If you hadn't been such an awkward, arrogant bitch, we could have been happy together."

I suppose it was the word 'ended' that alerted me to what I might see when we reached the attic.

It had to be that same room, didn't it? He couldn't have chosen one of the others. It had to be the room where Decima had spent so many sorrowful hours, waiting for the return of the man she loved, the man who never came back.

He kicked open the door and I saw that the room was bathed in pink and orange light, a legacy of the setting sun. He laid me on the unmade bed and as my head fell back on the pillowless mattress, I was forced to look up. It hung there above me, suspended from the beam on a huge hook, placed there especially for the purpose, spinning gently in the unseen draught.

He must have worked fast in between the police leaving and picking me up from the police station. I wondered vaguely where he had learned to tie such a professional looking hangman's noose. On the Internet, in all probability, I thought irrelevantly. After all, you could learn everything else from there – even how to make an A bomb, or so I had heard. The difficulty, apparently was getting hold of the plutonium. I wondered why I was thinking such nonsensical things when my ex-boyfriend was about to choke the life out of me at the end of a rope, but I couldn't help it. I seemed to have no more control over my thoughts than I did over my body. "The only thing left to contemplate, now, my darling Libby," he was saying softly, and I tried hard to focus on his voice to understand what he was talking about, "Is whether or not to have one final sex session before your trip to the gallows. Knowing what I do about your recent past, I suspect you would have the most exciting experience of your life, but it might be hard to explain away the DNA. This really will have to seem as though you had done it all alone – in despair at the loss of your dear old aunt – or guilt at having killed her."

I tried to beg him with my eyes, not being able, now, to speak a word, but he either did not notice my pleading glance, or he deliberately ignored it. He leaned over me and placed a kiss on my lips. I naturally didn't want to respond, but on the other hand, I couldn't pull away from his repulsive embrace either, "You know, sweetheart," he said softly, "I really couldn't just let you go off with another man – not once you had been mine. You see, only I can decide when a relationship is over. You are the first bitch who has ever tried to end it with me. Usually I'm the one who gets bored and has to kick the silly, clinging bints into touch. You hit me where it really hurts, walking away like that. And now you're going to pay."

He left me then, to watch in horror, wondering what he was going to do next. Jesus, I thought, he really is insane. I'm here, alone, in the hands of a psychopath, unable to fight, run, scream or even move. A nightmare come true.

He pulled a dining chair across the room and positioned it under the noose, then came to the bed to get me. I wanted to struggle – by God, I wanted to kick, bite, yell for help, flee, but I couldn't do a thing. I cursed myself for a fool for letting him trick me into this; I despaired that I would never see David again. I prayed that he would sense my distress and come galloping to my aid, on a horse across the hills, but my wish for my knight in shining armour was as lost and hopeless as Decima's had been before me. I was afraid, horribly afraid, not just of dying, but of the pain I would feel when the rope tightened about my neck. I had felt it before, in my dreams, and I never wanted to feel it again. It was agony, I knew it, but I was as helpless and empty as Decima had been. How ironic that I should end up by dying in the same manner as she had.

Brendan had my inert body slung over his shoulder as he climbed up onto the chair, and it wobbled slightly beneath him as he tried to get his balance correct so that he could lift me towards the noose. Panic swirled in my mind, swiftly followed by a hovering blackness which threatened to overwhelm me. I welcomed the thought that I might pass out. Better to be unconscious when he finally got the rope about my throat, than to feel the pull and drag of the rough fibres across my skin.

He had chosen a difficult task for himself. I could hear him grunting with effort as he tried to hoist me upright, whilst making grabs for the noose which now seemed to be swinging and dancing just beyond his reach.

I heard him whisper "Fuck!" under his breath as he scrabbled wildly for the rope, which now seemed to have a mind of its own. At last he caught it and he set me on my feet on the chair seat next to him, one arm firmly about my waist, holding me upright – or at least as upright as he could manage, for I lolled forward like a rag doll.

Suddenly the door swung silently open and with great difficulty I forced my eyes to swivel in my head so that I could see if it had merely blown open in the draught or if someone was there.

To my astonishment my sister Maddie stood in the doorway, Lil's shotgun clamped firmly to her shoulder.

"Let her down, Brendan, gently," she said loudly.

Brendan, perspiring and frustrated, hadn't even heard her come in. I felt him start violently at the sound of her voice, but he soon recovered himself when he saw who it was, "Go away, little girl, if you know what is good for you. This is between Libby and me."

"I'm warning you, you slimy bastard, put my sister down, or I'll fire this bloody gun right into your guts!"

He swung me around like a scarecrow so that my body shielded his, "You'll have to hit your sister first, my dear," he said smoothly.

"No, I won't," she answered and calmly walked across the room until the muzzle of the gun slid past my thigh and was pressing straight into his genitals, "You might want to rethink now, Brendan. Libby may get a bit spattered with blood, but I don't think she'll mind that, do you?"

Brendan wasn't mad enough to push her any further. He released me so that I slid gently to the floor and when I looked up, I saw his face was as white as a sheet, his hands in the air, like the baddie at the end of an old Western movie. He had every reason to be frightened, for I could tell by her set features and hard eyes that my sister was furious. Maddie took a couple of steps back, deliberately lowered the gun until it was in line with his knees, then she fired.

The sound of the shot resounded in the small room like cannon fire. Brendan disappeared for a minute in a cloud of smoke and when next he was seen, he was rolling around on the floor, clutching his legs and screaming in agony, "You stupid, fucking maniac bitch! You've shot my fucking legs off! I'll never walk again!"

"Oh shut up!" shouted Maddie, waving the gun under his nose, "It's only pellets. You'll live! Not that you deserve to, you bloody perv."

She left him bleeding on the floor whilst she helped me out of the room and down the stairs, more carrying me than anything, but fortunately her run in with Brendan seemed to have given her a hitherto unknown strength.

It was about two hours later before I could speak well enough to tell the police and my sister exactly what had happened, and Brendan had been long removed in an ambulance by then.

After my statement was taken and Inspector Goodenough, astounded to have been called to Hill Farm for a second time in the same day, was gone, I turned to my sister and asked her how she had come to be in the house in the very nick of time.

"After she had spoken to you this morning, mum had a call from the police, saying that you had been taken in for questioning about Lil's death, but that they had traced the anonymous call and it had come from her number. She knew at once that it must have been Brendan who made the call. She confronted him and he happily admitted it, then he reverted to type, called her a few choice names and walked out. She rang me and asked me to come up here the moment the police let you go. I was waiting outside the police station when Brendan brought you out. I followed you back here, but the Jag is a bit faster than my old crate and I was somewhat delayed. I seemed to miss every set of traffic lights and at one point was stuck behind a tractor for about five miles. By the time I arrived, Brendan had already dragged you off upstairs. I knew it would take too long for the police to get here and I also knew I was no match for Brendan on my own. Then I remembered you telling me about last week when Lil pulled her gun on him. It took me a while to find it, but fortunately not too long." I didn't recall having told her that; perhaps it was Brendan who had done so – but what did it matter?

I looked at my sister for a long time before I said, "Thanks, Maddie. I don't know what I would have done without you."

"You would have made a remarkably unattractive and macabre mobile," she said with grim humour.

"True enough." I smiled back at her, "Well, of all the people I expected to try and save me, Maddie, I have to admit that I didn't think of you. I'm sorry for not trusting you."

"I don't blame you. I've been a bitch – but you're my kid sister and I love you."

I'd never heard her say it before, and I don't suppose she'd ever say it again. "I love you too," I said, and then we hugged.

❦

Chapter Thirty

Chief Inspector Goodenough had insisted that I see the doctor, who arrived shortly after the police left.

It was the same doctor from that morning and he had the grace to look a little sheepish, "I'm sorry if I was brusque with you this morning, Miss Richmond. It's just that I knew Mrs. Farrell quite well and I liked her. The thought that someone might have ... well, you know what I mean."

I shrugged, "Think nothing of it, doc," I said. To be honest I didn't actually recall even speaking to him, nor he to me, but the whole day was becoming a bit of a blank.

He took my blood pressure, my pulse, shone lights in my eyes and asked interminable questions before finally declaring me fit, "You can't have had a full dose of the stuff he gave you, or you would still be out cold. In fact I'm surprised it had such a dramatic effect on you. You must be very susceptible to drugs."

"She is," interjected Maddie wryly, "I've seen antibiotics send her over the edge. God help her if she ever got caught up in the drugs culture. I reckon she'd last about ten minutes."

He laughed and looked at me, "Is that true?"

"I'm afraid so. Brendan knew what he was doing when he spiked my drink. He's seen me high on aspirin and coca cola."

"That's a fallacy, you know," he said seriously.

"Not for me, it isn't."

"Oh well, you should be fine now. Get a good night's sleep and I'll call back in the morning, just to make sure you are okay. Is your sister going to stay with you?"

I looked enquiringly at her and she nodded, "Sure. There's nothing to take me back home. I can ring work tomorrow and book a day's holiday. I'll get extra sympathy because of the family bereavement."

The family bereavement. Poor Lil. It seemed an eternity since I had found her this morning. I wondered where she was now, but decided not to ask the doctor. I didn't really want to know if she was in one of those dreadful metal filing cabinet fridges they always seemed to have in television police dramas.

Shortly after he left another visitor arrived. David. It seemed his staff had finally tracked him down and he had driven for hours to get home.

I wanted to throw myself at him, but Maddie's presence rather curtailed my enthusiasm. He seemed stilted too. I don't think there can ever have been a more awkward reunion.

Apparently the doctor had met him in the lay-by and had given him a potted version of my adventures. It was this which had rendered him tongue-tied. I think the reality of how close he had come to losing me was just beginning to kick in – at least I hoped that was the case. He certainly looked a bit green about the gills.

Maddie eventually decided to put us out of our misery and took herself off to make coffee so that we could be alone for a few minutes. The minute the door closed behind her, he crossed the room and sat on the sofa beside me, taking my hand in his. "I can't leave you alone for a moment, can I?" he asked huskily.

"It would seem not."

"I trust the police have Brendan securely locked up?"

"He's still in hospital, I'm afraid, having lead shot removed from his smashed knee-caps."

Evidently he hadn't heard this particular tit-bit and looked rather startled, "How the hell did that happen?"

"Maddie shot him with Lil's gun."

He began to laugh, "Oh my God! You actually have a sister who is worse than you are."

"Thanks a lot," I protested, but not really displeased.

Maddie returned, "What are you laughing about?" she said, rather aggressively. David turned and looked admiringly at her, "I was just complimenting Libby on her sister. I understand you knee-capped the madman."

"Well, he deserved it," she said defensively, "Libby is my sister and I reserve the right to be the only one who is allowed to torture her. Do you want sugar?"

He seemed a bit stunned by the sudden change of subject, "Er... yes, please, two." She nodded and was gone again.

"Sisters." he said, shaking his head.

"Yes, well, without that particular sister, I'd probably be in the police morgue with Lil by now."

He surprised me by reaching out and hugging me fiercely for a second, "Don't even say it," he whispered, "I wish I had been here. I'd have blown his bloody brains out."

Maddie came back bearing a tray and David hastily left me and went back to his chair.

"Anyway," he continued, in his normal voice, "tell me everything. For a start, how the devil did he keep getting into the house?"

"The police say they found a set of keys on him. They suspect he must have lifted the spare set from the key rack when he came the first time, had them copied, the returned the originals without Lil or me being any the wiser. We both tended to use our own sets from our own key rings, so neither of us would notice that the spares were missing. They were only there to give to the neighbours when she went away, so they could water her plants and keep an eye on the place. It just goes to show how easy it is to gain access when people are trusting."

"Frighteningly easy. No wonder he kept getting in even when you thought you had locked the place securely."

"Well, what sort of an idiot has their spare keys on show?" snorted Maddie, with her usual tact. Once upon a time I would have wanted to smack her for that, but not today. Today she could call me all the names under the sun, and I would only smile benignly at her.

"Yes, well one doesn't really expect to find one's ex-boyfriend has turned into a homicidal maniac," I answered calmly.

"I'd have expected it of Brendan," she said cynically, "I don't know what you ever saw in the little creep."

That was rich coming from someone who had been happily conspiring with him against me for the past fortnight.

"Neither do I, now, so can we drop the subject?" I asked. I was wrong about that smiling benignly. If she made one more of her bitchy comments, I really was going to lay one on her.

David evidently saw that this might be a good moment to distract us both.

"I still have your present from Rick Allingham in the car, Libby. Do you want to see it now?"

"Oh, yes! I'd forgotten about that. Hard to believe, I know, but I've had other things on my mind lately."

He was gone for a few minutes and returned bearing a large Harrods bag. Typical, I thought, Rick Allingham would have a posh bag on hand to put it in. If that had been me, it would probably have been at best Marks and Spencer, at worst a Co-op carrier bag.

He laid it on the coffee table in front of me and with trembling fingers I pulled my gift free from its covering. It was, as he had told me on the telephone, a portable writing desk, but it was far more ornate and heavy than I had been expecting. Bigger too. Mahogany with brass bindings, corner pieces and handle. When I opened it, with a small key presented to me with a flourish by David, I found it still contained all the paraphernalia required by any gentleman for his correspondence and his personal hygiene. In the desk section there were pens, nibs, inkbottles, penknife, silver scissors, a silver-handled magnifying glass, a wooden ruler, an ivory and silver-chased letter opener. There was a full complement of thick vellum paper, with the Allingham crest at the top, envelopes and sealing wax and a silver seal, similarly crested. That bit folded out into a sloping writing surface, lined with battered, scuffed leather. The other part was full of crystal bottles with silver lids (with crest and monogram, of course) which must once have contained Macassar oil, toilet water, and heaven knew what else. There was a pair of silver and ivory handled cut-throat razors, and a strop. A shaving brush with worn bristles and a crystal bowl to mix the foam from a stick of soap. My breath was taken away by the beauty of the objects and the generosity of the man who had given the thing away.

"Oh, David," I said, looking up for a moment, "It really is lovely. Surely I can't accept it. It must be worth a fortune."

He shrugged, "Rick was adamant. He seemed to think it ought to be with you. Perhaps because he knows Richard must have written to Decima using it. The desk did go to the Crimea with him, and was returned with his other effects after his death."

That, of course, made it even more special. Maddie peered at it with a marked lack of interest and grinned unkindly, "I suppose that is the Victorian equivalent of a lap-top computer." she said, with her usual stoicism and thus managed to break the spell, "You know, whenever you see those things on The Antiques Roadshow, they always have a secret drawer. I read someone found a bundle of old white fivers in one of those things."

"It wasn't one of these," I replied pedantically, "actually it was a bureau, but you are right about the secret drawers. I wonder if it has one."

"That's a bit far-fetched, isn't it?" asked David, just as Maddie began to roughly pull at any knobs, notches, niches and carvings she could find. My heart was in my mouth and I was just on the point of slapping her hand away, worried that she might break something off, when there was a tiny, barely discernible click and a drawer in the base slid open.

"How did you do that?" I asked, astounded. Maddie shrugged, "No idea. Is there anything in it?"

Of course there was. Bits of paper – or what could more properly be described as that mythical parchment, I suppose. Old anyway, and folded neatly. I emptied the drawer and pushed the desk aside whilst I unfolded the things carefully, my hands shaking with excitement.

"Makes me feel like one of the Famous Five," said Maddie, "Hurry up, Libby. Is it money?"

I read the first sheet with growing astonishment, "Oh my God!" I breathed.

"What?" she almost shrieked, her frustration showing only too clearly. I ignored her and looked into David's eyes, "It's a marriage license, David."

"Whose?"

"A contract of marriage between one Richard Allingham and Decima Watkins…"

He was as stunned as I. Maddie, of course, looked utterly blank, "What the heck…"

She might not have spoken. David said softly, "She didn't have an illegitimate baby. They were legally married. They must have eloped from here, covered by her grandmother. But why the hell didn't she say something? She could have saved herself all that heartache from her father if only she had told him that she wasn't a fallen woman. She might not even have been accused of murder if she hadn't had that stigma hanging over her, ruining her reputation."

"I think this was why," I said excitedly, gesturing to the yellowing paper in my hands, "Richard had the license, and had hidden it well. She had no proof of the ceremony and if his parents had discovered the truth, they would have used their influence to have the marriage annulled. She knew they were quite capable of doing that. I suspect she was merely biding her time until she could tell the truth. Unfortunately, events overtook her and she found herself facing a murder charge. That must rather have made her secret marriage take a back seat for a while."

"I suppose so. And I suspect the Allinghams knew of the marriage and were desperate to keep it hidden. That was why Decima found herself on a murder charge in the first place. The deaths of her sisters must have been Manna from heaven for Richard's father. A word or two in the right place, and the thorn in his side was removed forever. Inspector Lazarus himself said he saw no reason to suspect she had done anything wrong."

"And her father fed her to the wolves because he was still under the impression she had borne a child out of wedlock. I suppose he must also have believed she had poisoned her sisters too, after all, the accusation must have come out of the blue to him too," I added, carried away by our theories. Maddie dampened us for a moment, as usual, "This is all very well, but where is your proof? A scrappy old bit of paper which shows that Decima wasn't the tart they all took her for – but so what? It happened over a hundred years ago."

I looked at her for a moment, scarcely able to comprehend that she found the story less than riveting. As I gazed at her a sudden thought struck me and I found myself grinning like a mad woman, "Don't be so quick to dismiss the story, Maddie. If I'm right, Dad is the real heir to Havering Hall. And as the eldest, you will follow him."

For the first time in my life, I had the satisfaction of seeing my sister bereft of words.

I left her to mull over this startling revelation and turned back to David, "This also explains another little mystery," I said.

"And that would be?" he asked swiftly.

"The robbery that Decima's grandmother reported to Inspector Lazarus, after the execution. She said nothing was stolen, but the house was turned upside down. It must have been Allingham's henchmen, looking for the marriage license. After both parties were dead, they could not risk the license suddenly turning up and proving Decima's son to be the true heir. Mr. Watkins was hiding the child for his own reasons, but if he had known that the boy was heir to his old enemy's fortune and property, he would have brought him out into the open soon enough."

"Very true. But what do we do now? How do you prove all this?"

I was silent for a moment, then triumphant, "DNA," I said simply, "It was something Brendan said to me which reminded me – never mind why he mentioned it, it's not important. What is important is that Dad, Maddie and I will all share DNA with Rick Allingham, if we are related. And if I'm right about Decima being innocent of the murder charges, we could insist that her sister's bodies are exhumed and tested for poison. The graves must still be in existence, I imagine. They were a wealthy family and would have had a posh plot."

"Will the poison still show up after all these years?"

"Well, there have been enough documentaries on the subject of long-dead bodies and the causes of their deaths and illnesses in life. I've heard arsenic preserves bodies anyway. We can always try, can't we? It will be worth it, to see Decima cleared of blame, and her son restored to her, even if it is only on paper."

Maddie finally found her tongue, "I couldn't agree more. I think it an absolute scandal that the poor girl has been slandered all these years. I, for one, don't think we should waste another minute! We'll ring the newspapers, the television. It will be a smash hit. It's the least we can do for our beloved Great, Great Grandmother – or whatever she was."

I grinned at David, "I'm afraid our sudden elevation to the aristocracy has gone to my sister's head."

Now that our initial excitement had died down, he seemed rather sombre, "I'm not really concerned with your sister, Libby. It's you I'm interested in. Are you really all right after what that bastard did to you?"

"I'm fine. It's over now. Let's just forget it, shall we?"

"I don't think I can."

"You are going to have to try," I tried to sound light-hearted, but it wasn't easy. For me the bad memories were fading fast, thanks to the drug Brendan had given me, but God only knew if they would come back to haunt me one day.

And I doubted David would ever forget that he hadn't been here when I needed him the most.

Maddie had gone off to try and find the phone book so she could ring Channel 4 with a proposition for the rights to our story so I hoisted myself, with some difficulty, off the sofa and went to his side, "Everything that happened here had to happen, David. Decima needed me to clear her name and restore her place in our family history. I wouldn't change a moment of it – not even the frightening and dangerous parts, because if I hadn't heeded Lil's cry for help, I would never have met you…"

I didn't need to say anything else. He pulled me into his arms and began to kiss me, fevered, passionate, tender – everything a kiss should be and I was lost for a moment, until I heard a sharp intake of breath and my sister saying moodily, "For God's sake, Libby, show a bit of decorum. Kindly remember, our great, great Grandfather won a V.C!"

❦